About the author

Beverley Latimer grew up in a large working-class family in the city of Leeds, West Yorkshire. She now lives in a small rural village with her husband in North Yorkshire.

She has a grown-up family and five grandchildren.

Beverley has spent her career caring for others, first as a nursery nurse and later as a support worker.

She is now spending time writing, which has long been her lifetime ambition.

Hannah is her debut novel, and she is currently working on her second.

HANNAH

BEVERLEY LATIMER

HANNAH

Vanguard Press

VANGUARD PAPERBACK

© Copyright 2021
Beverley Latimer

The right of Beverley Latimer to be identified as author of
this work has been asserted by her in accordance with the
Copyright, Designs and Patents Act 1988.

A CIP catalogue record for this title is
available from the British Library.

ISBN 978 1 80016 158 0

*Vanguard Press is an imprint of
Pegasus Elliot MacKenzie Publishers Ltd.*
www.pegasuspublishers.com

First Published in 2021

**Vanguard Press
Sheraton House Castle Park
Cambridge England**

Printed & Bound in Great Britain

Dedication

For my children.

Acknowledgements

I would like to say a huge thank you to my husband, for his support, encouragement, patience, and understanding, during the writing of this book.

Chapter One
March 1976

Philip Turner strode out of the factory gates with his head held high. He walked with a swagger and was very arrogant in nature. Although he was tall and dark, he was nothing special, and yet, Philip believed himself to be God's gift to the opposite sex.

It was almost two-thirty in the afternoon, and, he had been working since six o'clock that morning, and so, he was gagging for a pint. He walked towards the Jug Inn, which was situated just around the corner from the factory. It had been a drinking hole for decades for the hundreds of men employed at the factory where Philip worked. He threw his cigarette on the pavement just before stepping inside the public house where he made his way towards the bar. The barmaid saw him and reluctantly tore herself away from the landlady, whom she had been in conversation with and walked across to serve him. Philip shamelessly eyed her cleavage as he asked for a pint of bitter, and a packet of cigarettes.

"Just finished for the day, have you?" she asked, in her usual friendly manner.

"Yep," he answered as he counted the change in his hand.

"Thought you would have wanted to get home to that pretty young wife of yours."

Looking up, Philip eyed the barmaid with contempt. "And what business is that of yours?"

The barmaids face fell, at the aggressive tone of Philip's reply. She handed him his pint, and his cigarettes.

"Just making conversation!" she snapped as she took his money. She returned with his change, which he took from her without speaking, not even to say thank you.

He chose a small table, next to the window. As he sat down, he poured half his pint straight down his throat before lighting up a cigarette. He took a long drag and blew the smoke back out through his nostrils as he brooded about his lot in life. He hated his job at the factory, hated being stuck indoors, and hated having a foreman breathing down his neck.

Philip preferred working outdoors. He was a bricklayer by trade, and because there was no building work in the area where he had recently moved to with his new wife, he had had to take any available job.

Philip finished his cigarette, before pouring the rest of his pint down his throat and went back to the bar to buy another, as the pub started to fill with more factory workers.

The same barmaid served him again, but she was noticeably huffy with him after the way he had spoken to her earlier. As he walked away, he heard her say, loud enough so that he could hear, "Thinks he's God's gift that one!"

Knowing her words were directed at him, Philip smirked as he went back to his seat.

The beer did nothing to lighten his mood. He was one of those men that got irritable with drink, and it always brought out the worst in him. He was twenty-three, newly married with a baby on the way, and stuck in a dead-end job.

This was not the way he had seen his life heading only a year ago. He spent the next two hours sitting alone, not wanting to get involved with the raucous laughter of the other men from the factory, as they laughed and flirted with the barmaids.

Philip poured pint after pint down himself until his money ran out. He was supposed to be getting a bag of coal for the fire on his way home, but he had spent every penny he had in the pub, and payday was still two days away. He didn't care, he had needed a drink after a heavy morning in the factory.

His house was a good twenty-minute walk from the pub, so as he left, he turned his collar up against the cold wind, dug his hands deep into the pockets of his overcoat and made his way home.

That same afternoon, Hannah had been standing at the living room window watching the dark clouds, as they were pushed across the sky by the cold March wind. It had gathered momentum as the afternoon had progressed and it was now a howling gale.

Hannah had been looking out to see if she could see her husband coming home from work, but there was no sign of him. He was already over half an hour late. Her heart to sank, as she began to realise that he had most probably gone straight to the pub after finishing work that afternoon.

She had then turned her attention to the large oak tree outside her front garden. She watched, as its branches were tossed about by the strength of the wind. The tree blocked out a lot of the light from the living room, which meant, that even during the summer months, the room was always shrouded in semi-darkness.

Her mood lifted as she noticed that the tree was in bud. Since early childhood, spring had been one of her favourite times of the year. It brought renewal and re-birth. It signalled, that summer was just around the corner, bringing with it the promise of, longer, brighter, and warmer days. The arrival of spring flowers and new-born lambs had always filled Hannah, with a feeling of joy, no matter how difficult life appeared at times.

She had a new life growing inside of her. Her baby was due in the middle of May, and so, she would soon have a spring baby to hold.

As she put a maternal hand on her stomach, the baby kicked hard, causing her to flinch. From the way her baby kicked, Hannah guessed that he or she was strong and healthy. She was secretly hoping for a girl, whereas her husband was hoping for a son. But whatever the baby turned out to be, Hannah knew she would love her child unconditionally.

Something caught her eye, causing her to look up — the neighbour in the house opposite was cleaning the inside of her bedroom window. Hannah had watched her mother do the same many times when she had been a small child. That had been when her mother had been a house-proud mother of six. Before everything changed, with the confirmation of a seventh pregnancy, and the onset of mental illness. At the age of eight, Hannah knew nothing about illnesses of the mind or postpartum depression. All she knew was that her mother had stopped caring for her children, had stopped caring for her home, and had become unpredictable and scary to be around.

When Lucy had eventually come along, Hannah and her eldest sister by four years had had to learn fast how to care for their baby sister, while their mother spent hours sprawled out on the settee.

Their father worked long hours as an HGV driver, meaning he was out of the house for up to twelve hours a day. He had been unaware of what was going on at home, during his long working hours. The girl's education suffered too, because Hannah and her older sister Carol were often kept off school to care for the baby, and to do household chores.

Hannah's mother had always been a mean-spirited woman who never had a good word to say about anyone. She had always taken pleasure in the misfortune of others while continuously complaining about her own lot in life. She had grown up in a household where she had been spoilt rotten by her father, and it had made her selfish and unempathetic towards others.

She had married Richard, Hannah's father, when they were both eighteen, after becoming pregnant with their first child. They had gone on to have six more children over twelve years. But it had been the confirmation of a seventh pregnancy that had sent Sue over the edge. She had not wanted the last four children she had given birth to, so, the thought of adding another child to her large brood, had had a catastrophic effect on her mental health. And it was her eldest children who had been expected to pick up the pieces, even though Hannah was still a young child at the time.

She had an older brother by three years, Stephen. He was their mother's golden boy. Thankfully, it hadn't made him mean towards his less fortunate sisters, but it had meant he had an easier time of things. Stephen had a mischievous sense of humour and he had been the only person who could put a smile on their mother's face, during those difficult years.

After having been stood at the window for some time, Hannah had realised she was cold. The fire had gone out almost two hours earlier because there was no more coal left to keep it going. She was expecting

Philip to buy some on the way home from work, and so she., was hoping he had not spent the last of his money in the pub. That would mean, there would be no coal and no fire to warm the freezing cold living room.

She moved away from the window and went into the kitchen to prepare their evening meal.

She closed the door and turned the cooker on to try and generate some heat, in the small kitchen. As she held her cold hands over the ring to warm them, she thought back to how she had once dreamt of being married to Philip. She was learning that the reality of married life was very different!

Chapter Two
July 1974

Hannah was on her way to her grandparents' house to borrow money for her mother, who had taken up drinking in the evenings. Sue used alcohol to calm her mind and help her sleep at night. She never drank during the day.

Sue's drinking brought more hardship for her children, because using money for essentials such as food and clothing were no longer her priority.

Hannah's father was a drinker too. So, almost every day, either Hannah or one of her siblings would be sent to their grandparents' house, a couple of streets away, to borrow money or food.

Hannah's grandparents were the only adults who Hannah and her brothers and sisters could rely on. Their grandfather had always been an excellent male role model for her brothers. He was hardworking and had been a good provider for his family. He was the one who provided his daughter's children with essential clothing, such as school uniforms, winter coats, and shoes. And a lot of the time, he provided food too.

Some major renovation work was being done to one of the large private houses, which lay halfway between Hannah's family home and her grandparents' house.

As she walked past where the work was being carried out, she heard a couple of loud wolf whistles. Not thinking for a single second that they were directed at her, Hannah turned around to see where the whistling was coming from.

She was surprised to see two men from the building site grinning back at her. One of them, the taller of the two, tipped his hard hat and called out, "Hello blondie."

She took note of his southern accent. Not knowing how to react, Hannah turned around and carried on walking amidst the sound of more whistles and laughter.

She spent a half-hour in conversation with her grandmother, before setting off home, with a five-pound note in one hand, and a pint of milk in the other.

She was nervous about walking past the builders again, becoming more self-conscious the closer she got to where the men were still working. As she got level with the house that was being renovated, she heard one of the men say. "Ey, Phil, Blondie's on her way back."

Hannah kept her head down and quickened her pace to get past as quickly as she could.

The one with the southern accent called after her, "Come back, beautiful, you're breaking my heart."

Hannah turned around and stared at the man who had just given her the biggest compliment she had ever had. He held a hand up to her, as if to wave, and smiled. She smiled back, before, turning away. She walked on, with her heart racing, as a feeling of excitement swept through her.

Hannah believed she was one of the plainest girls in her school, and so, the unexpected attention had taken her completely by surprise. She was not plain, in fact, she quite the opposite!

. At fourteen, Hannah was small, but she had the body of a woman. She was not aware that men looked at her whenever she walked past them, or that they stared at her, as they drove past her.

She had two more encounters with the builders over the next couple of days. She knew the tall one with the southern accent was called Philip, because she had heard his workmates call him Phil. He worked bare-chested, due to the hot weather. He was over six feet tall, lean, and deeply tanned from the sun. He appeared younger than his workmates, and he was better looking too, or so, Hannah thought.

Hannah became ever more willing to go to her grandparents' house, whenever she was asked, because it meant seeing him. He would whistle as she walked by, and throw compliments at her, while his workmates laughed at Philip's obvious interest in the young girl.

Hannah was shy, and so, she would blush, as she smiled back at him.

She found herself thinking about him all of the time. She even fantasised about becoming his girlfriend, even though she knew he was too old for her.

One Saturday morning, just three weeks after her first encounter with Philip, she had been sent to the local newsagents to buy her father his morning paper. She walked into the shop and stood behind a young man in the queue. She didn't recognise him because he was not in his work clothes, and he was not wearing his hard hat.

The young man turned around to look at something just above where she was standing, and did a double take when he looked down and saw her standing there. Hannah blushed when she realised who he was. Philip smiled, and held her gaze for several seconds, while Hannah's heart raced. He paid for his items, and then as he was about to walk out of the shop, he turned around and winked at her.

When Hannah came out of the shop, she noticed him leaning against a wall, smoking a cigarette. He walked over to her, and as he did her cheeks burned in anticipation of what he was going to say.

"This is a nice surprise, bumping into you this morning," he told her with a grin.

Hannah clung to her dad's newspaper, at a loss of what to say back. He looked around to see if anyone was about before asking. "Would you like to meet me later this afternoon?

Hannah couldn't believe that he wanted to meet up with her, but then her face dropped, when she remembered, she had chores to do that afternoon. "I can't this afternoon because I have jobs to do for my mother," she told him.

"Maybe tomorrow instead?" he asked, putting his head to one side as he allowed his eyes to wander over her body.

She nodded. "I could meet you tomorrow, but not here. Maybe outside the picture house, at one-thirty." Her heart was beating fast, as her spirits rose.

"Outside the picture house, it is… See you tomorrow, Blondie," he said, winking at her again.

"My name's Hannah," she told him in a quiet voice

"See you tomorrow, Hannah," he smiled at her before walking away, leaving her standing there, still clinging to her father's newspaper.

She had guessed him to be around nineteen or twenty, and so, she knew her mum and dad would go crazy if they were to find out, she was meeting a young man who, compared to her, was an adult.

Philip was already waiting for her in his van when she arrived the following day. He drove her to a park a few miles away, where they took a leisurely stroll around the large lake. He was funny, and he made her laugh. After a while he became more serious and asked her, "Are you still at school, Hannah?"

She nodded. "Yes, I am."

"How old are you?" he asked, turning to look at her face

"Nearly fifteen," she told him, even though her fifteenth birthday was six months away. He made no comment about her age, nor the fact that she was still at school.

They went to the lakeside café, where he bought coffee and chocolate cake for each of them.

He appeared to study the features of her face before saying to her.

"How old do you think I am?"

"About nineteen."

"I'm twenty-one, which is quite a bit older than you. People will say, you're too young to be out with me"

The smile fell from Hannah's face as her heart sank. He was older than she had guessed, and she feared, he was about to tell her that he couldn't see her again because she was too young for him.

Philip had seen her reaction, and it amused him. "Do you want to see me again?" he asked, smiling at her.

She lowered her eyes as she coloured up. "Yes, I do want to see you again."

He leaned towards her and asked, "Have you ever had a boyfriend?"

She shook her head. "No."

He leaned closer still, so that his lips were close to hers.

"So, you've never been kissed?"

Hannah's cheeks burned as she shook her head again. Philip brought his lips up closer so that they were now touching hers, and not caring who was watching, he gave her a soft lingering kiss on her mouth, sending waves of excitement throughout her entire body.

They arranged to meet up again the following Tuesday evening. Hannah normally went to the local Youth Club with a couple of her school friends on a Tuesday, so she would not have to explain to her parents why she was going out. She told Philip that she would have to be home no later than ten o'clock.

During that first couple of weeks into their relationship, Philip had gone on to make her all kind of promises. One being, that he would not touch her until she was sixteen, but he had lied. Hannah had been alarmed when just a week later he cupped a hand over one of her breasts, while they were kissing. She had not been expecting it, and the action caused Hannah to jump back, with a look of mortification. Philip apologised, but the following week he put his hand up her skirt while they were kissing. She pushed his hand away and told him very firmly, "No, please don't do that!"

He tried to seduce her by telling her that she was beautiful, and that she had a gorgeous body, and that was why he couldn't keep his hands off her, but that hadn't worked either.

One evening Philip took Hannah to his bedsit with only one thing on his mind.

After making the two of them a cold drink, Philip asked Hannah to join him on the sofa. Hannah felt uneasy, but she did as he asked. He playfully, pushed her backwards, so that she was lying down, before, he took hold of her.

Worried that he was wanting to take things further than she wanted him to, Hannah tried to sit up. Philip let go. He was clearly annoyed. "You know what you are, don't you?" he snapped. "A tease! You get me all worked up, and then you refuse to follow through." He turned away and began to sulk.

Hannah, shuffled to the edge of the sofa. She tentatively reached out and touched his shoulder. Philip rubbed his temple, thinking of his next move.

"I'm just not ready, Philip. The thought of it scares me," she told him meekly.

Philip knew which buttons to push. He narrowed his eyes, as his face darkened. "If you're not ready for a serious relationship, then we might as well call it a day." He enjoyed watching her squirm. "I might as well, look elsewhere, obviously you're still a little girl!"

Hannah's bottom lip trembled, as she tried not to cry.

Philip knew he was winning the game. Looking Hannah in the eye, he asked, "Do you love me?

"Yes, of course, I do." she whimpered.

"Then, show me!" He traced his finger down the side of her face, towards her chin, as he held her gaze.

And then, because Hannah feared she might lose the one person she believed loved her, she finally gave into him. Not because she wanted to, but because she believed that was the only way she would keep him.

It hurt a lot, and afterwards, she felt dirty and ashamed. But once she had given in to Philip's sexual demands, Hannah then felt that she had no other choice, other than to keep on giving him what he had wanted from her.

It would be many years later that Hannah would realise, that she had been sexually exploited and coerced into doing things that she had not been ready to do, by a man who had known exactly what he was doing!

When her parents had found out from a neighbour that Hannah had been seen getting into a young man's van on more than a couple of occasions, they had gone crazy. They had ordered her to stop seeing him immediately. But, because Hannah believed the two of them to be in love, she found all kind of ways to be with him, and Philip had been determined that her parents were not going to break them up.

One morning, just over a year into their relationship Hannah woke with a feeling of trepidation. She was skipping school that afternoon, to visit the doctor, for her test results. She had just missed a second period, and she was intelligent enough to know she was pregnant.

Philip had been careless about using contraception, and because, months had gone by without her getting pregnant, Hannah had convinced herself that she couldn't.

Later that afternoon, she cried when the pregnancy was confirmed. The doctor was very sympathetic and advised her to speak with her parents as soon as possible. Hannah told him that she couldn't speak to her mother, because she was a very unreasonable woman.

She did not mention the pregnancy to anyone, not even Philip, for the next couple of weeks, as she slowly came to terms with the fact that she was carrying his baby. Eventually, she knew she had to tell someone, so, she confided in her eldest sister, who promised to speak to their father, on her younger sisters' behalf.

Hannah trusted her father not to overreact, and she believed, he would know how to break the news of her pregnancy to her mother.

Hannah eventually spoke to Philip about the baby. Of course, he was shocked, but at his age, he should have known, that he had been playing with fire, when he had carelessly not bothered to use protection. He reluctantly agreed to meet with Richard in the local pub, at Richards request

Sitting himself down, next to Philip, the following evening, Richard put his pint down on the table, before speaking, "Right lad," Richard told Philip, "This is how it's going to be. You will marry Hannah as soon as she turns sixteen. If you don't stand by her, I am quite prepared to press charges against you, for having sex with an underage girl. So, you had better not try to run out on her." Then getting really annoyed, Richard said to Philip, "She's just a kid, for goodness' sake, couldn't you have looked for someone your own age?"

Philip could not look at Richard. Looking down, at the floor, he said, "I'm sorry, and of course, I will stand by her."

Richard shook his head, "What's done is done. You'll both just have to make the best of things."

Philip was just relieved that Richard hadn't attacked him for what he had done to his daughter. He also knew that he was backed into a corner. He had to marry Hannah as soon as she turned sixteen, or risk going to prison.

It was arranged that Philip and Hannah would move in with his parents in the South of England after the Christmas holidays, because Hannah's parents did not want their neighbours to find out about their teenage daughter's pregnancy. Arrangements were made for Philip and Hannah to marry in February, just a month after Hannah's sixteenth birthday. The baby was due in May.

Chapter Three
March 1976

Philip walked through the door at five in the evening. When Hannah heard the door handle turn, she immediately felt better. She had a welcoming smile on her face as he walked through the door. Her smile quickly fell when she saw that he had been drinking heavily.

"Did you get any coal?" she asked, knowing full well that he had not.

"No," He snapped, his face showing his irritation at the question.

"But the house is freezing! Have you not got any money left so that we can get some?" she wailed.

He banged his fist on the table, making her jump. "Don't you question me! I've been slogging my guts out in that factory, while you sit here all day like Lady Muck doing nothing. I am entitled to go out for a drink, and I am not going to answer to a bit of a kid like you. If you don't like things the way they are, then go, and run back home to your mother."

Hannah stood in shocked silence. It was the first time that she had ever felt afraid of him!

"No," he continued angrily, "the old witch wouldn't want you back, would she? Your one less mouth to feed as far as she's concerned. Be grateful that I was willing to put a roof over your head when your parents wanted rid of you!"

He slumped down onto the kitchen chair, took a cigarette out of its packet, and lit it with a match. The way he then looked at Hannah, made her shiver, as she fought hard to keep her tears at bay, just as she had done so many times as a child, when her mother was having one of her meltdowns.

After finishing his cigarette, Philip went to use the toilet while Hannah put their meal on the table. When he returned, they ate in silence.

He was in no mood to talk, and Hannah, was still reeling at how he had just turned on her.

After finishing his meal, Philip stood up and walked towards the living room, still wearing his outside coat. When he turned around to look at Hannah, she averted her eyes, as she used to do as a child, when her mother was being nasty to her. His tone of voice was a little softer this time. "I'll get some coal on Friday, after I get paid. Go to my mother's tomorrow and spend the day there until I get home."

"Okay," was all she said back to him.

She got on well with her in-laws, Frank, and Alice. Alice would not mind in the least if Hannah were to spend the whole day at her house the following day. She had welcomed Hannah into their family and she had been kind to her.

Alice was nothing like her own mother. She was kind-hearted and had a mild temper. She took pleasure in the small things in life and loved being surrounded by her family.

Frank was kind too. Alice had told Hannah how she had felt lucky to have met Frank, after her first husband had abandoned her and their two little boys two years earlier.

Frank was a Yorkshireman, and so he had felt akin to the little Yorkshire lass, who Philip had brought to live with them until, they found a place to rent, once they were married.

A week after the incident with Philip, and to everyone's surprise Hannah went into premature labour, at thirty-two weeks' gestation. After a long and exhausting labour, Harrison came into the world, weighing just four pounds. He was laid in his mother's arms for just a moment before being taken to the Neonatal Unit.

When Hannah had looked at her baby, for the first time, she was surprised to see that he had a full head of dark hair and his father's dark skin. She loved him instantly as she smiled at his little face.

After, Harrison was taken from her, Hannah, quickly fell into a deep sleep. The drugs she had been given during labour had not yet worn off, and so, she could not have stayed awake even if she had wanted to.

Hannah believed, childbirth had been the worst experience of her life, and although she had no wish to ever repeat the experience, she would go on to have four more children. But her fifth child would not arrive for another twenty years.

She was woken an hour later with the arrival of the porter to take her to the postnatal ward.

She was transferred into a bed next to where a dark-haired girl lay sleeping. Hannah watched her for a few minutes. She guessed the girl was probably just a couple of years older than herself, as she drifted back into a drug-induced sleep.

She was woken a couple of hours later with the clatter of breakfast being brought on to the ward. The girl in the next bed was awake and sitting up now. She asked Hannah. "Did you come in during the night?"

"Earlier this morning," Hannah told her.

"I'm Michelle. What did you have?"

"A boy... he's been taken to the Neonatal Unit, because he's eight weeks premature."

Just then, a young nurse came over with a breakfast tray.

"Michelle, will you go to the dining table, please?" she said, before turning to look at Hannah. She smiled. "You get to have breakfast in bed just this once since you have not long had your baby."

Hannah was all at once aware of how hungry she was. She sat up, wincing from the pain that her stiches were causing her. She gratefully accepted the tray of food. After she had finished eating, she was given a cup of tea.

As soon as breakfast was finished, Michelle was straight back over. She was a chatter box. She told Hannah, about how she had been abandoned by her baby's father, soon after she had told him she was pregnant. Just as Hannah was sympathising with Michelle, the babies were brought in from the nursery, where they had spent the night being looked after by the hospital staff, while their mothers had got some much-needed sleep.

Michelle lifted her baby girl out of the small crib, to show her off to Hannah.

"She's beautiful! What is she called?"

"Emma."

Hannah smiled, "My grandma's called Emma," she thought about her own baby and wondered if he was all right. "My little boy is called Harrison," she told the other girl.

"I've never heard of that name."

"It's not a very common name, but it was the only one that we could both agree on."

Before Michelle could comment further, the young nurse who had given Hannah her breakfast appeared at Hannah's bedside with a wheelchair, "I've come to take you to the bathroom. It's our policy that you don't use the bathroom by yourself on the day of your baby's birth. It's just in case you faint or start to bleed heavily while you're in there."

Hannah was mortified that she was going to have to undress in front of the nurse. But she did as she was asked. She got her things together and allowed the nurse to take her to the bathroom.

Things were quite different in the seventies to what they are today. Once in the bathroom, the nurse ran the bath, and taking note of Hannah's discomfort, she told her, firmly, "I do this every day, and you haven't got anything that I have not seen a thousand times before."

Once back on the ward, Hannah and Michelle spoke about how awful it was to have someone watch you take a bath. The only person who ever saw Hannah naked was Philip, and she was still shy about that.

Later that afternoon, Philip arrived with his mother. Hannah was embarrassed by his appearance. He had not shaved, his shirt looked creased, and he stank of stale beer and cigarettes.

A nurse appeared next to Philip with a wheelchair. "Would you like to take your wife to see your baby, Mr Turner?"

He looked at the nurse, in his usual arrogant manner, "She's had a baby, not major surgery, can't she walk?"

The nurses face, flushed red, as her tone of voice changed. "Your wife has had a very long and difficult labour, and she has several stitches. We would prefer her to be taken down to the Neonatal Unit in the wheelchair."

Looking Philip up and down, the nurse, turned on her heel and quickly marched away. Hannah could have died with embarrassment!

Alice looked at her sympathetically. "I'll push you, Hannah. I can't wait to see my grandson," she said, with enthusiasm.

Philip huffed and rolled his eyes.

Alice was unable to contain her emotions when she saw how tiny her grandson was. "He's so beautiful and look at all his hair Philip. He's the image of you, Philip, don't you agree, Hannah?"

Hannah nodded. Philip smiled at last. They each had a brief hold of the baby, before being asked to put him back in the incubator by the sister in charge. She explained that Harrison just needed to grow and get stronger before being allowed home.

While Hannah remained in the hospital, she visited her son, every morning, and every afternoon. Then she would spend another hour with him, when, Philip, Frank, and Alice, visited in the evenings.

When Frank saw Harrison for the first time, he had not been able to hold back tears of emotion, and yet, Philip had shown no emotion, when, he had seen his son, for the first time.

Hannah was discharged a week after Harrison's birth, while he remained in hospital for another three weeks.

When he was eventually discharged, Hannah took delight in looking after him. He was an easy baby to care for due to his placid nature. Philip, however, was not a good father. He got angry when Harrison cried in the night. He accused Hannah of giving too much of her time to the baby. He would have tantrums over it, accusing her of not caring about him now that she had the baby to care for.

It came as a shock to Hannah that Philip was jealous of his own child. She did her best to reassure him that she loved him, but he would disregard her words, and sulk for hours, leaving Hannah emotionally drained.

The summer of 1976 was a long hot one, and Harrison thrived during those summer months, while Hannah grew pale and skinny.

It had not gone unnoticed by Frank, who had voiced his concerns to Alice, one afternoon. "I'm a bit worried about Hannah. She's lost weight, and she doesn't look well."

"Just the demands of being a new wife and mother." Alice assured him, "Anyway, she eats like a bird, I'm not surprised she's lost weight. She's missing her family too, poor thing."

Frank nodded in agreement. "Philip should take her and the baby up there for a visit."

"He doesn't like them, Frank, and I get the impression that they don't like him."

"Well, he needs to think about what's best for Hannah, and less about what's best for himself," Frank told Alice, as he became annoyed over Philip's selfishness.

Not wanting to get into an argument about Philip, as they had done so many times in the past, Alice went into the kitchen to prepare their evening meal.

Although Hannah saw Frank and Alice a couple of times a week, it was her husband's company that she craved more than anything.

Philip took little interest in Hannah, even though he demanded her full attention on him, when he was home. When he wasn't at work, he spent a lot of time in the pub drinking and smoking the money away that was needed for more important things such as food, clothing, and rent.

Hannah found herself, spending most of her time alone with her baby, and by the end of the year, she was pregnant again.

Frank wasn't happy over the news that a second grandchild was on the way, because he was too concerned for Hannah's health.

Alice was equally concerned for Hannah's health. But her main concern was whether their daughter-in-law, who was still only sixteen, would be able to cope with two babies at such a young age.

Chapter Four
July 1977

Fifteen months after having Harrison, Hannah was back on the same ward, after having given birth to a second son, who they named Ethan. He had arrived eight weeks early, like his older brother, but he was a little bigger, weighing half a pound more. Hannah had had a much easier time of things this time. The labour had lasted only five hours, and she had not needed stitches.

Ethan looked just like Harrison had done as a new-born. He had the same dark hair and olive skin. And Hannah, felt the same, all-consuming love that she had felt for Harrison, when he had been born.

Harrison's hair had gradually lightened, and it was now a lovely honey blonde that complemented his soft hazel eyes. He was a chubby fifteen-month-old, who he was getting into everything, meaning Hannah needed eyes in the back of her head. He was staying with Frank and Alice while Hannah was in the hospital because she didn't trust Philip to look after him properly.

Harrison had brought a lot of love into Hannah's life. He was a smiler, who adored his mother. He would climb onto her knee, and plant wet kisses all over her face., while she laughed at his comical behaviour.

It had been Harrison who had got Hannah through each day during the months that had followed his birth, as she struggled to cope with the way Philip treated her.

She had soon realised, that she had swapped one bad situation for another.

Hannah had a wise head on her shoulders for her years, having had to grow up very quickly after the birth of her youngest sister. At seventeen, she still lived with the hope that Philip would grow up, and that her life would improve.

While, she was in hospital, she was recognised by the hospital staff from the previous year, who all made a fuss over her and her new baby. Still, when Hannah was out of earshot, they reminded one another how arrogant and rude her husband was.

As Hannah sat with her new baby, her mind travelled back to the first beating, she had received from Philip.

They had attended the wedding of his cousin. Philip, rarely took her out, and so Hannah had been really looking forward to it.

Alice had treated her to a new dress and a new pair of shoes. When Philip had seen her dressed up for the first time since their wedding day, he had whistled, while wrapping his arms around her waist. He had pulled her close, telling her how much he was looking forward to making love to her later.

Hannah had enjoyed her husband's attention. It took her back to the days before they had married to the days when he had made her feel that she was someone very special to him.

Philip's parents had left the reception early with Harrison, telling the younger couple to enjoy what was left of the evening.

The evening was coming to an end, and the last song had started to play, a slow one. Couples of all ages were getting up to enjoy a slow dance together, and Hannah had been looking round for Philip, hoping that he would take her onto the dance floor.

She had gasped when she had spotted him taking another young woman onto the dance floor instead. She had watched the two of them dance up close to one another, while her heart broke. She had felt so humiliated, knowing that everyone who was there, could see what Philip was doing right in front of her.

As they walked home afterwards, Hannah had not uttered a single word to Philip, but once they were inside, she had confronted him about it. "How could you show me up like that, with everyone watching. You have totally humiliated me!" she had cried at him.

"It was only a dance!" he had snapped, but then he had smirked, and Hannah had felt incensed.

"Who is she, and how do you know her?"

Philip's face had darkened, as the smirk was replaced with a look of contempt. Then without any warning, he had slapped her across her mouth. Hannah was knocked to the floor. As she fell, she had banged her head against the armchair she had been standing next to.

Philip had dragged her back up by her hair and had hit across her face with the back of his hand, catching her right eye as he did so. With a menacing look, he had warned her. "Don't you ever speak to me like that again," before throwing her to the floor again.

He had then kicked her in her back, with such force, that she had struggled to breathe.

She had heard him leave the room and stomp upstairs, while she had remained on the floor for quite some time.

She could hardly process the shock and devastation, that her husband had not only humiliated her in public, but that he had beaten her very badly too.

Hannah had believed that she had left a life of violence behind, when she had left home, to begin a new life with her baby's father. She had believed Philip, when he had promised to take her away from all that and give her a good life.

She was still only sixteen, still a child in the eyes of the law, and her husband, the man who was supposed to love and protect her, had beaten her black and blue!

She should have been dating boys of her own age, having fun with her friends, with her eyes fixed brightly on the future. She was far too young and way too sensitive, to be living the miserable existence that was her life with Philip!

After a long time, she had gone upstairs to get ready for bed. When she had seen her reflection in the bathroom mirror, it had been a shock. Her right eye was so badly bruised and swollen that it was almost closed. Her bottom lip was cut and badly bruised, and her back hurt from where Philip had kicked her.

The fear she had lived with as a child had returned and her heart was broken.

She had finished getting ready for bed before quietly slipping between the sheets next to where Philip lay sleeping peacefully, as if nothing out of the ordinary had taken place.

The next day he had made Hannah tell Frank and Alice that she had got so drunk at the wedding reception that she had suffered a bad fall on the way home. Frank had not been convinced, but he kept his suspicions to himself, while keeping a close eye on Hannah during the weeks that followed.

After the first beating, Philip had got into a habit of hitting her whenever she annoyed him. She had suffered another beating a few weeks after the first one, for daring to express her concern to him, over the amount of money he spent in the pub. He had made sure that he had avoided hitting her in the face that time, so that the bruises on Hannah's body, could easily be covered with clothing.

But at least he had not hit her since finding out that she was pregnant with Ethan.

Hannah's thoughts came back to the present time, and as she looked at her sleeping baby, she thought. *Is this going to be my life now, until I'm an old lady?* Her answer was no, it would not be!

Ethan was allowed home three weeks later, and Hannah settled into an endless cycle of feeding, changing nappies and housework. Things were easier when Philip was out at work. He drained her emotionally with his tantrums and dark moods.

Things were made much worse when three months after Ethan's birth. Philip was sacked from his job at the factory after verbally attacking the foreman. It was something that he had already received two warnings about. After the third verbal assault, he was given his marching orders from the factory manager.

Hannah knew that the loss of income would make her and Philip's life much harder than it already was. And she knew he would take all his anger and frustration out on her.

After starting and quickly quitting a couple of jobs, Philip eventually got a job as a taxi driver. The hours were long and unsociable, but he liked the fact that he didn't have a foreman breathing down his neck, and he liked staying in bed till late morning too.

He often didn't get in until after midnight, especially on the weekend. Hannah was usually in bed asleep by the time Philip got home, and so, if he was feeling amorous, he would wake her up, and she would never dare refuse him.

Philip was never gentle, never tender in bed, and after taking what he wanted, he would roll on to his side and go to sleep.

His days off, were every Wednesday, and every Sunday. But instead of spending time with his wife and children, Philip would spend the afternoons in the pub, where he would drink too much.

Those were the times that Hannah dreaded. She knew how the drink affected his mood and his temper. He didn't always hit her, but he would call her foul names to deliberately hurt her, telling her she was useless, that she was ugly, and that no other man would be willing to put up with her, before storming off upstairs to sleep the drink off, and leaving Hannah in tears.

She did not know what else she could do to please him; he certainly didn't try very hard to please her!

After a couple of hours, he would wake from his drink-induced sleep, and remain agitated for the rest of the evening, eating the meal that Hannah had put to one side for him in silence.

The next day, he could be all smiles, hugs, and kisses, while he tried to soft-soap Hannah after his vile behaviour. Other times his mood would continue well into the next day, or sometimes even beyond that.

Hannah clung to those small glimpses of how loving and tender he could be on occasions, as proof that he could change — the times when he was sorry, the times when he was more loving, towards her.

But the bad times always outweighed the good times. Philip was unpredictable like her mother, which meant that Hannah often found herself walking on eggshells around him.

She was exhausted at the end of each day, not realising how much stress she was under in caring for two young children, while putting up with an unreasonable and violent husband. It drained her energy, and Philip was sucking the life out of her!

Even if Hannah had wanted to leave, she had nowhere to go, and no money of her own. Even if she could afford the train fare back to

Yorkshire, returning to her mother's home with her small children was not an option.

Besides, Hannah had not admitted to any of her family, when she occasionally spoke with them over the phone, that her husband was a wife beater. How could she admit to her parents that they had been right about Philip all along, and that she had been wrong when she had argued with them that he was a decent man?

At the age of eighteen, Hannah was beginning to mature. She was turning from a girl into a young woman, and she was beginning to see her husband for what he truly was: an arrogant, selfish man, who had no empathy or compassion for anyone.

She was beginning to realise too, that most people did not like him. Yes, he had a couple of mates in the pub, who like himself, drank too much and then knocked their wives about, but he had no real friends to call his own.

What Hannah didn't know was that Philip had never had any intention of remaining faithful to her for the rest of his life. He wanted fun and the thrill of bedding other women, while he kept a tight grip on the one, he had at home.

He still wanted Hannah, but he knew that if the opportunity to sleep with other women behind her back presented itself, he would take it.

What Philip didn't know was that one day he would come to need Hannah more than she needed him, but he would realise far too late, and he would regret it for the rest of his life.

Chapter Five
July 1979

A German couple, Dieter and Ursula, had moved into the house next door to Philip and Hannah. They were both in their early forties and had moved to England after Dieter's job had been relocated there. They both spoke English fluently, albeit with a thick German accent. They had no children of their own, having given up the hope of having a child when Ursula had not conceived after many years of trying. Whenever they saw Hannah, either in the garden, or in the street they would stop and pass the time of day with her. It was clear to each of them what life was like for their young neighbour, from what they heard through the thin walls. Ursula had no friends or family in the UK, so she began to invite Hannah and her two children round to hers in an afternoon for coffee and cake. Hannah brought out Ursula's motherly instincts. She felt deeply sorry for the young girl, who looked as if she should have still been living at home, being looked after by her own mother. The boys who were now two and three, loved visiting the house next door because it felt safe and warm. Ursula would spoil them with strawberry milkshake and homemade cookies, always making sure there were a few extras for them to take home with them. Ursula quickly became a mother figure to Hannah. She was someone whom the young woman could trust and confide in, and someone who wasn't part of Philip's family. Although Hannah got on very well with her in-laws, she was always a little guarded about what she would tell them about Philip. With Ursula, she could really open up about her worries, and the two women, quickly, became close friends.

Ursula would tell Hannah stories from her childhood in Germany. She had been born just two years before the Second World War had begun.

Hannah found the stories of what life was like for a child growing up in Germany during the war years deeply interesting. Ursula had told her how her parents had been Jewish sympathisers, but that they had been too terrified of the Nazis to help their Jewish neighbours. Ursula spoke of the anguish she had felt for them, even though she had been a small child at the time.

She told Hannah about the wealthy couple who owned the jewellery store in the small town, where she had grown up, and how they had been rounded up with their teenage daughters and young son, by the German soldiers, along with the local butcher, his wife, and their small children. The elderly couple who had lived just a few doors away from Ursula's family home, had been dragged from the house they had shared all their married life.

With her eyes full of tears, Ursula spoke about how many more Jewish families from her local area had been rounded up like cattle, and how brutal the German soldiers had been. How they had kicked and punched men and women, while their children screamed in terror.

The memories still made Ursula cry, even after all these years. She told Hannah that none of the Jewish families had returned, after the war, so she and her parents had concluded, that they had all perished in the death camps.

Hannah had only ever listened to her parents' childhood memories of the war years. Getting a first-hand account from someone who had been a child on the opposing side during that time, gave her an incredible insight into the sufferings they had endured too.

At least Hannah's parents had not had to watch their neighbours and their children being dragged from their homes, beaten, and sometimes murdered right in front of their eyes.

Ursula also spoke of how she had loved Dieter for as far back as she could remember. At school, all the girls had liked him, and Hannah could see why. He was well over six feet tall, with a full head of blonde hair, and piercing blue eyes. He had particularly good bone structure, and Hannah could see how he would have slotted straight into the Aryan master race that Adolf Hitler had wanted to rule the world at that time.

Ursula was still an attractive woman, although a little overweight. But with her pretty face, chestnut brown hair, and brown eyes, she could still turn heads.

Over the last couple of days, Ursula and Dieter had agonised over something they had seen at the weekend. After talking it through over a couple of days, they had decided that Hannah had a right to know that Philip was cheating on her.

Ursula had invited Hannah round to hers to break the news as gently as she could, hating the fact that she was going to be the one to do it. It was made worse, because Hannah had confided in Ursula just the week before that her period was late, and she feared she was pregnant.

As Ursula carried the tray of drinks and snacks from the kitchen into the living room, she asked Hannah. "Has your period come yet?"

"No. I must be pregnant, it's the only time I'm ever late." She sighed.

Ursula sat down in the armchair next to where Hannah was sitting. She was hoping, with all her heart that Hannah was not pregnant. since she was just about to have her heart broken.

She spoke kindly and gently, "Hannah, I need to talk to you about something that Dieter and I saw at the weekend." She paused briefly before carrying on, as Hannah gave her a quizzical look. "We were in a pub in town on Sunday evening, and Philip was in there with a young woman. She was just a bit older than you, I would say." She watched the expression on Hannah's face change.

"Are you sure that they were together? I mean, he could have just been talking to her."

Ursula shook her head and continued, "No, Hannah, they were together all evening. He had his arm around her, and they were kissing one another... I'm so sorry to be the one to tell you this."

Hannah clutched at her chest as tears streamed down her face.

Ursula passed her several tissues from the box that was on the coffee table. "You know that we are here for you, don't you?" she told Hannah as she held her hand. Hannah nodded. She didn't like Philip at times, but she believed she still loved him.

He had put her through so much, but she never imagined for a minute, that he would be unfaithful. Now her future was beginning to look very bleak, especially if she was expecting another baby.

It was as if Ursula had read her mind. "You might not be pregnant, and if you are, you don't have to go through with it."

Hannah shook her head, she was a Christian, and a termination was out of the question.

The boys were becoming upset at seeing their mother cry. They stopped playing with the toys that Ursula kept at her house for them. Ethan climbed onto his mother's knee, while Harrison squeezed into the armchair next to her.

Hannah tried to pull herself together for their sakes. She took several, slow, deep breaths, to get her emotions under control. An hour later, she thanked Ursula for her hospitality, and took the boy's home.

"You must let us know if you need anything, no matter what time of day or night it is."

Hannah nodded as tears filled her eyes once more.

She stayed busy for the rest of the afternoon, before giving the boys their tea. She then got them into bed. Everything was done on automatic pilot, while Hannah, tried to cope with the devastation of what she had been told that afternoon.

Her heart was filled with a pain, that was so overwhelming, she felt sure she would not be able to bear it.

Once the boys were in bed, she sat herself down in the armchair next to the living room window and allowed the tears to come.

It was late in the evening when Hannah finally dried her eyes. Even though her head was throbbing, she decided to wait up for Philip and confront him about what she had been told.

He came through the door at ten minutes to midnight. He stopped dead when he saw that Hannah was still up. It was obvious to him that she had been crying.

At first, he thought that someone might have died, so without moving from the spot where he was standing, he asked, "What's wrong? Why have you been crying?"

"I know about your affair," she said firmly as she stood up and looked him straight in the eye.

At first, he pretended to be shocked. "Who's told you that?" he asked incredulously

"Is it true?" she asked calmly.

He did not answer.

"IS IT TRUE?" she yelled, too angry to worry about getting a slap.

A cruel smirk appeared on Philip's face. "So, what, if it is, you bore me. Look at you, you pathetic little tart!"

Hannah's face, reddened, as she glared, at her husband. She became consumed with a rage that she had never felt before. "How dare you call me a tart, when you are the one who is having an affair. YOU PIECE OF SCUM!" she screamed through her tears. "I want you to leave now, and if you don't, I will kill you, when you go to sleep." She finished her sentence in a voice that was heavy with emotion.

She watched Philip lunge towards her, and seconds later, she took the full weight of the blow to the side of her head. It knocked her across the chair she had been standing next to. Philip grabbed his jacket from the back of the settee and stormed out of the house, while Hannah wept uncontrollably.

She heard his taxi roar away a minute later. Five minutes after that, there was a tap on the living room window. Hannah was relieved to see Dieter and Ursula standing there, both in their dressing gowns. They had been woken by the taxi driver roaring his engine loudly as he sped away.

Ursula wanted to make sure that Hannah was all right and had got Dieter to go with her to check on the young woman.

Hannah opened the front door to let them in. When Ursula saw the state that her young friend was in, she rushed forward and put her arms around Hannah. "My poor dear," she said. "Dieter, go next door, and bring the bottle of sherry, please."

She took Hannah back into the living room and sat her down on the settee.

Hannah looked a wreck. Her eyes were red and swollen. Her head was sore from where Philip had hit her, and she still had the terrible headache, from earlier.

Dieter was back in less than ten minutes. Hannah noticed that he had got dressed. He poured each of them a glass of sherry, and as Hannah drank the warm sweet liquid, she began to settle.

"He called me a tart when he is the one that is cheating on me!" she told them tearfully. "I'm sorry, I can't stop crying."

Dieter leaned across and put his hand on the back of hers. "You've had a shock. Your husband is cheating on you, so naturally, you are terribly upset."

Ursula was nodding as her husband spoke. "He is no good, and you deserve better," she told Hannah, firmly.

The three of them talked for over an hour while they polished off the bottle of sherry between them.

It had calmed Hannah down quite a bit, and after her two neighbours left, she took herself to bed. She was exhausted from all the crying she had done that day, and so she quickly fell into a deep sleep.

She woke the next morning to the sound of the boys playing in their bedroom. All she wanted to do was pull the covers over her head and stay where she was for the rest of the day. Hannah forced herself out of bed and went into them.

"Mummy, why were you shouting at Daddy last night?" Harrison asked, his face full of concern.

"Mummy was a bit upset with him, that's all. Nothing for you to worry about."

"But you were crying. Did Daddy hurt you again?" Hannah's heart went out to him… A three-year-old should never have to worry about his mother, she told herself.

Ethan had wrapped his chubby arms around her legs, and had his face turned up towards hers. She bent down and picked him up.

"I'm fine, boys… Now, let's get you too washed and dressed and then we'll have some breakfast."

She tried to sound cheerful, but the pain in her heart was, unbearable, as she struggled not to cry in front of her children.

Hannah was too depressed to get washed and dressed, and so she stayed in her pyjamas until mid-morning.

She could not eat, in fact, she hadn't eaten since before finding out about the affair.

She drank a large cup of coffee, and while the boys played with their cars on the kitchen floor, she decided to ring Alice.

"Hello," she heard Alice say in her best telephone voice.

"It's Hannah. Have you seen or heard anything from Philip?"

"No, I haven't. Why are you asking me about Philip?

"He's been having an affair, Alice. We rowed about it when he got in from work, and he stormed out of the house. I wondered if he had gone to yours?" Hannah began to cry again. "He must be with her," she told Alice as she wept into the telephone.

"You don't know that he might have slept on a park bench for all you know... I hope he's all right." Alice sounded worried.

"Alice, have you not heard what I have just told you? He's been sleeping with another woman. Don't you care about what he has done to your grandchildren and me?"

"Have you been letting him have what a man wants, Hannah?" Alice asked, ignoring Hannah's question.

"WHAT?" Hannah was stunned at the implication. She instantly put the phone down on her mother-in-law and flopped down onto the settee. She put her head in her hands. She had developed another bad headache.

Alice had appeared not to care about what Philip had done to her and had even implied that it might be Hannah's fault that he was cheating on her.

Meanwhile, Alice had phoned Frank's work, after Hannah had hung up on her, and had asked if he could come home due to a family emergency.

Frank came flying through the door thirty minutes later, wondering what on earth could have happened to make Alice call for him to be sent home. When Alice told him about Hannah's call, he shook his head.

"I could knock his head off. What a selfish toe rag! Frank raged. He thought the world of Hannah, and unlike Alice, he could feel her pain.

"She put the phone down on me!" declared Alice angrily.

"Who's she, the cat's mother?" Frank threw back at her.

"You know who I'm talking about!" Alice shouted back, her cheeks turning red with anger.

"Yes, and let's remember who the victim is here, and it's not your bloody Philip!"

Alice knew that getting into a row with Frank was not going to help the situation. She continued in a softer tone. "Ring Hannah and tell her that we are coming over."

Hannah was just answering the door to Ursula when she heard the phone ring. She left her neighbour in the hallway while she took the call. Part of her was hoping it was Philip.

"Hello Hannah, it's Frank. I'm at home with Alice, and she's told me all about what's been going on. We'd like to call over just to provide a bit of moral support. That's if you don't mind?"

"That would be nice, Frank," she told him.

Despite what Alice had implied earlier, she knew Frank and Alice would want to help her. Frank was the one person in the family that she could always rely on to see her side of any situation.

She went back into the hallway to explain to Ursula that Philip's parents were on their way over.

"That's okay. I just wanted to make sure that you are all right."

"Can I come to yours this afternoon once they've left? I don't want to be on my own today."

"Of course, I'll be in all afternoon. Come around once Frank and Alice have gone. You and the boys are very welcome to stay and have dinner with us this evening." She gave Hannah a hug before heading back next door to her own house.

When Frank got off the telephone, he saw that Alice already had her coat and shoes on. "That lass is in bits over there, and all you can think about is him," he snapped.

It was obvious that Frank was seething over what Philip had done to Hannah, so Alice kept her mouth shut. They travelled to Hannah's house in silence. Frank could not believe how cruel Philip could be to his young wife. He believed that Philip had found someone special in Hannah, and he also believed she was far too good for him.

When Frank had got together with Alice, he had found Philip a difficult child. Despite being only three years old at the time, Philip appeared to have a spiteful nature. His older brother by two years had been a much nicer child, and Frank had found it hard not to show favouritism towards James. When his own children came along, Frank had kept an eye on Philip, knowing how spiteful he could be.

When they arrived at Hannah's house, Alice went rushing in like a bull in a China shop, and within less than five minutes, the boys knew that their father had left them. But they were too young to understand what it all meant. They were more concerned as to why Mummy and Nanna were both crying.

Frank did his best to distract them both while keeping an eye on Alice, to make sure she didn't upset Hannah more than she already had done.

A couple of hours later, Alice said that she wanted to get home, just in case Philip had tried to get in touch. Frank rolled his eyes and tutted.

As they were about to leave, he turned to Hannah and told her, "Ring us at any time, if you need us. Even if it's the middle of the night." He squeezed a ten-pound note into her hand and kissed her cheek before leaving with Alice.

After they had driven off, Hannah grabbed both boys and fled to Ursula's. Alice had completely drained her, and she did not want to be on her own with only two small boys for company.

Ursula cooked them a beautiful meal that evening, but Hannah could hardly eat anything. Every mouthful seemed to get stuck in her throat. Both Dieter and Ursula told her they understood and told her she was not to worry about it.

"But you must try to eat something," Ursula told her. "Try eating little and often, until you are feeling better. You need to keep your strength up to look after your little boys."

Hannah struggled to get through the next couple of days. She had to force herself to do even the smallest of tasks. She had no idea where her husband was, and he, hadn't let any of his family know where he was either.

Alice had rung the taxi firm that Philip worked for and had left a message for him to ring his mother, but he had not.

Hannah could not stop herself from imagining him and the other woman getting up to all sorts together.

Although she had lots of support from Philip's family and her neighbours, no one could take her pain away. At times she could barely breathe, so great was her grief and her mental turmoil.

Three days after Philip had stormed out of the house, and while Hannah was in the kitchen making herself a cup of coffee, he walked through the back door. The boys had been in bed for just over an hour. Hannah stood frozen while her heart hammered in her chest.

"Well," He asked, "have you calmed down yet?"

She was speechless, to begin with, he had been the last person she had expected to see that evening.

"It was nothing really." He had the cheek to tell Hannah. "I've told her it's over, and that you're the one I really want." He shrugged his shoulders as he finished speaking.

Hannah finally found her voice. She spoke quietly, but firmly. "You have broken my heart Philip, and now you expect to just walk back in here like nothing ever happened. You've been having sex with someone else... How do you think that makes me feel? How would you feel if it were the other way round? You called me a tart — me — your wife, who has never been with anyone other than you!"

She was trembling with emotion, and Philip was at a loss of what to say next.

He had used the other woman for a bit of fun, that was all, nothing more. She meant nothing to him. Standing here in front of him was the woman he loved.

He had known that he was not in love with Hannah when he had married her, but he realised now, that somewhere along the way, he had grown to love her, despite his cruel treatment towards her.

She was no longer the dumb kid that he once believed he had married. She was now a young woman with a mind of her own.

Hannah knew she couldn't force him to leave, and there was a part of her that was desperate to have him back, despite everything. They stood together in the kitchen in silence for a couple of minutes. Philip was the first to speak.

"I've been a fool... I don't want her, I want you. I love you, and I'm sorry."

It was the first time that he had ever told her he loved her. After all that he had put her through, him having an affair was the worst, and now he was telling her he loved her.

She wished that he was saying those three little words under different circumstances, then they might have had real meaning. Right now, she wasn't sure whether she believed him. Was he just saying it so that she would have him back?

Philip walked towards her and put both hands on her shoulders. Hannah moved away from him, but he followed her and took her face in his hands. "Come on, Hannah, let me make it up to you. It won't happen again. I promise you, it won't."

She pulled away from him again, the pain in her eyes, visible.

She walked out of the kitchen and towards the living room, but he caught her arm and pulled her gently but firmly up close to him. She looked up into his face and asked, "How can I trust that you're not still seeing her? In fact, how can I ever trust you again?"

"I will swear on the Holy bible if you want me to. I am not still seeing her!"

He bent down and kissed her more tenderly than he had ever done before. She didn't push him this time, but she sighed heavily. She still wanted him. In her young mind, she still lived with the hope that one day Philip would grow up and become a better man.

"I think I'm pregnant," she told him quietly as she wiped the last of her tears away.

"Even more reason for us to make a go of things," he told her, with a beaming smile.

Chapter Six
February 1980

Philip had been enticed by one of his cronies to take a job in Germany as a bricklayer, just a couple of months after he and Hannah had got back together, with the promise of earning double of what he could earn in the UK. Hannah was now towards the back end of her third pregnancy. The baby was due the first week in April, and it was now late February.

Philip had started his new job at the beginning of October. The pay was good, and although he was sending Hannah a decent amount each week, he earned a lot more than he had let on to her.

But because, Hannah now had enough money to pay all the bills and put food on the table, with even a little left over for new winter shoes and coats for herself and the boys, she was content with that.

The fact that she had not had to scrape together a few coppers, just to put a basic meal on the table for months, was a huge relief to her.

Her main worry was whether Philip would remain faithful to her. He would only be home for two weeks every three months, and so, Hannah, worried, that he would be tempted to stray. And despite everything he had put her through, she was missing him.

He had been home for two weeks over Christmas, and because they had more money than they had been used to, they had had a really nice time. They had spent Christmas day with Philip's family, as always, and the children had had a ball.

Just before Christmas, Hannah had received a card with fifty pounds inside it from her parents through the post. She knew the money had come from her father, not her mother.

There had been no invitation for Hannah, Philip, and the children to visit them over the holidays and no mention of her parents travelling to see her

After Christmas, Philip left to go back to Germany. Hannah had had an overwhelming feeling of melancholy. She felt the amount of time they were apart was too long, and because she knew that her husband had a large appetite for sex, she was sure he would not remain faithful to her.

Philip had not hit her since the night that she had confronted him about his affair.

The pregnancy had been confirmed a month after they had got back together, and although, Hannah, had not wanted another baby, Philip had seemed genuinely pleased by the news. He had taken the job in Germany a month later, meaning they had only spent two weeks together since October.

Hannah was practically bringing up her children alone. Still, at least she wasn't constantly worrying about putting food on the table, or how the rent and the bills were going to get paid. Nor did she have to put up with Philip's controlling behaviour.

When Philip was away, she had the freedom to see her friends and his family during the day. But, because she believed she still loved him, the weeks that he was away seemed to drag on and on.

It had been arranged that if she went into labour while Philip was in Germany, Hannah would ring Alice, and she and Frank would look after the boys until Philip could get back. Dieter and Ursula were on hand too, for if there were an emergency caused by Hannah's history of premature births.

It was the end of March when Hannah was woken up with a pain in her lower abdomen at two o'clock in the morning. She sat up in bed and looked at the clock. After ten minutes had gone by and no further pains came, she lay back down. Five minutes later, just as she was about to doze off, she had another. She sat up again and waited. Exactly fifteen minutes later, there was another one.

Because the baby was not due for another four weeks, she went downstairs to ring the maternity hospital. She was told that she had better go in.

Hannah rang Alice, who immediately began to fuss. She told Hannah they would be over in less than thirty minutes.

Hannah had already had her hospital bag ready for weeks just in case of a premature birth. She washed and put clean clothes on, before putting her coat, shoes, and hospital bag in the hallway.

Frank was already in the car with the engine running while Alice was dithering about. He got out of the car and called to her. "Come on, Alice, I don't want to end up delivering the baby in the blooming car!"

Alice rolled her eyes and quickly climbed into the passenger side next to him. "Come on then," she snapped, causing Frank to tut and roll his eyes before setting off.

Hannah was very relieved to hear them pull up outside. The contractions were now stronger and more frequent.

Alice went rushing in as if there was some major disaster about to take place. "Now, are you sure you have got everything you need?" Hannah nodded. "Are you absolutely sure?" Alice asked, her eyes darting about as she spoke.

"Yes, Alice, I have." Hannah felt a little exasperated, with Alice. "Help yourself to anything you want. I'll get the hospital to ring you as soon as there's any news." As an afterthought, she told Alice, "Don't ring Philip until tomorrow. I don't want him to be awake half the night when he has got to work on a dangerous building site in the morning."

"All right, I promise, I won't ring him, now go get in the car, Frank's already panicking that you might have it on the way!"

Hannah rolled her eyes at Alice before going out to the car. Frank put Hannah's bag in the boot.

Once Hannah was seated as comfortably as she could, he set off. The maternity hospital was a thirty-minute drive away, in the next town, and Frank was nervous in case things began to proceed quickly on the way.

They finally got to the hospital at three-thirty in the morning, much to Frank's relief. They went straight to the labour ward, where they were met by a softly spoken midwife. She showed them to a little side room and told Hannah to get as comfortable as she could. She turned to Frank, "And you are?"

Frank cleared his throat. "The grandfather." Looking a little embarrassed, he told the midwife, "I can't stay, I need to get back to my wife and grandchildren."

Hannah was mortified! How could he be anything else but the grandfather! Frank was only forty-seven, but to the twenty-year-old Hannah, he was nearly an old man.

"I hope it won't be too long for you, love. Get the hospital to let us know as soon as there is any news." He kissed Hannah on top of her head, before leaving her alone with the midwife.

At six o'clock in the morning, Sophie was born, weighing a healthy six pounds. She was handed straight to her mother by a beaming Sister Chadwick. "You have a beautiful little girl, Hannah."

Hannah was delighted, a little girl now made her family complete. She studied her little girls face, before taking hold of one of her tiny hands. Sophie, immediately, gripped her mother's finger.

She was so like her brothers, having the same full head of dark hair and olive skin, that they had both had, as new-borns.

Harrison still had honey blonde hair, but Ethan's hair had turned almost platinum blonde, the colour that his mothers had been as a child, except he had huge brown eyes, instead of her blue ones. Hannah was told that because the baby was a good weight, she would be able to go to the ward with her.

The midwife rang Alice, who had been dozing on and off in the armchair all night, while Frank had snored his head off on the settee. On hearing the phone ring, he was suddenly wide awake.

"Congratulations, you have a beautiful granddaughter. They are both absolutely fine and should be going up to the ward very shortly."

"A girl. How wonderful! Is she a good weight?" Alice asked while Frank listened, as he rubbed the sleep from his eyes.

"Six pounds, a good weight for her dates." Remarked the midwife.

It was now twenty past six, so Alice decided to ring Philip with the good news.

"Philip, you have a daughter. She was born twenty minutes ago, weighing six pounds." Alice gushed down the telephone.

"Why didn't anyone let me know that Hannah had gone into labour?" he snapped.

"Hannah didn't want you to be awake half the night because you have to go to work today… aren't you delighted at the news, Philip?"

"Yes, it's great news. How long was she in labour?"

Alice could sense that he was really annoyed that he had been told about his daughter's birth after his mother and Frank. "Only about three and a half hours, I think. When can you get back?"

"I don't know, I need to speak to my manager. Let Hannah know that I will ring the ward, at six o'clock this evening."

Alice could hear the boys moving about upstairs, so she hurried up to give them the news. They were both excited and wanted to go see their baby sister straight away.

"Oh, you'll have to wait until this afternoon. We're not allowed to visit this early." Alice told them both.

"Aww, that's not fair!" Harrison protested, while Ethan sat on the floor with his arms folded, looking really cross, at not being able to go and see his sister straight away.

The sight of him made his nanna want to laugh, but she held it in and kept her face straight.

Later that afternoon, Frank and Alice took the boys to visit their mum and Sophie. They were both beside themselves with excitement and so was Alice!

She went rushing over to the cot where Sophie lay sleeping, leaving Frank with both boys. "Oh, she is so beautiful, Hannah. She looks just like the boys did when they had just been born, except you can tell she's a girl," she added proudly.

Frank and the boys had caught up, and as Harrison peeked inside the cot at Sophie. Frank had to lift Ethan up to see her. "She's a little beauty, Hannah," Frank told her, smiling broadly.

"She's very small, Mummy," Harrison announced.

"Oh, you were much smaller than Sophie when you were born, and so was Ethan," Alice told him.

Ethan had climbed onto the bed, where he sat cuddled up to his mother. Harrison climbed onto the other side of the bed, and snuggled up to her. The boys weren't used to their mother not being in the house, and they had both missed her.

"Mummy, how did the baby get out of your tummy?" Harrison asked, with a serious expression.

"The doctor got her out," Hannah told him, hoping that that would satisfy his curiosity.

"But how did he?" he asked again while Ethan sat, listening, eyes wide.

Frank cleared his throat as he always did when feeling awkward. "Nanna will tell you later," he told his grandson.

Hannah wanted to laugh when she saw Alice's face.

"Thanks for that, Frank!" she told him, while looking anything but amused.

"Before I forget Hannah, Philip is going to ring the ward to have a little chat with you at six o'clock our time. He's pleased with the news, and he will speak to his manager today, about getting home a little sooner than planned. He was a bit annoyed that we hadn't told him that you had gone into labour."

Frank shook his head at Alice, while Hannah simply said, "Philip gets annoyed at everything!"

Alice raised her eyebrows and threw Frank one of her looks. Hannah asked Alice if she would ring her parents once they were back at her house, to let them know that she had had the baby. Alice nodded. She always felt annoyed whenever Hannah's family were mentioned, mainly due to their lack of interest in Hannah, and their grandchildren. Alice was a doting grandmother, and she could not understand Sue's indifference. Alice never voiced her opinion in front of Hannah, but she and Frank discussed it often. Hannah, however, was used to her mother's lack of interest, and generally took it in her stride these days.

At six o'clock, Philip rang the ward just as the patients were finishing their evening Meal. Hannah was told that they could have five minutes, otherwise, Philip would have to ring the payphone down the corridor. Hannah told Philip what the nurse had said. He told her five minutes would be enough.

"How are you both?" he asked.

"Really good. I can't wait for you to see her, she's so beautiful!"

"Hannah, I can't get back for another two and a half weeks."

"Why not?" she said, her face dropping with disbelief and disappointment

"I've been told that if I come home now, they will dock my pay, and I'll have to pay for my own flight. We can't afford it!"

His words stung. Hannah, felt badly let down by him, as she had so many times in the past.

"We can manage if we pull our belts in. I've got a little bit put to one side, and I'm sure Frank and your mum would help us out."

"No, Hannah, we will lose too much money. I'm coming home for a fortnight in just over two weeks. It really isn't worth it."

"Your daughter isn't worth it? Is that what you're saying?"

"You know that's not what I'm saying. Don't be so unreasonable, Hannah!"

"Me, unreasonable, that's rich coming from you!" She had forgotten that the nurses could hear her side of the conversation.

Philip slammed the phone down on her, leaving her reeling with shock. She gently put the phone down on the receiver.

The two nurses sitting at the nurse's station looked at her sympathetically as tears filled her eyes. She hurried to the toilet, and once inside, she wept for several minutes.

Having pulled herself together before someone came looking for her, Hannah, kept her head down as she went back to her bed. She picked up a magazine to hide her face while she pretended to read it. The young woman in the next bed could see that Hannah had been crying.

"Are you okay, Hannah?" she asked. Hannah nodded her head behind the magazine. "No, you're not all right, what's wrong, love?" the other woman asked kindly.

The other two patients that were in the same bay both looked over. Hannah could not hold her tears back. She threw the magazine on the bed, and sobbed.

The other two patients came over, and as the three of them gathered around her, Hannah explained that her husband would not be able to get back from Germany for another two weeks. She lied, and blamed his boss, not wanting them to know that it was Philip, who had decided not to come home until then.

She knew that the nurses would know the truth because they had heard her side of the conversation and had they had seen her face when Philip had slammed the phone down on her.

Philip had rung his mother and given his side of the story. while exaggerating Hannah's unreasonableness. So, when Alice and Frank had visited her the next day, Alice had scolded Hannah for upsetting Philip the way she had. Hannah had burst into tears because Alice always took Philip's side no matter what. Whereas Frank always took Hannah's.

"Alice, she's just had a baby, for goodness' sake! She's entitled to be upset if Philip can't get home. Think about what you were like with your hormones, after having Alex and Jane."

Alice gave Hannah a half-hearted apology. Hannah continued to cry, causing the other patients and their visitors to look over towards her.

Harrison and Ethan had both became very subdued. Ethan cuddled up to her while Harrison just sat and watched his mother with sadness in his eyes. "Are you coming home soon, Mummy?" he asked after several minutes.

"Yes, darling, hopefully, the day after tomorrow. Come and sit up here with me," she told him. He climbed onto the bed and snuggled up close to her. She kissed the top of his head and put her arm around him.

"Don't be worrying about these two," Frank, reassured Hannah, "we'll look after them for as long as is needed."

"Thanks, Frank. You've both been wonderful," she said, looking from Frank to Alice. She could not fault Alice as a grandmother or as a mother-in-law. It was just that when it came to Philip, she appeared blind to his true nature

The next day, the doctor told Hannah that he was happy enough for her and the baby to be discharged. She rang Alice, who told her she would get Frank to pick them up from the hospital as soon as he had finished his early shift.

Frank arrived to collect them at three-thirty in the afternoon. When he pulled up outside Hannah's house, the door was flung open. The boys were jumping up and down excitedly next to their nanna. Alice ushered Hannah into the house with Sophie. She began to fuss over the two of them so much, that she made Hannah's head spin.

"Give her a chance to catch her breath, Alice," Frank told her. Alice ignored him as she took the baby from Hannah's arms.

Frank made coffee for the three of them, and then he entertained the two boys while Alice continued to fuss.

"Now, Hannah, I have cleaned the house throughout, and I've bought enough groceries to last the week. There is a casserole in the fridge that you just need to heat up... Make sure you rest as much as possible over the next couple of days... I'll come over tomorrow afternoon to give you a hand."

Hannah tried to digest all that Alice was telling her. "Thanks, Alice, you've been wonderful. Let me give you the money for the groceries."

"You certainly will not! If we can't help family, then who can we help?" Alice told her in a strict voice. "Don't be overdoing things when we leave, especially with these two," Alice said, gesturing towards the two boys with her head.

"We'll get going in a minute, give Hannah a chance to get herself settled," Frank told Alice.

She gave him one of her looks. She was enjoying holding the baby and wasn't ready to go home just yet. Frank ignored the look and gestured that it was time to leave as he drained his cup. Alice reluctantly put Sophie down in her Moses basket and put her shoes on.

"Ring us day or night, Hannah, if you need anything at all," said Alice.

After Hannah's in-laws had seen themselves out, she suddenly felt very alone and overwhelmed.

There was a tap at the back door. Ursula had been waiting for Frank and Alice to leave, before popping around to see the baby.

She had crocheted a lovely white shawl for Sophie, and she had bought the two boys a little treat each, which Hannah told them they were not allowed to eat until after tea.

Ursula went over to the Moses basket and peered inside. When she saw Sophie, she was overcome with emotion. "She is beautiful, Hannah... boys, what do you think of your little sister?"

"I love her," Harrison told Ursula with a huge smile.

"Me too," Ethan added, with the biggest smile ever.

"It's so good to see you, Ursula," Hannah told her, with a sigh., "Alice has completely drained me. She fusses far too much… I'm a little bit out of sorts, to be honest."

"Tell me what you need me to do. I'm here to help in any way I can?" Ursula reassured her.

"Alice has done everything. She's even cooked a casserole that I just need to heat up for tea."

"It will keep in the fridge until tomorrow, right?" I will take the boys off your hands for a couple of hours. They can have dinner with Dieter and me, and I'll bring some round for you later, when we bring them back home."

The boys were immediately excited at the thought of having their tea next door. They both went to get their shoes without having to be asked.

"That would be a huge help. Thanks, Ursula."

Ursula thought Hannah looked pale and tired. She was a constant worry to the older woman.

"My pleasure! I will want a little cuddle with this one when I come back later," she told Hannah with a wink.

As Hannah sat alone with her baby, her thoughts turned to Philip. He hadn't bothered to contact her since the day of Sophie's birth. She knew that was his way of punishing her over what she had said to him over the telephone. He was such a brat at times! He was twenty-seven now, and Hannah felt that he should have behaved more maturely over her becoming upset that afternoon.

Although she had only just turned twenty, she knew that she was outgrowing him in many ways, and at times she felt confused as to what her feelings were for him these days. She had forgiven him over his affair, but she would never be able to forget it. The affair had changed her feelings towards him somewhat. At times she loved him desperately, and at other times she disliked him intensely. Today she felt a mixture of both!

She remembered how Philip had been in a hurry to get her into bed the night he had gone back to her. Still, all she had been able to think about was that he had been doing the same thing with someone else, perhaps only a few days earlier.

The thought of it had caused silent tears to run down her face as he had made love to her, and Philip had been too busy enjoying himself to notice.

She had been devastated at the pregnancy test results, and now she felt riddled with guilt as she looked at her baby girl.

The telephone rang, interrupting her thoughts, and making her jump. It was Philip.

"Hello, Hannah, I've not been able to get to the telephone until today. Mum's been on the phone to let me know that you're back home. How are you both?"

Hannah knew he was lying about not being able to use the phone, until today. Philip told so many lies, that Hannah believed that he sometimes didn't know himself, whether he was lying or telling the truth.

"I'm okay," she answered in a cool tone.

"You do understand the situation, don't you? If I could be there, then I would be."

"I'm sure that you would be here if you really wanted to be."

"Aww, Hannah, for goodness' sake, be an adult!"

Ignoring his comment, she told him. "Sophie's fine. Ursula has taken the boys to hers for their tea, so that I can get myself organised." Her tone was still cool, but civil.

"I'll be back two weeks on Saturday. I'll get my mum to babysit, and I'll take you out somewhere nice. It will be really nice to have some time on our own, just you and me."

She knew he was soft-soaping her. "That sounds really nice," she replied, but Hannah wore her heart on her sleeve and was unable to hide how she was truly feeling.

"You don't sound good."

"It's just my hormones, that's all."

Instead of staying on the phone to give Hannah support and reassurance, Philip told her that he needed to go because someone else was waiting to use the telephone. He had taken note of the icy tone to Hannah's voice at the beginning of their conversation, and it stuck with him for the rest of the evening, so, he made a point of ringing her the following two evenings to soften her up.

She did soften towards him in the end. She even asked herself if she had been too unreasonable, in expecting him to lose two weeks' wages to get home to see Sophie, but deep down, she didn't think she had been.

Hannah could not shake herself out of her present mood. She had felt anxious and tearful over the last twenty-four hours, and now, she was worried as to how she was going to cope over the next few days, if she continued to feel the way she was just now.

A lot of it had to do with Philip. They should have been sharing the excitement of the birth of their first daughter together. Instead, he was in another country, behaving like a single man, and getting up to goodness knows what, while she shouldered all the responsibility of the home and the children.

The years of abuse, along with disappointment after disappointment, were taking their toll on Hannah's emotional wellbeing. It was her children who kept her going each day, along with support from her friends next door, and Philip's family. But it was Philip's love and support she had yearned for since marrying him. She had begun to realise more and more, that she would probably, never have it!

Dieter and Ursula came back at six-thirty with the boys, who had both been spoilt rotten by Dieter, who was looking forward to seeing the new addition to Hannah's family.

"Mummy, can Uncle Dieter get us ready for bed and then read us a story... please?" Harrison begged.

"Pease, Mummy." Ethan echoed. He still couldn't pronounce his L's.

"That sounds like a good idea, don't you think, Hannah?" Ursula suggested. You will be able to eat your meal in peace, while I have a little cuddle with the baby."

Hannah smiled and nodded.

"Yeah!" The boys cheered as Dieter chased the two of them up the stairs, causing them to shriek with laughter.

Ursula could tell that Hannah had been crying, so she asked, "Are you all right, my dear?"

"Just the baby blues. I'll eat later if you don't mind?"

"Of course. May I have a little hold of the baby?"

"Yes, of course you can. She's due a feed soon. You can feed her if you like."

"I would love to… Now, what is really the matter, Hannah? I know that you don't cry over nothing."

Hannah poured everything out to Ursula, including the conversation she had had with Philip on the day Sophie had been born.

"Of course," Hannah, told her, "Alice had taken his side as usual."

Ursula listened and as she did, she shook her head. Hannah felt better for getting everything off her chest.

Dieter came down after tucking the boys into bed.

Ursula was only just finishing feeding Sophie. Dieter smiled at his wife, but at the same time, his heart ached for her. She would have loved a child of her own, and so, at that moment Dieter felt a deep sadness, that it was now too late and that it would never happen for them.

Hannah left them both with Sophie while she went to say goodnight to her boys.

Dieter was holding Sophie when Hannah came back downstairs. He looked scared to death, fearing that he might drop her at any second.

The look on his face made both Hannah and Ursula laugh. Ursula took Sophie from him and settled her back down in the Moses basket. She told Hannah, "We will go now, but please ask if you need any help."

After closing the door, Hannah ate half of the meal her neighbour had cooked for her.

The telephone rang just as she had decided to get an early night. It was Gill, her sister-in-law. Gill was married to Philip's older brother James. She had called to say that they would call round after tea the following day to see the baby.

Hannah found Gill a bit of a busybody and could have done without having to entertain her the following day.

Philip's brother James was the only person who Philip looked up to. He was nothing like his younger brother, neither in looks or personality. James was a gentle giant. He was blonde and blue-eyed, whereas Philip was dark with brown eyes.

Philip disliked Gill with a passion, and she disliked him in equal measure.

They arrived the following day just as Hannah was clearing the dishes away from tea.

Hannah was very tired, having been woken several times during the night by the baby, and could have done without Gill's company. Gill walked straight over to the Moses basket and lifted the sleeping baby out, without even asking Hannah if it was all right to do so. It made Hannah bristle.

The boys jumped up at James, who picked one up in each arm. They loved their uncle. He was funny and great fun to be around. He would play fight with them and tickle them both into submission.

He was not like their father, who could turn nasty halfway through playing with them.

Hannah made a tray of drinks and took it through to the living room. James had sat down in one of the armchairs, and the boys had squeezed in either side of him, making Hannah smile.

They had bought Sophie a beautiful lemon dress that would hopefully fit her in the summer, and they had brought treats for the boys.

Hannah handed each of them a cup of coffee and offered the biscuits round.

"When's his lordship going to show his face?" Gill asked with a sniff. Hannah went red in the face, having been caught off guard.

"Gill let's talk about something else," James suggested. He could see by the look on Hannah's face that she did not want to discuss Philip.

"I see Alice is making excuses for him, as usual," Gill said, ignoring James.

"For goodness' sake, Gill, just drop it!" James told her.

Hannah felt tearful, so she excused herself and went into the kitchen to try to get her emotions under control, but she found she could not

"Don't bring the subject up again, Gill," James warned his wife. He knew what his brother was, and he knew Hannah could have done a lot better for herself.

She was still very young, and James, like Frank, hoped that his selfish younger brother would not succeed in destroying her.

When Hannah had not returned after several minutes, James told Gill and the boys to stay where they were while he went into the kitchen to see her. She was, using the tea towel to wipe her eyes.

"What's wrong, Hannah?" James asked gently, putting his hand on her shoulder. Hannah could not look at him because she was embarrassed that he had found her crying.

"It's just my hormones. I'll be all right in a minute or two."

"Are you sure that's all it is?" he asked empathetically.

"Yes, honestly." Hannah tried to force a smile on her face.

"We'll come over on Saturday and take Harrison and Ethan out for the day if you don't mind, that is? It will give you a bit of a break."

"They will love that, James. Thank you"

He looked at her with fondness, "We'll go and leave you in peace," he told her kindly

"You don't have to leave, have your coffee first."

"No, we'll get off and we'll see you on Saturday. You might feel more like having company by then."

He put his arms around her in a brotherly manner and held her for a couple of minutes.

It felt good to be held in the arms of a man, not that Hannah had any improper thoughts towards James. She just really needed to be held and having James' arms around her for just a minute or two was really comforting.

As usual, Philip was not there to provide what she so desperately needed.

After they had left, Hannah got herself and the boys ready for bed. She was so exhausted, that she decided to take herself to bed as soon as Sophie had finished her feed.

As she lay in bed, she thought about her reaction to James's hug earlier, but she quickly put it down to her hormones, and dismissed it from her mind.

Two weeks later, Philip arrived home. He found Hannah a little distant, something about her had changed. He tried to be on his best behaviour, but then he had had a couple of tantrums when he felt he was not getting enough of his wife's attention.

So much of her time was taken up caring for the three children, and it never entered Philip's head that if he were to help her with them, she might have had more time for their relationship.

Philip felt Hannah was slipping away from him, and so, he had even considered staying in England and finding another job. But the thought of losing a really good wage and all the freedom he had, while Hannah shouldered all the responsibility of the children, was too much for him to give up.

He was used to doing what he liked, when he liked, and with whom he liked. He wanted the best of both worlds. He enjoyed his one-night stands on a Saturday night, knowing that Hannah would never find out, but he also wanted Hannah waiting for him at home. He didn't want to give up either of his two worlds, so he went back to Germany as soon as the two weeks were up.

Hannah had mixed feelings about Philip returning to Germany. She felt that she was losing him, and she was worried that eventually he would meet someone new She felt something between them was changing, and she believed their marriage would not survive the continuous distance between them.

What Hannah would come to realise several weeks later, was that it was, she who was changing. She had been mostly independent for several months, and emotionally she had begun to move on.

The realisation brought its own sadness, for how she had once loved him!

Little by little, Philip's bullying, along with his total selfishness, had chipped away at her feelings, and now, Hannah felt she had nothing left to give. Still, despite everything that she had been through with Philip, the realisation, brought its own feeling of loss.

Chapter Seven
1981

Sophie was now a year old and had just learnt to walk. Harrison was almost five and had started school the September just gone. Ethan would be four that coming July and would be joining his brother in the local primary school that coming September. Hannah had made friends with a woman called Debbie, who lived just around the corner from her. They had got into conversation several times while walking to and from school with their children and had become close friends. They would often go to a local coffee shop after dropping their children off at school. Ethan went to the school's preschool class each morning until lunchtime, so Hannah made the best of the mornings when she only had Sophie to look after. Debbie was a few years older than Hannah, but the two women had similar interests and could spend up to a couple of hours talking about all kinds of things. Debbie had a great sense of humour, and she brought a lot of laughter into Hannah's life. She would sometimes invite Hannah's boys to hers after school to play and have tea with her children, who were just a little older than Harrison and Ethan.

Hannah found that she was getting used to life without Philip more and more. She was her own person when he was away, and so, she was finding it harder to tolerate him when he was home. The last time he had been home, he had slapped her hard across her face one afternoon after accusing her of having an affair. The accusation was ridiculous! She never went out without at least one of the children with her. The only people she saw were Ursula, Dieter, Debbie, and Philip's family.

It had happened because Philip had sensed that Hannah was different towards him these days, and to his mind, the only explanation was that she must be seeing someone behind his back.

The simple truth was that she had stopped loving him. And now, whenever he was home, it felt like he was intruding on her and the children's space. She didn't want him there, and she had been glad when the time came for him to leave.

The bombshell came several months later. It was September, the first day of the new school year. Ethan had been overcome with excitement that morning because he was starting proper school for the first time. Hannah and Debbie had doubled up with laughter as he had tried to hurry everyone in his eagerness to get to school. Ethan had a very intense nature for such a little boy. He was very much a child that was driven by his emotions.

After, leaving the boys at school, Hannah had gone straight home because Debbie had an appointment with her GP.

She had been in the house less than five minutes when she had received a call from Philip to tell her that he had been sacked and sent off-site, having been accused of being drunk.

Of course, he had told her that it wasn't true, but Hannah knew him and believed that if he had been accused of being drunk, then he most likely had been.

She imagined that he had probably been drinking well into the early hours and had not had long enough to sober up before starting work the morning after.

It felt like the bottom had dropped out of her world! She flopped into a chair with the telephone in her hand.

They were going to lose a good income, and Philip would be back home for good. She put the phone back down and sat with her face in her hands, trying to absorb the shock of what was happening.

Philip was going to be back that evening. He had managed to get a cheap flight home, and he would be back just after tea.

Hannah knew what Philip was like when money was short, and so, she was all at once filled with a dread that she had not felt for a long time. She picked Sophie up and went next door to Ursula, who on seeing the stricken look on Hannah's face, knew straight away that something was very wrong. She swept Hannah and Sophie inside.

Hannah took a seat, in the familiar room, that always smelt of furniture polish and coffee. "I don't want him at home all the time,"

Hannah told her friend. "He'll be in a right mood when he gets home, and I know he'll take it out on me."

"When are you expecting him back?"

"This evening, around six." Hannah's insides were churning as Ursula handed her a cup of coffee.

Sophie was busy playing with the toys that Ursula had emptied onto the floor for her.

"I've got so used to life without him, and I'm so used to not being constantly under his control. I hate his dark moods and his nasty temper. And I don't love him any more, Ursula."

Ursula wasn't surprised, she had watched Hannah, blossom, over the last eighteen months. Her confidence had grown too. She had realised the last time Philip was home, that Hannah's feelings towards her husband had changed, by the way she had spoken about, her being glad when the time came for him to leave again.

"You need to tell him to find himself somewhere else to live." Ursula told Hannah firmly.

Hannah's eyes widened, and she gave a half laugh, as she looked at her neighbour as if she had gone out of her mind. "I can't tell him that! You know what he's like. He'll beat me to a pulp if I tell him to leave!"

"You cannot stay with a man that treats you the way he does just because you are afraid of him. You are young, you still have the rest of your life ahead of you. Hannah: you deserve so much more from life. Speak to a solicitor and get some free advice... please don't waste your life on a man like Philip."

Hannah knew that what Ursula was saying was true.

"Can't you go back to where your family live?" Ursula asked. Hannah shook her head.

"No one would have any room for us. Nor would my mother want us turning up on her doorstep. I've told you what she's like."

Hannah could feel panic beginning to rise inside her. Her chest felt tight, and so did the back of her head. Ursula looked alarmed.

"Are you all right?"

"I think I'm having a panic attack... I've had them before." She took several long deep breaths to try to calm herself down.

Ursula poured Hannah a tumbler full of sherry and handed it to her. "Drink this, it will help." As Hannah gulped a large mouthful, she started to settle. She took another large gulp.

"You will make yourself sick if you drink it like that," Ursula warned her.

Hannah finished the drink, and then said, I need to go and get the house cleaned from top to bottom."

Philip always expected the house to be spotless when he was home.

Although Hannah kept the house clean, she didn't mind if there was a bit of a mess from the children. She told Ursula. "I don't want to give Philip an excuse for having a go, when he gets back."

Ursula tutted, "Leave Sophie with me for the rest of the morning. You go and do what you have to do."

Every time Hannah thought about Philip coming home, she felt sick.

She knew he would be angry over losing his job, and she hoped he would not upset the children once he arrived home.

After finishing her cleaning, she collected Sophie from next door and gave the little girl her lunch before putting her down for her nap. She wondered about how the children would cope with their father being at home permanently. He was practically a stranger to Sophie, and the boys' memory of him being at home all the time would be faded by now.

It was almost two years since Philip had taken the job in Germany, and Hannah knew that she and the children had moved on. She knew too that they all deserved so much better, but how she would ever get the courage to tell Philip that her feelings had changed, and that she would prefer him to live elsewhere?

She decided that she could do nothing about the situation today. She said a silent prayer in her heart for strength and wisdom in dealing with the situation over the coming days.

Debbie was shocked too at the news, that Philip had been sacked and of his imminent return to the UK.

It had been several months into her and Debbie's friendship before Hannah had told her about her marriage problems.

"How are you going to manage?" Debbie asked out of genuine concern.

"I really don't know. But I do know that I don't love him. That died just a few months after having Sophie."

Debbie was slowly shaking her head, "Well, he has only himself to blame for that. I wouldn't treat an animal the way he's treated you over the years!"

Hannah sighed heavily as they approached the school gates. They changed the subject, not wanting anyone to overhear their conversation.

When Hannah got the boys back home, she told them that Daddy was coming home for good. She was surprised that they didn't seem even a little excited at the news, but they both had memories of their father's treatment of their mother, and Philip had become a stranger to them.

As the time ticked away, Hannah became increasingly apprehensive.

She had just cleared the dishes away when she heard his key turn in the lock. She took a deep breath while her insides churned.

She forced a smile on her face as she went into the hallway to greet him. He looked at her with a look of despair as he gave the boys who had both appeared, a hug each. Sophie toddled out of the room, but she clung to her mother's side. She hardly knew her father and so she was shy of him.

Hannah felt genuinely sorry for him when she saw the look on his face.

"Is there anything to eat? I'm starving," he told her. He too, looked as if the bottom had dropped out of his world.

"Yes, I've saved you some tea. I'll just warm it through for you," she said.

"Don't I even get a kiss from my wife?" he asked as he walked towards her.

She forced another smile on her face as he took hold of her and kissed her. It turned her stomach, using the excuse, that the children were in the hall and watching. She said, "Philip, the children," as she pulled away.

Philip followed her into the kitchen and sat at the kitchen table with his head in his hands. "I could kill that bloody site manager," he told her. "He's had it in for me for ages. I wasn't drunk, Hannah. Honestly, I wasn't. Do you believe me?"

Hannah nodded, she knew not to disagree with him, but she did not believe him.

While Philip ate his meal, she got all three children ready and settled into bed for the night a little earlier than usual just in case Philip got into one of his moods, as he often did when things weren't going his way. When she came back downstairs, Philip had his coat and shoes on.

"I'm off to see Jim to see if I can get my old job back."

Hannah was immediately encouraged. If he got another job straight away, they would not be in such dire straits financially, and it would put Philip in a better mood.

She smiled, so as to not give away, her true feelings. "That's a good idea." she told him. Even though she knew that he would most likely stay in the pub all night and drink himself into oblivion!

Hannah took herself to bed once it turned ten.

She had a terrible feeling of hopelessness, over her new set of circumstances. How long would she be able to keep up this pretence? She asked herself.

She hoped that Philip would crash on the settee when he got home, as he often did after drinking all evening.

She was woken by the sound of him coming up the stairs sometime later. Hoping he would go straight to sleep, she lay completely still, pretending to be asleep herself. But Philip had other ideas. He grabbed hold of her and pulled her underneath him. His breath stank of stale beer and cigarette smoke. It turned her stomach so much, she almost gagged. There was no tenderness, no gentleness, as he slammed himself inside her with such force that it caused her to cry out in pain. He had not even tried to arouse her, and neither did he stop when she cried out.

After he had taken what he wanted, he rolled off and turned onto his opposite side, where he fell into a drunken sleep.

Hannah was filled with loathing towards him. She was his wife, and he had just used her as if she were a nothing more than a street walker who he had paid for her services!

The next morning, Philip finally got up at twelve, while Hannah and Sophie were having their lunch together. He set about making tea and toast for himself.

"You, okay?" he asked Hannah, noticing her coldness towards him.

"No, I'm not okay! You really hurt me last night, and I'm sore."

Philip had forgotten about what he had done because of the drink. It all came back to him as soon as Hannah reminded him what he had done to her.

"I'm sorry, I'd had a lot to drink." He came over to the table and kissed the top of his daughter's head. She blinked up at him with the sweetest smile. Hannah did not want to put Philip in a bad mood, so she asked in a much softer tone. "Did you manage to get to speak to Jim last night?"

"Yes. I start back next Thursday. That's good news, isn't it? I won't be earning anywhere near what I was in Germany." His facial expression changed to one of indignation towards the man who had sacked him.

Hannah was just relieved that Philip would soon be back at work. Still, she was afraid that he would be in the pub most days, during the coming week, spending the money that they needed, for other things.

It was obvious that Philip had a drinking problem. He used it as a crutch when things were not going the way he wanted them to.

Hannah told him, "Your mother's going to be over in an hour. She knows that you've lost your job, but I haven't told her that you've been sacked. It's up to you what you tell her."

Philip put his cup down and rolled his eyes, he was not in the mood for his mother today.

Hannah put Sophie down for her afternoon nap just as Alice arrived.

She went straight through to the living room, where Philip was sitting, and smoking a cigarette.

"Philip, what's happened with your job?"

"We've all been made redundant." He lied, straight-faced. Philip was so good at telling lies!

"Oh, just as the two of you had got on your feet," Alice replied, pouting as she always did when showing sympathy to anyone.

Hannah walked back into the living room. After she said hello to her mother-in-law, she looked across at Philip, who quickly told her. "I've just been telling Mum about the redundancies."

Hannah raced her eyebrows and turned back towards Alice, who had just started to say, "Isn't it awful for you both? But it will mean that you'll see a lot more of each other, which will be nice for you all."

Hannah thought to herself, *Will it, indeed?*

"I've managed to get my old job back with the taxi company I used to work for. I start next week."

"Well, there you are then, things are not as bad as you think." Alice beamed as Hannah went into the kitchen to make the three of them a drink. Alice had no idea how much Hannah's life would be affected by Philip's permanent return and that it would not be for the good!

After Alice had left, Hannah left Sophie with her father while she went to collect the boys from school. She met Debbie on the corner of Debbie's street, as usual.

"How's it going?" Debbie enquired.

"He's managed to get his old job back. He went to see his old boss last night," she lowered her voice. "He was very drunk when he got back last night. I pretended to be asleep, but he grabbed hold of me and forced himself on me. He was very rough, and it really hurt." Hannah's eyes filled with tears as she looked at Debbie's horrified expression.

"That is barbaric! No one has the right to do that to you, not even your own husband." Feeling sorry for Hannah, she said, "Come back to mine for a coffee after we pick the kids up."

Hannah shook her head. "No, he'll go mad if I don't get straight back, especially as I've left him looking after Sophie."

"Oh, Hannah!" was all Debbie said in response as she shook her head.

After tea Philip appeared restless and a bit agitated. The truth was that he was used to his freedom, and he felt hemmed in, at home. He told Hannah that he needed to meet Jim later to discuss his hours and rota etc. She knew that he was probably lying because he wanted to get out of the house, but Hannah was used to being on her own most evenings and so, she was happy for him to go. She just hoped that there was not going to be a repeat of last night's performance.

When he got back that night, he did collapse onto the settee, being too drunk to even walk up the stairs. He stayed there until six in the morning. After waking, to use the toilet, he crept upstairs and crawled into bed next to Hannah while she lay sleeping. Again, he stayed in bed until lunchtime.

Hannah had been up for hours. She had dropped the boys off at school and had enjoyed a long chat with Debbie on the street corner. Knowing that Philip would not be up for at least another couple of hours, she had popped into Ursula's to have a quick coffee and a catch up about how things were going with Philip at home.

She told Ursula about the lie he had told his mother and that he had been drinking more than usual since getting back home. She also told Ursula how he had used her on the night of his return.

"You should tell him, NO!" Ursula told Hannah passionately.

"He would kill me if I did that! You know him, he would beat me black and blue, and then take what he wanted anyway."

"No!" Ursula said firmly, becoming quite worked up, "you need to see a solicitor and get some advice. Find out what your rights are. You cannot carry on living like this!"

Hannah decided that it would not hurt to get some advice on her rights if she found that she could no longer go on living with Philip. She rang a local solicitor's office and made an appointment for Friday morning.

Hannah had a plan. She would go to see the solicitor, after she had dropped the boys off at school. Philip would be told that she was going into town to get some shopping. It was arranged that Ursula would meet her outside the solicitor's office and would watch Sophie while Hannah had thirty minutes of free advice.

On the way to pick the children up from school later that day, she told Debbie. "I've got an appointment with a solicitor on Friday morning. Apparently, I can have up to thirty minutes free advice. I just want to find out what my rights are in case things turn really ugly with Philip."

Debbie's face brightened, "You are definitely doing the right thing, Hannah. You need to know what help you will be entitled to, if you need to get Philip out of the house."

"It's terrifying, Debbie! I know he won't go without a fight, and I'm so scared about what he might do to me!"

Putting a hand on Hannah's arm, Debbie looked at her with understanding. She told her, "I know this is going to be really hard for you, but it's something that you will have to go through. It's one of those things that you can't avoid if you are to get to where you want to be. Try not to fret about it until after you've had a chat with the solicitor on Friday."

Hannah nodded, while wishing there was an easier way.

As they strolled home with the children, the two women didn't talk about Hannah's appointment, in case one of the children overheard, but as they parted company, Debbie squeezed Hannah's arm and kissed her cheek. "Good luck," she whispered.

That morning Philip had told Hannah that once he had finished breakfast, he was going to go see his mother. Hannah knew full well that he was going to the pub yet again. She knew all his tricks. Saying that he was going to his mother's was just an excuse for him to get out of the house. She hoped that he would not be drunk when he got back that afternoon. Philip could be violent without a drink, but he was a monster once he had a drink inside of him, especially if he were that way out! He never stopped to think about how his behaviour affected his little family, nor did he seem to care.

In the beginning, Hannah had wanted nothing more than to be loved and treated kindly by him. Now he had three adorable children who only wanted the same, but they too had been very badly let down by Philip over the years. He never stopped to consider that his wife might not put up with his behaviour forever or that she would ever contemplate leaving him. He was far too arrogant to think that.

Hannah arrived back with the children just thirty minutes before Philip. She was standing at the kitchen sink peeling potatoes when she saw him walking up the garden path. Obviously, he had been drinking, and by the look on his face, he was not in the best of moods.

Hannah's legs had already turned weak. Her heart thumped in her chest as she watched him from the window. He threw the door open and glared at her. She had not seen him as bad as this in a long time. Sophie, who had been sitting in her highchair babbling away to her mother while her brothers watched their favourite TV programmes in the living room, squealed, "Daddy!" as he walked through the back door.

"Shut up, you little brat!" he yelled at his little girl. Sophie jumped, and then her face crumpled, and she began to cry as she held her arms out towards her mother.

Having heard their father, Harrison and Ethan were frozen to the spot as their little hearts raced. They hoped he would go straight up to bed as he often did after being in the pub.

Hannah rushed over to her baby and lifted her out of the highchair.

"No, you don't," Philip roared at her, "these kids are all ruined because of you."

He tore Sophie out of her mother's arms and dumped her down on the floor while she continued to scream for her mother.

The boys were both on their feet and had begun to cry, but they stayed where they were, as they feared for their mother's safety.

Philip hit Hannah across her face with the back of his hand, causing her to fall onto the table that she had already set up for tea. Some of the crockery fell on to the floor and smashed. Fortunately, Sophie had toddled over to the corner of the kitchen where she stood screaming as she watched her father attacking her mother.

Philip dragged Hannah up from the table by her clothing, tearing the blouse she was wearing as he did so. He punched her in the stomach and then in her face before throwing her onto the floor. "I hate you, you ugly little witch! You have ruined my life, and I wish I'd never set eyes on you!" he screamed, as saliva sprayed from his mouth. All the anger he felt over his being sacked was now being poured out, and it was his wife and children who were suffering for it.

The boys were now in the doorway, crying uncontrollably because of the vicious attack on their mother.

Philip stormed out of the room and went straight upstairs to sleep off the drink as his injured wife lay on the floor, still trying to get her breath.

She felt sick from the blow to her stomach and her face throbbed as her children cried all around her.

Hannah forced herself up off the floor. Although she was in a lot of pain, she tidied up the broken crockery from the floor to prevent any of the children from cutting themselves on it.

She had been hoping that Ursula was in and that she would have called the police, but unfortunately, Ursula had gone to meet Dieter from work. They were having dinner out together that evening.

Hannah was afraid that she might have a broken rib or something worse as she gave the children their tea. She was far too upset to eat anything, herself.

She felt it would be best to get the children into bed a little earlier than usual so that they would be out of the way once Philip got back up. She knew there was every possibility that he might start again once he was up.

She heard him moving about not long after she had settled the children down for the night. She had saved him some tea, not wanting to give him any excuse to start again.

He ate his meal in silence in front of the TV and ignored Hannah for the entire evening. He still wanted to punish her, even though she had done nothing wrong.

At ten o'clock, Hannah stood up to go get herself ready for bed. "Goodnight Philip, I'm going to bed," she told him so that he could not accuse her of ignoring him.

He ignored her, not even turning to look at her.

Her face was a mess. She had a swollen and blackened eye, and her cheek was badly bruised. Her stomach hurt like nothing she had ever experienced before, causing her to fear that she may have a serious injury.

The next morning when Debbie saw Hannah's face, she was outraged. "What did you do to deserve that?"

Of course, she knew full well that Hannah would have done nothing to deserve it.

While Debbie's children stared at Hannah's injured face, Harrison spoke up. "Daddy did it. He hit Mummy really hard, and when I'm big, I'm going to hit *him* really hard."

"Harrison!" Hannah said sharply.

"You can't blame him for feeling that way. Children should never have to watch their mother being beaten in front of them!" Debbie told her crossly.

Hannah sighed heavily and acknowledged that Debbie was right. She could have died with shame as she saw the other parents and their children staring at her as they approached the school. There was no way she could hide the bruises. She knew all the adults would conclude that she had received a beating from her husband because that was always the conclusion, she came to herself, if she saw a woman with a battered face.

The boy's teachers tried not to stare at Hannah's face as she took Harrison and Ethan to their classrooms.

Hannah hated the fact that she would be the topic of discussion in the staffroom, that day.

On the way home, she told Debbie all that had gone on the day before while she wept. Debbie listened with compassion as they stood on the corner of the street. "Come to mine and have a cup of coffee, Hannah."

She shook her head, "I'd better not, he might be up, and I don't want to start him off again." At that moment, she felt hopelessly trapped.

Debbie had never in her life felt such anger towards one individual as she did towards Philip Turner. Watching Hannah, holding her stomach, she asked. "Why do you keep holding your stomach?"

Hannah lifted her jacket a little and showed Debbie the large, bruised area. Debbie gasped. "You should go and get that checked out. You could have internal bleeding or anything. The maniac. I could smash his face in!"

"Don't make me laugh, it really hurts when I laugh," Hannah told her as she held her injured stomach.

"It's a good job you're seeing a solicitor tomorrow. All the evidence he needs is right there, and not just on your face!"

They said their goodbyes to one another and went their separate ways.

On reaching her house, Hannah saw Ursula coming out of her front door. She held her hand up to her mouth when she saw Hannah's face.

"Come inside for a minute, dear," she told Hannah, her eyes filling with tears at the sight of the injuries to Hannah's face. Hannah held her finger to her lips and whispered to Ursula that Philip was in the house.

"I can only come in for a minute. I don't know if he's still in bed or not," she whispered again. She gave Ursula a brief version of what had gone on the day before. "I was hoping you were in, and that you would call the police!"

"I'm sorry, dear, I was out till much later in the evening. But if I hear anything today, I will ring the police straight away. I'm popping out for about half an hour, but then I will be in all day. Just wait there for a few seconds," she told Hannah. She came back with her camera and photographed Hannah's face. "Evidence," she told Hannah. "I will see you tomorrow outside the solicitor's office."

"You will," Hannah told her, before hurrying next door to her own house.

She was relieved to find that Philip was still in bed. He finally got up around eleven-thirty as she was preparing some lunch for herself and Sophie. She turned around to look at him when she heard him enter the kitchen. He looked surprised at the sight of her badly bruised face.

Sophie had been very clingy all morning with Hannah, but when her father walked into the kitchen, she clung even tighter to the back of her mother's legs and hid her face from her him.

"What's wrong with her?" Philip snapped.

Not wanting to cause an issue, Hannah told him. "She's just a bit clingy today, that's all."

Hannah felt really emotional, but she swallowed her tears down, so as not to give him reason to ridicule her, as he had often done in the past after he had made her cry.

He made his usual tea and toast for his breakfast, as Hannah sat Sophie in her highchair. She took the chair next to her little girl.

Sophie appeared anxious as her father joined them at the table. She grabbed her mother's hand and held it tightly as she ate her sandwich, while Hannah hoped that Philip would not cause a scene and frighten Sophie more than he already had done.

Not only was he practically a stranger to his daughter, but he had hurt the most important person in her world and so, she was naturally frightened by his presence at the table.

They all sat and ate in silence for several minutes. Philip, who had been surreptitiously studying the bruises on his wife's face, was the first to speak. "What are you going to tell my mother if she comes here and sees your face?"

"What do you want me to tell her?" she asked quietly, avoiding eye contact with him.

"Tell her you fell down the stairs."

"Do you think she'll believe that?"

"She might, but that's the story we're going to stick to if anyone asks," he told her abruptly.

Hannah nodded her head in reply. "I'm taking Sophie up for her nap," she told him wearily.

Philip drank his cup of tea as he sat brooding over what had taken place the day before.

He normally avoided hitting Hannah in the face to keep the evidence of his brutality hidden, but he had been in such a rage the day before that he hadn't cared.

It had not gone unnoticed by him that Hannah kept holding the left side of her stomach. He remembered how hard he had punched her in it the day before. He knew too, that she had not deserved it, and now he was concerned about how severely injured she might be.

Hannah had just settled Sophie down in her cot and was closing the door behind her when Philp appeared on the stairs. She was startled because she had not heard him. He stepped onto the landing and lifted her top to have a look at her injured stomach. Hannah saw shock flash across his face when he saw how badly bruised, she was. He touched the injured area of her stomach, causing her to hold her breath as her body stiffened.

"I'm not going to hurt you," he told her quietly, as he let go of her top.

She went to walk past him, but he took hold of her. "I'm sorry I hurt you. You must hate me?"

Hannah knew she needed to tread very carefully. A wrong word or the wrong facial expression could cause him to turn on her again. She had learnt over the years how to humour him, to protect herself, so she told him, "I don't hate you."

He took hold of her more gently than he usually would and kissed her mouth softly. "Come to bed with me for an hour while Sophie's sleeping," he whispered into her ear as he brushed his lips against it.

Hannah was alarmed. She could feel his breath warm against her ear, but the last thing she wanted was to go to bed with *him*.

"No, I can't. I'm in agony, Philip." Her legs had started to tremble while she tried not to let the fear show on her face.

Philip's face was a picture! She held her breath as she turned to walk down the stairs, hoping that he would not attack her again.

She was in far too much pain to even consider entertaining him in the bedroom, and even if she wasn't, she hated having any kind of intimacy with him these days.

He grabbed her arm, making her jump. She turned around and held her breath again as she looked at his face. To her absolute relief, he told her, "Go on, get out of my *sight*." His voice expressing his displeasure.

She went downstairs and into the kitchen to clear the dishes away, but her heart was beating so fast that she felt sure she would faint. She sat down on the kitchen floor. Today had been the first time she had ever refused Philip since the day they had married, and she was sure at some point there would be consequences.

He had brutally attacked her the day before, and now all he could think about was sex!

Sometimes he was sorry after he had beaten her, but there were more times when he was not. He would go on and on about if she were a better wife, he would not hit her and that it was her fault he behaved the way he did.

Hannah knew she was a much better wife than he deserved, and that it was him who needed to improve his behaviour, not her!

Philip walked into the kitchen five minutes later, stopping dead at the sight of her sitting on the floor. "Why on earth are you sitting on the floor?" he asked with a frown.

"I feel faint," she answered quietly and breathlessly.

He was all at once concerned that she might have a serious injury. He went over and sat on the floor next to her. He knew he should be seeking medical advice over her injury. Still, he also knew that if a doctor were to see her injuries, he would know where they had come from, and Philip was too much of a coward to allow that. So, he told her to go lie on the settee, while he got her a pillow and a blanket.

He disappeared upstairs and was back in less than five minutes. He put the pillow under her head and covered her with the blanket. He sat on the floor next to her, stroking her hair and kissing her face. Hannah felt nothing but repulsion, but she didn't let on.

This was a side of Philip's nature that didn't show itself very often. Still, Hannah knew that he was more than capable of going back to the pub that afternoon, before returning home to repeat yesterday's performance all over again.

He was often unpredictable, and that made living with his Jekyll and Hyde character scary.

"I'm starting work tomorrow instead of next Thursday," he told her as he continued to stroke her hair. "Someone's off sick, so I'm covering over the weekend."

"It's really good that you've been able to walk straight into another job," Hannah told him quietly, pretending to be happy for him.

He nodded, while he chewed his fingernail. He knew he could have killed Hannah the day before, and he feared that one day, in a drunken fit of rage, he might just do that.

He knew he needed help; that much, he did know, but he was too proud to admit to anyone, that he had a problem.

"I'll collect the boys from school today, and I'll get some fish and chips for tea later. Lie here and rest while Sophie has her nap."

She smiled at him. "Thank you." It was an act. She was just going along with him. It was a self-preservation technique that she had developed over the five-and-a-half years that they had been married. She was determined to keep her appointment with the solicitor the following morning because she knew the situation was becoming critical, and that she needed to get herself out of the situation before he ended up killing her. She just didn't know how she would do it, or even if it would be possible.

Chapter Eight

The following morning as Hannah met up with Debbie on the street corner. Debbie told her, "Boy, am I glad to see you this morning! When I saw Philip collecting the boys yesterday, I was afraid he'd done something really bad to you. In fact, I was going to ring you this morning if you'd not turned up."

"Oh, he was all over me yesterday afternoon. Couldn't do enough for me. It won't last, it never does... can you believe he wanted me to climb into bed with him while Sophie was having her nap, after what he'd done to me the day before? I told him no. His face was a picture!" Hannah giggled.

Debbie laughed out loud, picturing his face in her mind.

"I'm very apprehensive about this morning's appointment. I've a huge knot in my stomach, and I feel sick."

Debbie turned to her. "Hannah, you *must* go to the appointment. You need to know what your legal rights are if you were to break up with Philip."

She had lowered her voice considerably so that the children who were all walking in front of their mothers didn't hear their conversation.

"I am going to the appointment. I'm just very nervous. Ursula is going to meet me there, so I won't be on my own."

After the children had been dropped off, Debbie told Hannah, "You are absolutely doing the right thing. Please, ring me to let me know how it all went."

"I'll ring you, once Philip has left for work." Hannah walked away, and made her way to the solicitor's office

Hannah arrived at the solicitor's office, and found Ursula was already waiting outside for her. The two of them went inside together with Sophie, who had fallen asleep in her pushchair.

They had only just sat down when a door opened and a very good-looking man of around forty called Hannah into his office. She was immediately intimidated by his good looks and charm. He introduced himself as Alan Sinclair and gestured for Hannah to take a seat.

He tried not to let his shock show at how young the battered girl in front of him appeared to be.

"I'm Alan Sinclair, but please call me Alan... how can I help you?"

"Well, I'm obviously in an abusive marriage," she told him quietly as she pointed to her face. She chewed her bottom lip for a couple of seconds. "I need some legal advice as to what my rights are concerning getting a legal separation, custody of the children, etc."

Alan studied the young woman's battered face for a few seconds before asking, "May I call you Hannah?"

She nodded and gave him a weak smile.

How old are you? I'm guessing about eighteen?"

"Twenty-one. I'm twenty-one," she answered.

Alan sighed heavily and shook his head.

Hannah wanted to run from his office because of the deep shame she felt about her situation. As if he could read her thoughts, he gave her a reassuring smile before speaking again.

"The first thing I would suggest is that we go for an emergency injunction. It would state that your husband would have to leave the marital home and would not be allowed within a certain radius of it while you and the children are living there. How do you think Mr Turner would react to such an order?"

"He would go crazy! He'd probably kick the door in, and I dread to think what he would do to me. He is a very unreasonable man. And I'm afraid of him," she finished quietly, averting her eyes away from his empathetic gaze.

The solicitor could see that the idea of an injunction, and the difficulties it could bring her were causing the young woman some distress.

"I have another suggestion, which under the circumstances might be the better option," he told her carefully. "I have the telephone number of an organisation that helps women in your situation. They have several refuges dotted around the country. They may be able to find a place of safety for you and your children, although I'm afraid it could be anywhere in the country. But they would support you in getting financial help, a place to live, and they would even support you in court if it should come to that."

She gave him another weak smile. "That would be really helpful. I've got nowhere to go," she told him sadly. "So, if they could help find somewhere safe where the children and I could all be together, then that would be more than I could hope for."

Alan took a card from one of his drawers and wrote the number of an organisation, that helped women who were suffering domestic abuse. His wife worked for them, and she often spoke to him of the evil things that happened to some women inside their own homes.

Alan handed the card to Hannah.

As she took the card from him, Hannah thought he had the kindest eyes that she had ever seen. He was probably twenty years older than she was, but she found him incredibly attractive.

It was the first time since meeting Philip that she had ever looked at another man in that way. She found herself blushing as he stood up to show her out. He shook her hand, it felt warm, strong, and masculine.

"Please, ring the number I have given you as soon as you are able," he told her with genuine empathy, "Don't hesitate to call me if you need any further help or advice."

Hannah smiled and thanked him before leaving his office.

Once they were outside, Hannah told Ursula everything that the solicitor had told her.

She asked Ursula to keep the card in her purse because she did not want Philip to accidentally find it. The plan was that once Philip had gone to work, Hannah would go to Ursula's and ring the helpline. She felt hopeful that she would be able to get the help she so desperately needed.

She bought a few groceries to take home because that's what she had told Philip she was going into town for. When she got home, Philip was still in bed. She gave Sophie a drink and a snack, while she did her best despite her injury to tidy up downstairs.

She was just in the middle of changing Sophie's nappy when she heard Philip getting up. He was still in a reasonably good mood, causing Hannah to feel a little guilty about her plans to rid herself of him for good.

Sophie was still very anxious around her father, and it really got to him that she would not go to him when he put his arms out for her.

"Just give her time. She just needs to get used to having you at home," Hannah lied. She knew that Sophie was frightened of Philip because of what had gone on the other afternoon.

Hannah sat and had a cup of tea with him while he ate breakfast. She knew exactly what he would do to her if he knew what she was planning. An hour later, he was ready to leave. He took hold of her and pulled her up close to him. She gasped. "Careful, Philip, my stomach."

He had forgotten for a moment, and so he quickly let go of her. She could tell what he was still in the mood for, and she knew what he would want once he got in from work that night. Any other man would not have expected his injured wife to make love with him until she was much better, but Philip was too selfish to think that way. The thought of it made her feel sick. She knew too, that he would not allow her to refuse him a second time!

After he had left, Hannah went straight next door to ring the number she had been given that morning. Ursula jigged Sophie up and down on her knee while Hannah rang the number. A female voice on the other end answered. "Hello, Jenny speaking, can I help?"

"My name is Hannah Turner. I was given this number by a solicitor this morning. I'm a victim of domestic abuse, and I really need some help."

"Are you in danger right now, Hannah?"

"My husband is at work just now. He gave me a severe beating just two days ago, and although he was in a good mood when he left for work, that could have changed by the time he gets home."

"Do you have children, Hannah?" Jenny asked.

"Yes, I have three young children. My eldest is five, and my youngest is nineteen months."

Jenny explained to Hannah that if she could get herself to a family member or a friend's house with the children, it could be arranged for them to be picked up from there by one of their support workers. She warned Hannah. "It could take anything from thirty minutes to several hours to find a refuge that could take you in. But I must warn you that it could end up being somewhere in another county."

Hannah's heart sank at the thought of leaving her two best friends behind, and of course, she would miss Frank and Alice too.

She knew how devastated Alice would be if she wasn't able to have contact with her grandchildren. Even though Hannah knew that she needed to get away from Philip, her heart ached for what it would do not only Alice but for what it would do to Frank too. They were excellent grandparents, and Hannah could already feel the pain they would suffer.

Hannah gave Jenny Debbie's telephone number and told Jenny that she could be picked up from there, but she would need to get her eldest two children back from school first.

Hannah knew that she did not even need to ask Debbie. Debbie would be only too pleased to help her escape from Philip. Jenny arranged to ring back in an hour to give Hannah time to get herself organised. She was shaking. "It's all happening, Ursula. Can I ring Debbie?"

"Of course, ring whoever you need to," she told Hannah.

Hannah rang her friend with trembling fingers. After quickly explaining everything to Debbie, Hannah asked. "Would you go and collect Harrison and Ethan from school for me? I'll ring the school and tell them that we have a family emergency and that you will collect the boys for me in about ten minutes."

Debbie said, "Of course, I'll do whatever you need me to do."

After putting the phone down, Hannah picked it up again and rang the school. When the school secretary answered, Hannah tried to steady her voice as her emotions began to rise. "This is Mrs Turner, Harrison and Ethan's mum. We have a bit of an emergency at home, and I need the boys to come home. Mrs Debra Clarke is going to collect them for me in about ten minutes."

"Oh, dear, I hope everything is going to be all right."

Of course, the news had quickly spread around the staff at the school about the state that Mrs Turner had turned up in, the day before.

"I'll make sure the boys will be ready to be collected straight away," she assured Hannah.

Hannah's head was in a whirl as she tried to think what she needed to do next.

Sophie had fallen asleep, and Ursula had laid her on the settee with a cushion under her head and had put her own cardigan over her. Hannah told Ursula, "I need to go home and quickly fill a bag with a few bits to take with us."

"You go. I'll look after the baby."

Hannah went home and took a large holdall from the top of the wardrobe. She put two changes of clothing in it for each of them, including underwear and pyjamas — nappies for Sophie and each of the children's favourite teddy.

Hannah's heart was beating at a rate of knots. She kept imagining Philip bursting in at any second and finding her in the middle of packing. As soon as she had finished, she rushed back to the safety of the house next door. Ursula poured each of them a small glass of sherry once Hannah was back. Her nerves were as frazzled as Hannah's. Jenny rang back as she said she would.

"Great news Hannah," she said, sounding very pleased, "there is a refuge just forty miles away from where you are. If you give me the address of your friend, someone will pick you and the children up in an hour. Does that give you enough time?"

"Yes, it does." Hannah gave Jenny Debbie's address before thanking her and telling her how grateful she was.

She felt a bit shellshocked. It was all happening so fast! She stared at Ursula. "Someone is picking us up from Debbie's in an hour."

"That is wonderful! Oh, I am going to miss you all so much!" Ursula began to cry as she hugged Hannah to her. "Now, take no notice of me, you need to do this. You can ring me later and let me know that you have arrived safely."

Ursula carefully lifted Sophie from the settee and laid her down in the pushchair. The two women got their coats and shoes on and left

Ursula's house to walk around the corner to Debbie's house. Ursula pushed the pushchair while Hannah struggled with the holdall because of her injury.

On the way home, the boys had asked why they were coming home. Debbie had told them that they were going on a little holiday and that Daddy couldn't go because he had to work. She hoped that she had told them the right thing because they had both become overly excited at the thought of a little holiday with just their mummy and Sophie. "Daddy would spoil it anyway, because he can be mean," Harrison told Debbie with feeling. She smiled inwardly, knowing that Philip was about to get his just desserts!

Hannah and Ursula turned up with Sophie a little while after Debbie had got back with the boys, who were jumping up and down with excitement and asking their mother where they were going on holiday. Hannah looked across at Debbie with a quizzical expression. Debbie winked before speaking. "I was telling the two of them that they are going on a little holiday with you, but Daddy can't go because he has to work."

"Well, boys, you will have to wait until you get there, otherwise, it will spoil the surprise. Hannah told them while she hoped that wherever they were going would be a nice place and that the boys wouldn't be disappointed once they got there.

Sally arrived bang on time to collect the little family. She was a retired social worker and had worked with lots of victims of domestic abuse throughout her career. She had taken early retirement and now worked part-time at the refuge. She worked just two days a week. There were times when there was great sadness attached to the job. Still, she felt that providing shelter to women and children who desperately needed help always brought more happiness than sadness.

There were lots of hugs and tears between the three women. Ursula and Debbie told Hannah to ring as soon as they arrived to put their minds at rest. They made her promise that she would always keep in touch. Debbie had pushed ten pounds into Hannah's pocket. Ursula had already insisted on giving her twenty pounds to help her over the first few days.

Once all four of them were settled in the car, Sally set off. As Hannah waved to the best friends she had ever had, she felt as if her heart had been ripped out of her chest. She did not know how she would ever get used to life without them. She cried quietly all the way to the refuge. Sally handed her some tissues and told her. "It is perfectly normal to be upset. You are leaving your friends and your home. You will even feel some sadness at leaving your husband, even though he has treated you so very badly. But you have made the right decision, and believe me, that takes guts!"

Hannah nodded as she wiped her eyes and nose.

They pulled up outside a large, detached house with large electric gates for added security for its residents.

The house looked as if it was probably at least a hundred years old.

The gates opened for Sally's car to drive through. A very jolly woman of around fifty came out to meet them. She was the owner of the house. It had been left to her by her late parents.

Because Brenda already owned substantial property, she had wanted to use the house to help women who were victims of domestic violence. Her own mother had been beaten often in front of Brenda as she had grown up. And now, she was very passionate about helping other women.

Her mother had suffered thirty years of abuse, before her father's untimely death from a stroke. His death had given her mother fifteen years to enjoy a life free from violence before she died too. But it still hurt Brenda that the best years of her mother's life had been made a misery by her father.

She helped get the children out of the car. She had Sophie in her arms as she watched the young, battered woman climb out of the car with great empathy and compassion. She remembered how her own mother had often had similar bruises, to the ones, Hannah bore. She was taken by surprise at how young Hannah appeared to be.

"I'm Brenda," she told Hannah with a huge smile as she swept the two boys towards the large front door with Sophie still in her arms. Sally followed with Hannah, who was carrying the holdall.

The house could only house five families at a time. There were four large doubles bedrooms and a small box room. Each double bedroom could accommodate a mother and up to four children, while the smallest bedroom could only house one woman and one child. There were three bathrooms that all had to be shared.

Hannah was introduced to the other four women. Tracy was in her mid-twenties and had three children, a girl and two boys like Hannah. Another woman, Julie, looked around forty and had two teenage daughters with her. Jane was around thirty and had two small boys.

A young girl was sitting quietly in the corner of the room, holding a young baby. She looked around thirteen, but Hannah later found out that the girl, Becky, was sixteen. She had been a victim of both physical abuse and sexual abuse.

Hannah was horrified to find out later that Becky's father was the father of her baby.

She had escaped one afternoon when she had been left at home alone with her baby. She had run with her baby in her arms to a neighbour's house and had begged them to help her. The police had been called, and Becky had been assisted to travel over sixty miles away from her father house to the refuge where she had been living for just over two weeks. Her father had been arrested and was awaiting trial.

Sally made a plate of sandwiches for the new arrivals. She gave the children a cup of milk each while Brenda showed Hannah to her room.

Even though the furniture was old and worn, the room was bright and clean. It had a lovely floral smell. There were four single beds and a small cot, as well as two large sets of drawers. Hannah was told that she would have to share the bathroom with Becky, who occupied the box room next door.

Hannah put the holdall on one of the beds and decided that she would unpack later.

Brenda took Hannah back downstairs into a large farmhouse-style kitchen. In the centre, there was a huge farmhouse kitchen table with eight chairs around it. Hannah was told that each family were allocated two cupboards each for their food, but the large fridge freezer had to be shared, and that each family labelled their own food to avoid food getting mixed up.

After they had finished their late lunch, Hannah was taken on a tour of the downstairs. There was an office, which was for the use of staff only. It was explained that there was a total of five staff members who all worked part-time except for Brenda, who was there each day, Monday to Friday, from nine-thirty until four-thirty. Each staff member had to take their turn at being on call in case of an emergency during the night. The name and telephone number of whoever was on call that night, was displayed on the board in the kitchen.

Besides the office, there was a large playroom that the children were only allowed to use if they were accompanied by an adult. There was a utility room with two washing machines, two driers, two irons and two ironing boards. At the front of the house was the main lounge, which was light and airy. It had a television in one corner.

Harrison announced to everyone that he was going to like this holiday and then went very red in the face when all the adults laughed over his comment. Hannah looked across at him and gave him a reassuring smile.

She had been given some emergency food and toiletries to tide them over until Hannah could get to the shops the following day.

After tea, she decided to let the children watch some television with the other children for an hour before getting them ready for bed. Harrison and Ethan had so many questions that they sent her head into a whirl. She explained that they may be here for a while but did not tell them just yet that they had left their home and their father for good. She decided to leave it for a couple of days to give the boys a chance to settle in first.

That evening she sat and chatted with the other women. They swapped stories with each other, about their lives as victims of violence.

Hannah could feel the strong atmosphere of camaraderie that existed between them all.

Her eyes kept wandering over to Becky, who appeared quiet and withdrawn. The girl was stick-thin, with a pale face. Her eyes were large and dark, which made her resemble a bush baby from the Australian bush.

Hannah thought about how often she had suffered at the hands of her mother as a child, but she had never experienced sexual abuse from a family member during her childhood, and so, she could only try to imagine what Becky must have suffered

After a while, Hannah went to use the pay phone to let both Ursula and Debbie know that they had arrived safely and that she would be in touch again after the weekend.

At nine-thirty in the evening, Hannah found that she could not keep her eyes open, so she apologised to the other women and took herself off to bed. The day had flown by, but it had been exhausting. She and the children were in a place of safety, and it had all happened so fast.

As she lay awake, her thoughts turned to Philip. He would not yet know that she had left him. Friday nights were busy, and he probably wouldn't get in until two in the morning.

She thought about Frank and Alice and decided that she owed it to the two of them to let them know that she and the children were safe and well. She would ring Alice and let her know that they were okay the following morning.

Later that night, Philip decided to finish a little earlier than he normally would. So, at one o'clock in the morning, he drove home. He went straight into the bathroom to use the toilet, wash his hands and face and clean his teeth. When he had finished, he walked into his and Hannah's room. He stopped dead at the sight of the empty bed. He panicked! His first thought was that Hannah may have been taken to hospital because of the injury to her stomach.

A cold hand of fear gripped his heart. *Was she alive? Was she dead? Had she been suffering a slow internal bleed from where he had punched her?*

He gripped his head with both hands before running his fingers through his hair. He imagined himself spending the next twenty years in jail for manslaughter while his mother and Frank raised their motherless children.

He knew Hannah was very friendly with the German woman next door, so he decided to knock her and her husband up because he had to know what had happened and why none of his family were in the house.

He hammered on their front door while his heart and mind raced. "Please, God, let her be all right." He kept repeating to himself.

Dieter eventually opened the front door with a scowl on his face as he looked Philip up and down.

"I am really sorry to get you out of bed, but I've just got in from work, and I've found the house empty. Have you any idea why Hannah and the children are not at home?"

Just as he had finished speaking, Ursula walked up behind her husband, wearing her dressing gown.

"Hannah has left you. She and the children were picked up by a woman this afternoon, and Hannah told me that they were being taken to a refuge several miles away."

Ursula kept her face straight to hide the pleasure she was feeling at breaking the news to Philip, that the young woman he had treated so badly was now safely out of his reach.

The look on his face was priceless. He had not seen this coming. Everything had appeared normal that morning. She'd taken the boys to school, which meant she must have taken them out again later that day, before school had finished.

Philip felt as if he'd been hit in the face with a shovel as he went back to his own house. He dialled his mothers' number as he frantically lit a cigarette with shaking hands. It rang for quite some time before he heard his mother's voice.

"Hello, can I help you?" she asked.

On hearing her speak, Philip began to cry like a child. "Hannah's left me," he told her, "She's gone off in a woman's car with the kids. She told the next-door neighbour that she was going to a refuge and that she won't be coming back."

"Oh, no, Philip. I'll wake Frank up, and we'll be with you as quick as we can. Just stay where you are!"

"Okay," Philip told his mother as he continued to weep.

Alice frantically ran up the stairs to Frank. She shook him roughly to wake him. Frank sat up, wondering why Alice was in such a state.

"Hannah's left our Philip. She's taken the children, and no one knows where she's gone." Alice was gripping her chest and pacing up and down in the bedroom. "We'll have to go straight over, Frank. Our Philip's in a right state. How could she do such a thing?"

As Frank was getting out of bed to put his clothes on, he told Alice, "Because the poor lass has finally had enough, Alice. You know how he treats her, and don't tell me that you don't know that he hits her." Frank's words cut through Alice, who did not want to face the truth about her son.

"Just get dressed Frank!" she told him irritably. Alice could not get to her son quick enough. When Philip let them in, she could see that he had been crying. It broke her heart to see him like that.

"The sly little bitch!" Alice spat the words out of her mouth.

Philip put his hand up. "Don't call her that, Mum. It's my fault." he had started to cry again. "I was really angry about losing my job, so I went out on Wednesday afternoon and got drunk. I came home and took it out on her. I really hurt her, Mum." Alice held one of her hand across her mouth. Frank was outraged!

"You hit that little lass, who has never done any wrong to you in all these years? YOU BLOODY COWARD!" Frank roared at his stepson.

"Frank, this is not helping, he knows he's in the wrong."

Alice tried to reason with him, but Frank was not in the mood to hear about how sorry Philip was. He loved Hannah as if she were his own daughter, and he adored his grandchildren. Now, he knew he might never see any of them again because of Philip.

Frank rang the foreman who was working the night shift to say that he wasn't well and would not be at work the following morning. He needed to get his head around what had happened, and boy, did he need a whiskey right now!

After they had all taken several minutes to calm down, they decided that they would take Philip to theirs because Alice was worried that Philip would do something silly. He had told his mother that he could not face a future without Hannah in it.

Once they were back home, Frank and Philip drank far too much whiskey between them. Frank told Philip some home truths about his treatment of his wife. The two of them had almost come to blows a couple of times, so Alice was very relieved when Frank finally decided to go to bed. Philip repeated his threat to do away with himself if he couldn't get

Hannah back. His mother sat with him until he finally fell into a drunken sleep at five in the morning.

The following morning Hannah had got up early with the children. After they had all been washed and dressed, she took the three of them downstairs for breakfast.

It appeared that they were the only ones up. It was Saturday, so she assumed everyone was having a lie-in. After they had all eaten, she took the children into the lounge so that they could watch Saturday morning TV while she braced herself to call Alice.

The house was quiet, so she decided it was a good time to ring, even though it was only eight in the morning. She picked up the receiver of the pay phone in the hallway. She had several coins in her hand but only intended to have a quick chat with Alice. She dialled the number. Alice answered the telephone. She started to cry as soon as she heard Hannah's voice.

"Oh, Hannah, where are you?" Alice wailed down the phone. "Philip is in a right state. He's been talking about doing away with himself because he says he can't go on without you."

Hannah was immediately alarmed. She did not want the death of her husband on her conscience for the rest of her life.

"Alice, I'm only ringing to let you know that we are safe and well. I don't want to get into an argument over Philip. He will never stop hitting me, and I can't take it any more!" Hannah was crying now as she put another coin in the machine.

"Oh, Hannah, please just talk to him." Alice cried.

Philip had woken on hearing his mother wailing down the phone. He felt as if a steam roller had run over his head from all the whiskey, he had drunk the night before.

When he heard his mother say Hannah's name. He jumped off the settee, and ran into the hall, grabbing the phone out of his mother's hand.

"Hannah, don't put the phone down," he begged. "I am so very sorry for what I did to you on Wednesday and all those other times that I've hurt you. Please come home... Give me a chance to prove to you that I can change... Please, Hannah." He begged as tears ran down his face.

"No, Philip, you've gone too far. You terrorised the children on Wednesday by what you did to me, and you didn't even care!"

Philip wept into the phone while his mother's heart broke as she watched him.

"Hannah, I love you, I need you. Please give me just one chance… I can change. I'll have therapy, go to marriage guidance counselling — anything! I need you here with me. I don't want to live without you. I can't live without you!" he told her between sobs.

Hannah panicked. *What if he did kill himself? How would she be able to live with that for the rest of her life?* She could not bear to hear him cry it ripped her insides apart. Neither could she cope with his pain because she could feel it in her own heart. But did she want to go back.

"I need to go, Philip," she sobbed.

She was too compassionate a person to cope with hearing him weeping.

"No, Hannah, don't hang up. Please stay on the phone."

"I need time to think, Philip. I can't turn my feelings off and then just switch them back on again as if nothing's ever happened."

Philip was desperate, but he knew he had to let her go and think things over, otherwise, he was in danger of blowing any chance of getting her back.

"Will you call me tomorrow morning before lunch?" he asked, before continuing. "Just think about what I've said. I will do whatever you want me to do. This has been the kick up the backside that I've needed for a long time. Will you ring me tomorrow, please?"

Hannah's mind was in turmoil and she couldn't think straight. She found herself promising to ring him the following morning before insisting that she really needed to go.

"Okay, darling. I love you, Hannah. Much more than you could ever imagine."

"Bye, Philip," she told him before she put the telephone back on the receiver.

She was shaking with raw emotion. And she was all at once so very unsure of everything. Was it possible for someone like Philip to change? Maybe if he got the professional help that he had promised to have, he could be helped to change his behaviour. She did not want Philip to harm himself, and she found herself fretting over his threats to kill himself.

She checked on the children, who were all deeply engrossed in their favourite Saturday morning TV show.

She went into the kitchen to make herself a cup of tea, just as other household members were appearing one by one to have breakfast. Everyone could see that Hannah had been crying.

Once everyone had eaten breakfast, the women sent the children into the TV lounge so that they talk with Hannah.

They all gathered around the kitchen table as she told them about the conversation she had just had with her husband. She explained that she had not expected Philip to be at his mother's house when she rang just to let her know that she and the children were safe.

"They all cry," Jane told her while the rest of them nodded their heads in agreement. Jane continued, "They promise you the moon, and the stars, and their undying love, and then once they've got you back, it all starts again."

"Don't fall for it, Hannah." Tracy warned her.

But Philip had sounded broken. She was convinced that he had meant every word that he had spoken to her. Maybe this was the lesson he had needed? She had never seen or heard Philip cry, not ever. If he did kill himself, she knew that she would never be able to live with the knowledge that she had caused it.

She got through the rest of the day on automatic pilot as she kept going over and over everything that Philip had said to her that morning.

By the next morning, she had made her decision. She had to give him at least one chance to prove that he could change. He was her husband and the father of her children. If he could be the husband that she wanted him to be, maybe she would grow to love him again. But if he did not change his ways, then she would leave him for good.

Hannah explained to the other women that she had decided to give her husband just one chance. She could see that they were all mortified with her decision, but they all knew that it had to be her decision and that she would learn the hard way as most of them had done.

She rang Philip and told him he would be given only one chance to prove himself and that if he did not stick to the promises he had made, then their marriage would be over.

Philip was so relieved that he would have agreed to anything just to get her back.

She told him that she wanted Frank to pick them up, not Philip, at the bus station in the town where she had been staying. She gave him the address of the bus station, and it was arranged that Frank would meet her there in two hours.

Hannah did not want to risk Philip finding out where the refuge was for the sakes of the other families that lived there.

Tracy helped Hannah with her bag and the children to get to the bus station.

Frank was already waiting, and when he caught sight of them, he got out of the car to help with the children. Tracy hugged Hannah and each of the children before turning around and walking away. She believed Hannah was probably making one of the biggest mistakes of her life, and she would live to regret the decision to go back to her husband.

"Are you sure that this is what you want?" Frank asked her earnestly, "He doesn't know where you are, and he doesn't have your number."

"I have to give him this one chance, Frank."

Frank nodded. "Okay, love," he said as he climbed into the car. Once Hannah and all the children were seated properly, Frank drove off. He was glad to see them all, but he felt deep within himself that Hannah had made the wrong decision in going back to Philip.

It had been planned that the three children would stay with their grandparents for two nights to give their mum and dad some time alone, to talk things over, and hopefully have some quality time together.

A bag had already been packed for the children, and Frank would take them with him after dropping Hannah and the holdall off.

The children loved sleeping at Nana's and Grandad's house, so it was an extra treat for them.

Hannah walked through the back door, not knowing if she had made the right decision. Philip walked over to her and swept her up into his arms. She gasped because of her injury.

"I'm so sorry, I forgot," he said as he quickly let go of her. He took her face in his hands and kissed her mouth. She couldn't help pulling away from him. She watched his face drop as she did so. "Philip, please give me a chance to get into the house." The tone in her voice had not gone undetected by him.

She looked around the kitchen that she had believed she would never see again with a sinking feeling in the pit of her stomach. "Philip, we have a lot to talk about before we get into any physical stuff."

"I just want to hold you, that's all."

"Can you only ever think about sex?" Hannah snapped.

There it was again, that irritation in her voice.

He walked into the sitting room and sank down into one of the armchairs, sighing heavily.

Hannah followed him and sat herself down in the chair opposite him. He looked across at her with a sorrowful look. "Of course, I want to make love to you. I love you, and I thought I'd lost you for good," he told her miserably.

Immediately her heart went out to him. "Philip, I need time. I know you're disappointed, but I'm not ready for any of that just now. You've let me down so badly over the years, and it's affected my feelings for you."

She spoke as gently as she could as she watched his eyes fill with tears. She felt dreadful because she knew he was hurting.

He couldn't stand to hear that she had stopped loving him, even though he knew it was his fault. He didn't know how to make things better between them. He wanted to go out and drink himself into oblivion, but he knew that would certainly end his marriage. He also knew that he needed to tread very carefully just now, otherwise, she would take off again.

They sat in silence for several minutes.

Hannah knew in her heart that this was not where she wanted to be and that she had been too hasty in her decision to go back. She had panicked over his threat to do away with himself.

Because she had always been an empathetic person, she had put Philip's pain ahead of her own welfare.

But she had made her decision, and now she needed to try to make it work.

"Philip, if you get the help that you promised you would, I feel we could make a go of things. Will you get professional help?"

"I will. I'm really going to try to make things up to you. Please don't ever leave me again."

That was something that she could not promise. Everything hinged on how things progressed over the coming days, weeks, and months.

Philip went out and bought them a takeaway and a bottle of wine from the local Chinese restaurant. They enjoyed the meal and shared the bottle of wine. They talked more than they had done in years, and by the time they had finished, they both felt better than they had done earlier.

Philip went over and sat down on the settee next to her, causing her body to stiffen.

"Just let me hold you. I'm not expecting anything more. I just want to hold you, please."

Hannah allowed him to put his arms around her, but as she sat in his arms, she knew for sure that whatever she had felt for him in the past had gone. It just wasn't there any more.

She felt utterly depressed as she struggled to hide her true feelings from Philip.

They went to bed later, and as they lay side by side, Philip wanted more than anything to make love to her, but neither did he want to do anything that would make her leave again. He had got her back, and he did not want to risk losing her.

He realised too that she was no longer completely under his control, and the thought both angered and terrified him at the same time.

Hannah knew that at some point, she would have to be intimate with her husband if their marriage was going to work. It was a huge mess with three young children caught up in the middle of it all.

Later as Philip lay sleeping next to her, she cried silent tears into her pillow. She had reached a place of safety, and now she had just probably made the biggest mistake of her life all because she had panicked. All she could do was hope that he would keep the promises that he had made to her, and, that things would work out for the best.

Chapter Nine
Three weeks later

Philip had been trying hard since Hannah had gone back to him. He had cut right back on the drink and tried to be a better father to his three children. At times though, the strain on him was noticeable, causing Hannah to worry as to whether he would be able to keep it up. She was doing her bit by allowing him the intimacy that he craved from her. It was not easy for her because she neither loved him nor was she attracted to him any more. She had become good at faking it, and of course, Philip hadn't a clue!

Philip had done well to have not lost his job after Hannah had left him because he was supposed to cover the entire weekend but had only worked the Friday. Jim had given him the benefit of the doubt and had kept him on, but he had given Philip a stern warning not to let him down again.

Today was going to be a real test. Philip was going to the pub with his brother James to watch the football, while Hannah and the children spent the afternoon with Alice and Frank.

Hannah was very apprehensive about how Philip would be with several pints inside him. She had woken that morning with a real sense of foreboding.

She had been struggling emotionally ever since she had gone back to him. The thought of spending the next fifty years with a man she no longer loved made her feel hopelessly depressed.

Once Debbie had got over the shock of Hannah going back to Philip just a day after leaving him, she had told her that once you had fallen out of love with someone, it would be very unlikely that you would ever fall back in love with them.

Ursula had been furious with Hannah for going back to Philip. It had taken a fortnight before she was all right with Hannah again.

She had never been in Hannah's shoes, so she was unable to understand Hannah's reasons for giving Philip a second chance. Ursula knew nothing about being a victim of abuse, neither did she have any insight into the self-doubt, the low self-worth, and the belief that somehow it was all your fault that victims of abuse often experienced.

Debbie had been much more understanding, but she felt sure that Hannah would live to regret going back to the man that had been the cause of so much misery in her life.

The children had had a lovely afternoon at their grandparents' place. Frank always spoilt them with too many treats, and Alice was very much the doting granny, always providing lots of love, hugs, and kisses.

The time had run away, and it was after four when Hannah noticed the time. She knew that Philip was probably at home already, so she asked Frank if he would quickly run them home.

It was almost four-thirty before they arrived home. She walked into the house with the children hoping Philip had gone to bed to sleep the drink off. She walked into the living room and found Philip sitting there with a face like thunder.

"Where the hell have you been?" he roared.

"Your mother's," she answered, as she began to feel the usual weakness in her legs while her heart thumped in her chest.

"You knew what time I'd be in, so why you weren't back here in time?"

"I simply lost track of time, that's all."

Hannah could see that the children were looking frightened. They all jumped when he suddenly got up and marched out of the room and upstairs to bed.

The relief washed over Hannah, but she was still very shaken over what had just taken place as she put the children's coats and shoes away.

They had had so much to eat at Frank and Alice's that she just gave them a sandwich and some chopped fruit for tea. She decided to get them into bed at the earlier time of six-thirty instead of seven. She wanted them all safely tucked up in bed before Philip woke from his alcohol-induced sleep.

She was just cooking one of his favourite meals, chicken curry and rice, when she heard him coming down the stairs at around seven. She held her breath as he walked into the kitchen, not knowing whether he would still be in a foul mood. She thought back to what Jane had told her only three weeks earlier. *They promise you the moon and the stars and their undying love, but once they've got you back, it all starts again.*

Philip had been really trying, but was that all going to change today?

He walked up behind her while she braced herself. She was surprised when he snaked his arms around her waist while kissing the back of her head. "Sorry about earlier. I panicked because I thought you had gone again, but then I rang my mother, and she told me you were on your way home."

Hannah forced a smile on her face before turning to look at him. "I've made your favourite tea."

"I don't deserve you," he told her as he smiled down at her.

And I don't deserve to be married to the likes of you! She thought to herself.

She made the best of what was left of the evening with Philip, making him laugh over the antics of Frank and the boys that afternoon and about how Frank had been scolded like a naughty child by Alice. But Hannah's mood remained low. She had tried to kid herself that things would get better. The truth was, she felt trapped in her relationship, and she had begun suffering mild anxiety attacks because of it.

Of course, Alice was delighted that Philip and Hannah were back together. Still, everyone else, including Frank and even James, had thought that she had been a fool to go back to Philip, and Hannah knew it.

She knew that they stood a much better chance of making it as a couple if Philip could stay off the drink, but she also knew that he would not be able to stop drinking completely.

There had been another episode the following Sunday. Philip had met up with a couple of his old drinking buddies, and he had had way too much to drink. He had come home and had shouted at the children over nothing. Hannah had tried to humour him, but he had rounded on her angrily, shouting at her over having left him a few weeks earlier. "You ever pull a trick on me like that again, and I will find you and kill you!" he had yelled at her.

She and the children had all been afraid of what he might do next and had been relieved when he had stormed upstairs to bed.

She had got the children into bed just minutes before she heard him moving around. She berated herself over how stupid she had been to have gone back to him.

Philip had only been to one marriage counselling session, saying it was a waste of time. He had not gone on the anger management course that he had promised to go on either.

Hannah felt she was struggling to keep her head above water at times. She thought about leaving again, but there was the threat that he might kill himself if she did, and there was also the real threat that he would find her and kill her if she dared to leave him. Hannah had taken both threats very seriously, causing her to feel more trapped than ever.

When Philip got back up, Hannah, saw that his mood had not lightened. He ate the meal that she had kept to one side for him in silence. He ignored her attempts to have some light conversation with him.

Hannah thought back to the early days of their marriage and how that kind of behaviour had made her sad and desperate for his affection. Now it just angered her. It made her want to wring his neck. She was no longer the child he had married, who would have done anything to please him. She was a woman. Her circumstances had made her grow up fast, and she was far more mature than Philip, despite their age difference.

Hannah thought back to how Debbie had laughed when she had told her that she feared that Philip would have killed himself if she had not gone back to him. Debbie had said that someone so self-centred would never do such a thing. But then she had apologised on seeing the stricken look on Hannah's face.

Hannah had given Debbie and Ursula the money back that they had given her on the day she left to go to the refuge. She had not touched any of it because she had only been gone just over twenty-four hours.

Philip sat and stared at the TV for a good hour after he had finished his meal. He suddenly turned to her in anger. "You think you've got the upper hand, don't you?"

"No, I'm just trying to make this marriage work for all our sakes," she answered, trying not to let her fear show.

"You ever pull a trick like that on me again, and I will kill you. Wherever you go, I will track you down. You will never be free of me!" he growled

Hannah's legs were trembling, and she could hear her heart pounding in her ears.

Here was the nasty side of Philip's nature, rearing its ugly head again. She fully believed that he would carry out his threat if she were ever to leave him again. She was in such a state of anxiety as she sat listening to his threats that she felt that she would go completely mad at any second. Fortunately, Philip did not say another word for the rest of the evening.

Hannah knew that he was not going to be able to live up to the promises that he had made to her just a few weeks ago and that it was only a matter of time before she would be on the receiving end of one of his beatings.

A few days later, her Health visitor called round. She knew that Hannah was struggling since returning to her husband. She had wanted Hannah to join a mother and toddler group set up by social services, which was the reason for her visit.

The group was aimed at giving support to young mothers such as Hannah, who were struggling with life under difficult circumstances. Its aim was to provide an environment where they could express their worries and difficulties, in a place where they would receive support through group discussion. It would be run by two social workers, May, and Pat, who both had years of experience in helping and supporting young families.

The children would play in one room, where trained staff would look after them, while the mothers could have a couple of hours of adult conversation. Hannah said that she would like to give it a try.

May and Pat called round to have a chat with her a few days later, and two weeks later, the group was up and running.

It was held in a day centre every Thursday afternoon.

May and Pat introduced the seven young women who had been invited to attend the group, to one another.

There was a woman there called Helen, who Hannah immediately recognised as having a Yorkshire accent. It turned out that Helen was from a city less than ten miles away from where Hannah had grown up. It was lovely to hear a Yorkshire accent again. She had not been there since Ethan had been a baby. Philip did not like her going, and her mother had never made her feel welcome, and so she had just simply not been. Before she knew it, years had passed by, and she had not seen any of her family for a long time.

The two hours flew by. Hannah had been interested to hear that Helen had been a victim of domestic violence, and that she had fled to the small town where Hannah now lived, because she had feared that if her husband ever found her, he would kill her. Helen told the group that she had known, that it would never have crossed his mind to look for her in a small town in the south of England.

Hannah shared her recent experience with the group. It was good to get it all off her chest to a group of women who fully understood why she had made the decision she had made They did not judge her for the huge mistake she had made. Each of them had made their own mistakes in dealing with similar circumstances. In fact, Helen had told the group that she had gone back to her husband three times before finally leaving him for good.

Hannah felt supported and encouraged by the group. It was just what she needed, and she was looking forward to going again the following week. She had found somewhere where she didn't have to pretend that everything was okay, and where she could openly admit that she had made the worst decision that she had ever made when she had gone back to her violent and unpredictable husband.

As Hannah was walking out of the day centre, Helen caught up with her. "Hannah, can I give you my telephone number?"

"Yes, of course." She smiled.

Helen scribbled it on an envelope that she had taken from her bag. "If you need anyone to talk to at any time, ring me. I will not break your confidence. I know exactly what you are going through, and I know it's tough!"

Hannah wanted to cry, but she held on to her tears. She left the day centre that afternoon feeling that she had found an ally in Helen.

There were still days when Philip appeared to be trying, and on those days, he was quite pleasant to be around, but then without warning, he would turn.

He was drinking heavily again on his days off. Those were the days that Hannah dreaded the most. He hadn't hit her since she had gone back to him, but she knew he had been close to doing so, on more than a couple of occasions.

He had smashed a vase against the wall one afternoon, and another time he had thrown his plate at the wall and had then screamed at her to immediately clear up the mess.

Hannah's nerves were suffering from the stress of it all. She knew that she needed to get away from Philip before he succeeded in destroying her.

She had started meeting Helen for coffee once a week outside of the Thursday afternoon group. She was blessed with some wonderful friends. Friends that she did not want to lose. She sometimes felt that it would be better to put up with Philip than move away and lose her support network of friends.

It had been her friends and never her family who had been there for her, and as much as she hated her life with Philip, she couldn't cope with the thought of no longer having them in her life.

Chapter Ten
November

The first week in November, Hannah was told the devastating news that Ursula and Dieter were moving back to Germany the third week in November. Dieter had received a promotion, but it meant relocating to Cologne in Germany. The couple had known for just over two weeks, and the two of them had worried about how Hannah would respond to the news. She had not been herself recently, and Ursula was worried about her. So, she arranged to call round to see Hannah one evening when Philip was out working, and the children would be in bed to break the news to her. Hannah had felt like she had been slapped in the face at the news that her two friends would be moving away in less than three weeks. Both Ursula and Hannah had cried and vowed to keep in touch with one another. Ursula had told Hannah that she and the children were very welcome to visit any time. Still, Hannah knew that that would never happen while she remained married to Philip.

After Ursula had gone home that evening, Hannah had gone to bed exhausted from all the tears she had cried. She felt as if she would never get over Ursula moving away. They had been extremely close friends for over three years, and Ursula was more like a mother than just a friend.

She spent the next two weeks helping them pack and get ready for the move as much as her relationship with Philip would allow.

The night before they were due to move, Hannah had cooked a special tea and had Dieter and Ursula round while Philip was working. She had bought them a small gift each, and they had bought gifts for Hannah and each of the children. Hannah's gift was a small gold locket that held a tiny photo of Ursula and Dieter. She felt like her heart was breaking as she thanked the two of them for such a lovely gift. They were leaving early the next morning before Hannah, or the children would be up.

Hannah felt totally consumed with the devastation of her loss. Knowing that Ursula would not be living next door after tomorrow made her feel as if she were drowning in a sea of heartbreak and misery.

It was about a week after they had moved that she noticed Philip was acting a bit strange. She had heard him humming a little tune to himself in the bathroom. It had made her laugh.

When he appeared downstairs, she saw that he had taken a lot of care over his appearance. Sometimes he would go to work without bothering to shave, but that morning he had shaved and had one of his good shirts on and even a little aftershave.

"Where are you going?" she asked.

"To work," he told her, looking very pleased with himself.

"You don't normally go to so much trouble when you're working."

He took hold of her around her waist and told her, "I don't want you going off me, do I?"

Too late for that! She thought to herself. He gave her a lingering kiss on her mouth, leaving Hannah to wonder what had got into him. She was meeting Debbie later for coffee before they picked the children up from school.

"Hey, his Lordship was very pleased with himself this morning. All smiles, hugs and kisses," Hannah told Debbie as they sat down in the tea shop.

Debbie looked puzzled. "I wonder what he's up to."

Hannah shrugged her shoulders and changed the subject to avoid any awkward questions. It had crossed her mind that he might have his eye on someone at work, but it had only been a few weeks since he had threatened to kill himself if she didn't go back to him. He had sworn his undying love for her so, surely, he would not risk losing her for a bit on the side.

Debbie did not tell, Hannah, that she had heard a rumour just a couple of days earlier that Philip had been seen with a blonde woman who was not his wife. She had ignored it, telling herself that there might be a perfectly innocent explanation. And like Hannah, she had told herself that it had only been five minutes since he had cried and begged and pleaded with Hannah to go back to him. But now, after hearing what

Hannah had just told her, she wondered if there was any truth in the rumour. Of course, she had no intention of saying anything to Hannah just now. Hannah was still struggling over Ursula having moved back to Germany, and Debbie did not want to add to her woes with something that might not even be true.

Harrison and Ethan were going to Debbie's to play and then have tea after school that afternoon. They had been over-excited about it over breakfast and had nearly driven Hannah mad. Debbie's husband Kenny would drop them both back home at seven, so it would be just Hannah and Sophie at home for tea that evening. Sophie was a real chatterbox these days, but only Hannah could understand much of what she said.

She made her mother laugh every day with her comical little ways, and it was these small pleasures in life that got Hannah through each day.

She felt sad that her boys couldn't have Debbie's boys around to their house to play. Neither Kenny nor Debbie would allow it just in case Philip came home and had one of his meltdowns in front of their children.

Hannah's boys were still as high as kites when they got back in from Debbie's house. They both kept talking over the top of one another in their hurry to tell their mother everything that they had done at their friend's house.

Sophie was already in bed, and it was well after eight before she managed to settle the other two down.

After she had settled them both, she decided to have a hot soak in the bath and listen to some music. She took herself to bed at nine-thirty and quickly fell into a deep sleep. She was woken by Philip getting into bed. She could smell beer on him, which was odd because he didn't usually have a drink after work, due to everywhere being shut by the time he finished his shift.

She pretended to be asleep as always, hoping that he would not want the usual. As she was dozing off again, she could have sworn that she had got a whiff of a woman's perfume as Philip turned over. What she did not know was that it was three in the morning. Philip had gone back to one of the female driver's house for a couple of drinks after work, and he had already had sex before going home to Hannah. Philip went to sleep feeling very pleased with himself, knowing that Hannah had no idea of the time or of what he had been up to.

The next morning, she heard Philip humming again in the bathroom. He took a lot longer than usual getting ready as he had done the day before.

Hannah was suspicious of her husband's behaviour. He was not a morning person, and so, he would often be grumpy on getting up. When he eventually came downstairs, Hannah questioned him about why he was so happy, and why he was dressing much smarter than he would normally do just to go work.

Philip was a convincing liar, he told her that the boss had asked each of them to dress a little smarter for work because it was good for business, with the promise of a pay rise in the new year, which had put him in a good mood.

Hannah was not convinced that he was telling her the truth, but she let it go for now. He pulled her up close to him and kissed her as he had done the morning before. Yes, Philip was good at deceiving people!

It was only a couple of weeks later that Debbie had asked Hannah to go to hers on the pretence that she wanted Hannah's opinion on some new wallpaper she was thinking of buying. Hannah knew that Philip wouldn't be up before eleven, so she went to Debbie's with Sophie straight after the school run.

Sophie got involved with pulling everything out of the toy box, which sat in the corner of the room, while Debbie and Hannah sat down with a cup of coffee each.

Debbie looked serious as she leaned forward towards Hannah. "You know that I'm your friend and that I would never do or say anything to deliberately hurt you, don't you?"

Hannah frowned, and eyed her friend. "Debbie, are you about to tell me that Philip is having an affair?"

Debbie looked at her, gobsmacked! "How did you know?"

"I didn't, I just guessed. He's getting dressed up to go to work, arriving home after work smelling of drink and a woman's perfume. It doesn't take a genius to work it out!"

Debbie sat with her mouth wide open, still staring at Hannah.

"How did you find out?" Hannah wanted to know from Debbie

"Kenny saw them together on Sunday evening. Philip doesn't know that Kenny saw them. There's been a rumour going around for a couple of weeks, but I didn't want to tell you until I was certain that it was true."

"So, as usual, the wife is the last to know!" Hannah said, angrily.

There were no tears of devastation this time, just anger. Hannah could have been well on the road to a new life with her children. Less than three months ago, he had convinced her that their marriage was worth another try. He had sobbed down the phone, telling her that he could not go on without her. He was probably laughing up his sleeve, believing that he has the best of both worlds, she told herself. She was furious that he was deceiving her yet again. She wanted to scream from the rage she was feeling inside, as she continued to rant to Debbie.

"How could he have behaved so desperate to have me back and do this so soon after? He said he would kill himself if I didn't go back!"

"Emotional blackmail." Was all Debbie said, as she slowly shook her head.

Hannah was now up on her feet, pacing up and down Debbie's living room. "He told me he was, oh, so sorry for everything he had done to me. He sobbed like a child, begged me not to put the phone down on him."

"You're his possession, a possession that he can't live without. He believes that he owns you while he does exactly what he pleases."

"Debbie, will you come to mine and babysit the kids for an hour tomorrow night? It's his day off. He told me that he's going out for a game of darts with Jim, which is where he was supposed to be last Sunday when he was with her! I'm going to catch him red-handed, and let's see how he manages to lie his way out of that one."

It was arranged that Debbie would get to Hannah's house twenty minutes after Philip had gone out. She would ring Debbie to let her know that the coast was clear for her to arrive.

Hannah got back home just after ten-thirty. She had spent much longer at Debbie's house than she had intended to do, so when she got back, she was surprised to find Philip already up. She could barely look at him when he walked through from the kitchen.

"Where have you been?" he snapped.

She felt like shouting that it was none of his business, but she knew she could not give him an inkling that she knew anything.

"I've been to Debbie's for a cup of coffee," she told him flatly.

"That's right, just go gallivanting with your mates when you should be here looking after this house," he told her, obviously annoyed that she had not gone straight home after dropping the boys off at school.

"It was only a cup of coffee," she snapped back.

"Hey, who do you think you are talking to. You watch your tone with me, Madam!"

She wanted to rip his lying, cheating face off, as she struggled to calm her temper. She looked right through him, thinking about the shock he would get the following evening, when she walked into the pub, where she would catch him with her.

Philip eyed her suspiciously, wondering if she knew something as he drank what was left of his cup of tea. He decided that he better go straight home after work that night just in case she was waiting up for him like the last time. Of course, he would deny it to her face if she were to question him about it.

Hannah did not know how she had managed to keep her cool that morning, all she wanted to do was tell him that she knew exactly what he was up to.

After he had left for work, she rang Helen and told her what she had found out that morning. She also told Helen about her plan to catch him out in the pub the following evening.

"What will you do if you catch them together?" Helen asked.

"Tell him that we are finished, and if he refuses to leave, then I will."

"He won't leave, Hannah, I'm telling you now, he won't. He likes a bit on the side, and the thrill and excitement of having the best of both worlds. You are the one he can't live without, the one he loves. He doesn't want her, he's using her. I know what I'm talking about, Hannah."

Helen was eight years older than Hannah, and she respected Helen's opinion. What she did not understand, was if all that Helen had told her was true, then why did Philip treat her so badly, and why would he risk their marriage to have a fling with someone he couldn't care less about? None of it made sense.

When she could not stand her own company any longer, she put Sophie in her pushchair and went for a walk around the shops. Every time she thought about what she was going to do the following night, she felt sick.

Philip would be at home the next day, and she would have to put on an Oscar-winning performance all day. She could not risk him knowing that she knew about his affair.

She was still awake when she heard him come in, but she pretended to be asleep. She had no idea that Philip had not been getting in until two or three in the morning, after spending two to three hours in the bed of the other woman, up to three or four nights a week.

She realised that he had not been near her for almost three weeks, and so she realised that must have been when he had started sleeping with his tart.

After climbing into bed, Philip started stroking Hannah's inner thigh while kissing the back of her neck. She was disgusted that he should touch her when he had been getting up to all sorts with someone else. She moaned, "Don't, Philip, I've been really sick tonight, and I don't want you to catch it." He ignored her at first. "No, Philip, I feel really sick."

He stopped what he was doing and turned over onto his other side, huffing and puffing as he did so.

The next day was difficult. Hannah found it hard to be civil towards Philip, but she knew she had to be, otherwise he would realise that she knew something.

He had asked her how her stomach was. She told him it was still a little upset, hoping that would explain why she was quiet and why she had eaten nothing all morning.

Philip lounged about on the settee all afternoon smoking cigarettes and drinking copious amounts of coffee while watching daytime TV. Even though he believed Hannah to be under the weather, he did nothing to help her in the house. He didn't even offer to collect the boys from school. He really was the most selfish individual!

Finally, the time came for Philip to get ready to go out. He showered, shaved, and spruced himself up while Hannah got the children ready for bed.

Knowing that he was doing all that for someone else filled Hannah with disgust, as she struggled to keep her feelings in check.

She had managed to fool him into believing that she really had got a stomach upset because she had not been able to eat anything at teatime due to her anxiety levels.

Philip left at seven, not suspecting a thing. On his way out, he stopped. "Hope you're feeling better by the morning. Have an early night. A good sleep will put you right." He kissed the top of her head before walking out the door.

Once he had left, Hannah rang Debbie to come around.

She got herself washed and changed into her best dress. She put on a little makeup and some of the perfume that Alice had bought for her last Christmas.

Debbie warned Hannah to be careful. She gave her a five-pound note and told her to take a taxi back home, after the deed had been done.

Hannah arrived at the pub where she knew her husband drank, twenty minutes after he had.

You could have heard a pin drop when she appeared in the doorway of the main lounge. As she walked towards the bar, Philip saw her. The woman he was with was small, like Hannah, but she had short blonde hair, whereas Hannah had long blonde hair. From the back, she looked to be in her mid to late twenties. Hannah was still twenty-one.

Philip took a cigarette out and lit it up. He looked at the woman who appeared to be saying something to him. Everyone in the room knew that Hannah was his wife. It had given Philip a thrill to be seen with this other woman knowing no one who drank in there would tell his wife what he was up to.

Hannah ordered a pint of lager and a double gin and tonic. She drank the gin straight down and then walked towards where her husband stood watching her, while the woman still had her back to Hannah. Before Philip could stop her, she poured the entire contents of the pint glass over the woman's head. The woman spun around and tried to catch her breath while she looked at Hannah with a horrified expression as the freezing cold liquid ran down her face.

"I'm Hannah, Philip's wife and the mother of his three children," Hannah told her with a look of pure satisfaction.

The woman ran out of the pub while Philip stood motionless for several seconds. Hannah lifted her chin and looked at him with a look of defiance. He looked her in the eye with a look that could kill before he turned around and marched out of the pub.

The barman gave Hannah another gin and tonic. "On the house, love. I bet you need it after that?" She drank it down quickly to settle her shaking hands.

As she turned to leave, she heard one of Philip's cronies say, "She'll be in for a right battering tonight."

Hannah turned and looked at him with a look of utter contempt, before lifting his pint glass off the table and throwing what was left of its contents in his face.

A huge roar of laughter went up in the room as Hannah turned and walked out of the pub.

She saw Philip and his floozy up the road having words with one another, so she flagged a passing taxi down to take her home.

Debbie could not believe what Hannah had done in the pub, but now she was worried about what the consequences of her actions would be later.

Hannah did not expect Philip to come home that evening. She was fully convinced that he would be spending the night with his bit on the side.

She took herself to bed just before ten, feeling exhausted from all the stress of the last couple of days. She must have dozed off quickly because she was woken by the sound of him coming up the stairs, and when she looked at the time, it was only ten minutes past ten.

He walked into the room and looked at her with a look that could kill. He had a bottle of whiskey in his hand that he had bought from the off-licence on his way home.

"Thought you were really clever tonight, didn't you?" he hissed in her face. Hannah was all at once very afraid, and her legs had started to tremble under the bed covers. "Well, it's over now because of your childish prank," he told her. His voice and his facial expression showing the strength of his anger towards her. "I thought you were supposed to be ill. You lied, didn't you?" he asked through gritted teeth.

"Why did you take her where everyone knows that you are married to me? Did you not think that someone might tell her? Or were you wanting me to find out?" she asked, mustering up as much courage as she could. "Why did you beg me to come back to you less than three months ago? You threatened to kill yourself if I didn't come back." Believing that she was going to get battered anyway, she told him, "It's over, Philip. I can't live like this. If you loved me, you wouldn't treat me the way you do, and you would not be sleeping with another woman."

"You really are a piece of work. You little witch. I could kill you," he hissed as he grabbed hold of her throat with one hand.

As Philip tightened his grip on her throat, Hannah became terrified, as she watched his expression turn more menacing. He brought his face up closer to hers. "You will never be rid of me!" he growled through gritted teeth. "Wherever you go, I will find you, and when I find you, I will kill you. I will never allow you to live without me, nor will I ever allow you to belong to another man!"

Hannah was convinced that he would kill her, and as she feared for her life, she feared for her children too. What would happen to them if she was no longer around to take care of them after tonight? So, she begged him. "Please let me go, Philip, please!"

He looked as if he had completely lost it when a smirk appeared on his face. He began to taunt her. "I could just snap your neck, or I could just keep squeezing your throat until you are gone."

His smirk turned into a grin. He spoke in a hushed tone that sent an icy shiver down Hannah's spine and made her blood run cold. Every part of her body was convulsing with terror as she struggled to get enough air. "Please let me go. Think about the children, Philip, please."

She could barely speak as he kept a tight grip of her throat. Just as she felt that she might black out, he tightened his grip a little more for just a second. The grin left his face, and he let go of her. "You need to be taught a lesson to never cross me the way you have tonight."

He yanked the bed covers away from her before pinning her down. She struggled to get free, but she could not match his physical strength. He placed one hand over her mouth to stop her from screaming while he used his own weight to hold her down. He subjected her to a violent sexual assault, and then he raped her, so violently, that she was almost sick.

When he had finished, he lay on top of her for several minutes before eventually rolling off to adjust his clothing.

Hannah lay completely still, too afraid to move. She was deeply traumatised, and every part of her body trembled, while she feared what he might do to her next.

She had not believed him capable of behaving in such a depraved and sadistic manner until tonight. Her throat hurt, and other parts of her body were severely bruised.

Philip knew he had gone way too far and that he had been far too brutal. As his temper began to calm, he began to feel shame and deep regret, realising for the first time in his life that there was something very wrong with him. There had to be because his actions tonight had not been the actions of someone who was normal.

Lying next to him was the woman he loved, but the power he had held over her, along with the terror he had seen on her face as she begged for her life, had aroused in him an animalistic sexual urge, that he had not tried to control.

He knew there was no getting back from this because what had been done could never be undone. He felt sure that what he had just put Hannah through had just ended their marriage.

They both lay in silence for what felt like an age.

Hannah needed to use the bathroom, and so, with shaking legs she forced herself up off the bed to make her way to the bathroom, hoping that Philip would not start again. She felt very unsteady as she made her way along the landing.

Passing urine was excruciating, so much so, that she felt as if she was going to faint. She clung to the sink for support and only just managed to get her head far enough over it, as she began to vomit.

Philip heard and quickly ran to the bathroom. He rinsed the vomit from the sink while Hannah still clung to it.

She felt helpless as Philip washed her face and her mouth with a cloth. He lifted her up and carried her through to their bedroom, where he laid her on the bed before pulling the covers over her. Hannah could not look at him.

"I'm sorry. I'm sorry," Philip told her repeatedly as he buried his face in her hair, "I don't know what's wrong with me. Please forgive me," he begged as he cried.

Hannah was still in shock. She did not want to look at him, nor could she bear the touch of his hands on her. The feel of his breath against her as he wept and begged for her forgiveness made her feel sick again, she hung her head over the side of the bed as she began to vomit once more.

Philip was afraid that there might be serious consequences to his actions if he had severely injured her. He lifted his head and watched her as she continued to tremble.

She lay her head back on her pillow, but all the while, she kept her face turned away from his.

He took the bottle of whiskey, and after unscrewing the top, he took a couple of large mouthfuls to settle his nerves. He forced Hannah to drink some, telling her it would settle her nerves and make her feel better. Although she did not like the taste or the way it burned her throat, it did help.

Philip was beside himself. His biggest fear was, that she might tell one of her friends what had taken place that night. He did not want anyone to know what he had done to her, especially his own family. His mother would be appalled and would never forgive him if she were to find out.

It would be many years before rape within marriage would become a criminal act, but if Hannah had serious enough injuries, he knew she could press charges against him over them, even if she could not have her own husband charged with rape.

She got herself further under the covers after the whiskey settled her nerves, and by some miracle, she even managed to get some sleep. Philip decided that he would not go to work in the morning. He not only needed to make sure she was all right, but he needed to prevent her from leaving him too.

He would tell Jim that Hannah was terribly ill and he needed to be at home to look after her and the children. He would take the week off while he tried to think of a plan to prevent her from leaving. But he would not be able to watch her every minute of every day, and so, he knew he would have to come up with something. He had another couple of swigs of the whiskey before cleaning the carpet where Hannah had been sick.

When Hannah woke early the next morning, she pulled away from Philip, who was lying up close to her with his arm across her. The memory of the night before came flooding back. Physically she was injured, but emotionally she was completely broken!

She didn't want to do anything other than stay in bed and sleep, to keep the thoughts of the previous night out of her head. She pulled the covers over her head and tried to go back to sleep. She had suffered a huge trauma, and that was her body and her mind's way of dealing with it.

For the first time since they had married, Philip had to take responsibility for the children. He told them that Mummy still had a poorly tummy and was staying in bed.

"I heard Mummy being sick last night, and she was crying. I always cry when I'm being sick," Ethan told him.

Philip looked at his young son and hoped that was all he'd heard. "She'll be better soon," Philip reassured the children.

After they were all ready, Philip went up to check on Hannah before they set off to school. She was in bed with the covers over her head. He gently pulled them back and found her asleep.

He kept the covers away from her face and gave her a light kiss on her head. He wanted to weep, because he could tell there was something very wrong with Hannah, and whatever it was, it was he who had caused it.

Debbie was immediately concerned when she saw Philip with the children and no sign of Hannah. On the way home, she hurried to catch up with him. "Where is Hannah?" she demanded to know.

"She's in bed with an upset stomach."

"What have you done to her?"

"ME? I haven't done anything to her."

"You never take the boys to school, so you can come off it. I know all about your tart, and I also know that Hannah caught you with her last night. I looked after your children while she followed you." She was so angry that she wanted to slap Philip's face.

"Look, I don't have to explain anything to you, but Hannah drank a lot of whiskey last night after we had rowed. She's in bed with a raging hangover. She's been sick all over, and she's in no state to look after the kids. I have to take the day off work to look after not just the kids, but her too."

Debbie did not know whether to believe him or not. She decided she would ring Hannah at teatime to check that she was okay.

When Philip got back with Sophie, he sat her down on the floor and put Tots TV on for her to watch while he went back upstairs to Hannah. She was still sleeping, he decided that it was probably best to let her sleep.

She was having all kinds of weird dreams, all of which involved her husband in one way or another.

Philip went downstairs and lit a cigarette as he tried to think about what he should do. Should he ring his mother, and confess to her what he had done, so that she could help, or should he keep quiet and hope that Hannah would snap out of it?

He watched Sophie as she held her doll while she watched TV. He asked himself how he would feel if someone in the future was to do to her what he had done to her mother. He knew that he would want to kill them.

He tried to contemplate a future without Hannah in it and found that he could not. He had meant every word when he had begged her to go back to him a few weeks earlier, but he had failed to live up to his promises simply because he just couldn't. He did not know why he couldn't control his anger or why he could not control his violent behaviour towards his long-suffering wife. Maybe he just liked hurting women, he told himself.

He liked to have rough sex with other women. Rachel, the woman Hannah had caught him with, liked it rough, and he had not been able to get enough of it.

What he had done to Hannah, the previous night, was unforgiveable, and he would never be able to undo what he had done. He did not care about Rachel! She was not fit to lace Hannah's boots. He had used her to provide him with the kind of dirty sex that he would never expect from his wife.

Hannah had never wanted anything other than to be loved by him. He was the only man that she had ever been with, and the thought that one day she might leave him and meet someone else was more than he could bear to think about.

Hannah woke halfway through the morning, needing the loo. She felt strange and wobbly as she made her way to the bathroom. Passing urine was still excruciating. She held her breath until she had finished. After washing her hands, she went back into the bedroom and crawled back into bed.

Everything around her felt strange and unreal, and she had a very unpleasant feeling in the pit of her stomach. Just then, Philip appeared in the bedroom.

"Are you okay, love?" he asked, knowing full well that she was far from okay.

"No," was the only answer she gave him.

"Come downstairs, Sophie is asking for you. Please, look at me when I'm speaking to you."

She shook her head as she continued to look at the floor. "You have degraded and humiliated me most disgustingly and appallingly, and now you want us to go on like it's never happened."

The look on her face spoke volumes.

"I know I've treated you really badly, and I know that I really hurt you last night. What I did to you is unforgivable, but I was really angry over what had happened in the pub."

She lifted her face to look at him for the first time since the attack. "YOU RAPED ME!" she screamed at him.

Philip was speechless from the impact of the accusation. Sophie, who had heard her mother scream at Philip, had started to cry.

"Go and see to your daughter!" Hannah told him, the disgust she felt toward him clearly visible on her face.

Philip left the room, shocked that she had even dared to speak to him in such a way. He picked Sophie up and tried to sooth her. She put her little hand on his cheek.

"Want Mummy. Want Mummy," she repeated over and over while her bottom lip quivered.

"Mummy isn't well, darling. She'll get up later today."

"Want Mummy!" Sophie wailed as tears poured from her eyes.

"Hey, Sophie, guess what? I know where Mummy hides her chocolate. Shall we see if we can find some for Sophie?"

A smile appeared on her chubby little face as she blinked away her tears.

"Here it is." Philip handed his little girl some of the chocolate that he found in Hannah's hiding place. She appeared to be consoled for now. He poured her a cup of milk while he poured himself a large whiskey to calm his nerves.

Hannah lay on the bed, trying to push the memory of the night before out of her head. She could still smell the beer and cigarettes from his breath as he abused her in the most appalling manner. The memory made her feel sick. She felt like she was going mad. Strange feelings swept through her mind, making her feel panicky, as she struggled to keep a grip on her emotions.

Later that afternoon, Philip brought the boys home from school.

"Is Mummy up yet? I've made her a get well soon card. Look." Harrison showed the card to his father, who gave him a weak smile and told him it was a nice card.

"Is Mummy better, Daddy?" Ethan asked.

"No, not yet. She might get up later." Philip realised just at that moment, that Hannah had not eaten or drunk anything all day. Once they were home, he poured a glass of water and took it to her. He found her awake but still lying-in bed, staring at the wall.

"I've brought you some water. Try to drink it, you haven't had anything all day." She ignored him and continued to stare at the wall.

Philip was scared, really scared! He sat on the floor with his face up close to hers and stroked her hair as he had done so often in the past when he was trying to get around her after he had hurt her. "Please come downstairs. The kids are desperate to see you. Please for their sakes, not mine."

Hannah got out of bed without looking at her husband and went downstairs to her children. She looked a mess. She hadn't washed, cleaned her teeth, or combed her hair, all of which was very unlike her.

She sat partly on her side because sitting was painful. Harrison gave her the card he had made and planted a wet kiss on her cheek. Ethan watched her anxiously, as Sophie climbed on to her knee. Hannah was not her usual self. Her strange behaviour was frightening the boys, and Philip could tell. He walked across to her and took hold of her hand, telling the children that him and Mummy were going to make tea together as he led her into the kitchen. Once they were in the kitchen, he told her. "Hannah, you have to pull yourself together. You're frightening the children, and you are scaring the hell out of me!"

Fresh tears ran down her face, she was not herself at all, but she could not snap out of it. She felt as if she was losing her grip on reality, while fearing that this might be how a person feels just before they were about to go insane.

All the trauma and disappointments that she had suffered since she was eight years old had come crashing down on her. She had a feeling of hysteria that kept building and then receding as she fought to keep herself under control.

Philip really should have had the sense to call a doctor, but how could he, when he knew it would all come out. And he was afraid of facing criminal charges for assault and battery, so he carried on trying to deal with the situation himself.

Hannah took things out of the cupboards and the fridge on automatic pilot, while Philip helped for the first time in over five years of marriage. He kept glancing at her as they prepared the evening meal. He told her,

"You need to get a bath and change that nightgown once the kids have gone to bed."

Once the meal was ready, Philip called the children to the table. He lifted Sophie into her highchair; even she appeared subdued.

As they all sat around the dinner table, the tension in the room was palpable. Hannah stared at her plate while she moved her food around with her fork. She ate nothing. Philip watched her anxiously, and the boys watched her with knots in their stomachs.

The phone suddenly rang, making them all jump. It was Debbie, who was so disappointed on hearing Philip's voice on the other end of the line. "How's Hannah?" she asked, trying to sound polite.

"Not good," he told her truthfully.

"Can I speak to her?"

"She's not able to come to the phone just now. Could you call back tomorrow?" he asked, trying to buy himself some time.

Debbie could have screamed with frustration. She was desperate to know if Hannah was all right, but all she could do was hope that Hannah would turn up for the walk to school the following morning.

Helen had been expecting a phone call from Hannah all day, but on not hearing from her, she had rung just a few minutes after Debbie, but had got the same response from Philip, that Hannah was unwell and not available to come to the phone.

Helen's instincts told her that something was very wrong, having lived with domestic violence herself. Helen decided to try again the following day, while she hoped that Hannah wasn't trapped at home, seriously injured.

Once the children were all in bed, Philip ran her a bath. He sat on the bathroom floor with his face in his hands. He was not going to leave her to have a bath alone because of her strange behaviour.

As Hannah climbed into the bath, the hot water touched where she was injured, causing her to gasp loudly. Philip flicked his head up at the sound. Hannah closed her eyes as the pain slowly subsided. She washed as quickly as she could before climbing out and drying herself. She dressed into the clean pyjamas that Philip had got out for her to wear.

She cleaned her teeth and brushed her hair before walking back into the bedroom.

She had not uttered one single word all evening to her husband. She climbed back into bed and took the glass of watered-down whisky from him. She hated the taste, but she needed something to help her nerves. After she had drunk it, Philip poured her another, telling her it would settle her and help her to sleep. She still could not look at him. He poured himself a large glass as he worried about what tomorrow would bring.

After Hannah had fallen asleep, Philip went out to the local off licence to buy cigarettes and another bottle of whiskey. When he got home, he emptied what was left of the other bottle into his glass. He stroked his chin with his other hand as he wondered how they were ever going to recover from this. He told himself that she would snap out of it eventually. He knew Hannah loathed him just now, and he knew that it was what he truly deserved.

That night he hardly slept, Hannah kept moaning and crying out in her sleep throughout the night, and when he tried to hold her, she pulled away from him.

The next morning, he made her get up and get washed and dressed. He thought that if she got back into her normal routine, then she might snap out of her present state of mind. He had got her to wear her polo neck sweater to hide the pale purple mark on her throat.

As they walked to school, Debbie caught up with them. "Hi Hannah, are you feeling better?"

Hannah wanted to beg Debbie to help her. She wanted to tell her that her husband had raped her in the most violent way and that she felt like she was losing her mind, but she couldn't because Philip was right by her side.

Debbie could see that there was something very wrong with Hannah, but there was nothing that she could do, because if she tried to interfere, it could make things a lot worse for her.

Debbie stood from a distance watching Hannah as Philip helped the boys change their footwear. Hannah was standing with a blank expression on her face. Her arms hung limply by her sides, and she looked totally defeated! Debbie cried once she was home because she had no idea what to do to help her best friend.

Philip and Hannah walked home in silence. Hannah didn't want to talk, and Philip was at a loss as to what to say. Once they were back in the house, he told her very sternly. "Hannah, you need to snap of it. People are going to think you are mad if you keep carrying on this way, and I don't know what to do with you!" His voice rising as he finished his sentence.

All at once, blind panic swept through Hannah. She couldn't breathe. She felt like she was drowning. She ran upstairs with Philip behind her. She sat on the bed with her arms wrapped around herself, and as she rocked back and forth, she wailed loudly. Philip wrapped his arms around her. He could hear Sophie crying in her pushchair, but Hannah was his priority right now. He tried to calm her down, but he couldn't.

She did not push him away this time because she needed someone to cling to, even if it was him. He had to leave her while he rang his mother, asking her to get to theirs as quickly as possible. Frank was at work, so Alice took a taxi.

When Alice arrived, she found Philip waiting for her at the front door with Sophie crying in his arms. Alice heard what sounded like an injured animal coming from upstairs and was horrified to be told it was Hannah.

"Philip, ring the surgery, and tell them we have a medical emergency here, and we need a doctor immediately." Philip did as he had been asked, as Alice hurried upstairs to Hannah.

"What is it, sweetheart? How can I help?" Alice asked, her heart full of fear as she went towards her daughter-in-law. Hannah continued to weep loudly, unable to speak. Alice held her and rocked her slowly in her arms as you would a small, injured child.

The doctor arrived less than thirty minutes later. After giving Hannah a strong sedative, he explained that she was in the middle of a breakdown, and that she may need to be admitted to a psychiatric hospital. Philip's face fell, he held one of his hands against his forehead, the shock of what he was being told, knocking the wind out of him.

Alice told the doctor. "No way! If she goes into the hospital, she may never come out. No, we will look after her and the children."

"Okay, but if her condition deteriorates, then she may have to be sectioned, and I'm afraid that if that happens, it will be taken out of your hands." The doctor, said, as he carefully observed Hannah.

Philip was rocked to his very core. He had not intended for any of this to happen. How he wished that he could turn the clock back so that the events of the night before last had never taken place.

The doctor gave Philip a prescription for some strong tranquillisers, telling him to get them immediately. He told Philip and his mother that under no circumstances was Hannah to be left alone. He explained that he would call again tomorrow.

Alice stayed with Hannah and Sophie while Philip went and got the medication.

He had been practically chain-smoking all morning, so he bought himself two more packets of cigarettes. He could have killed for a pint, at that moment because his nerves were completely shattered.

While Philip was out, the injection had started to do its job, and Hannah had started to calm down considerably. Alice had gone downstairs to make her a cup of tea, but Hannah had fallen asleep on the bed, still wearing her coat and shoes.

When Alice got back upstairs, and saw that Hannah was now asleep, Alice told herself that it didn't matter, so long as Hannah was no longer in the terrible distress, she had found her in.

Alice really needed Frank home, so she rang his work and explained that someone in the family was very seriously ill and Frank needed to get to his son's house as soon as he could.

Philip was a little worried that Hannah may have told his mother what he had done to her, so he was greatly relieved when he returned home, to be told that Hannah was now sleeping and that she had told his mother nothing.

Frank arrived nearly thirty minutes after Alice had rung his work. As soon as he got there, Alice broke down and told him all that had happened. Frank immediately put the blame for Hannah's illness down to Philip's behaviour. When he managed to get Philip on his own, he had asked him what he had done to Hannah to cause her to be so distressed. Of course, Philip said that he could not believe that Frank was blaming him. Frank had looked at Philip with contempt and simply told him, "The truth will out!"

After Frank had arrived, he took charge. "I'm owed some holiday, and under the circumstance, I'll be able to take the rest of the week off. The children will have to come to us, Alice, for the rest of the week, and we'll have to set up a family rota so that Hannah always has someone with her. Philip can't do it all by himself. I know James and Gill will want to help."

Their daughter Jane was only twenty, but she could help with babysitting at the weekends. They decided not to tell their son Alex because he was away at university. Nor would they tell Hannah's family just yet.

Alice was very relieved that she would have Frank at home during the coming week.

"The doctor was talking about having her sectioned," Alice told him tearfully.

Frank patted her hand. "We won't let that happen. She'll be fine. She just needs a lot of support and no stress." As he finished speaking, he looked in Philip's direction. Philip said nothing, but he knew Frank's words were directed at him.

Helen rang just before lunch. Alice took the call.

"No, Hannah is extremely ill just now and won't be available to speak with you for a while to come. No, I can't give you any details, except that Hannah is being well looked after by her husband and his family."

Helen was more than just a little alarmed. She was convinced that Hannah had been severely injured by Philip after she had followed him the other evening. She had been fine when Helen had spoken with her that afternoon. Helen decided to get in touch with either May or Pat, who ran the Thursday afternoon group, to discuss her concerns over Hannah.

Debbie was given the same response from Alice when she had called just a little while later.

When Kenny came home from work that evening, Debbie had cried in his arms over her worries that Philip had done something terrible to Hannah. She knew that her hands were tied for the time being. All she could do was hope and wait.

Mid-afternoon, Hannah woke as the powerful drug she had been given had begun to wear off. She was surprised to find herself still wearing her coat and shoes. She could hear people talking downstairs as she sat up. She had a strong sense of foreboding in her chest and stomach. Nothing felt real. She didn't feel real. Terror began to fill her heart and mind once more. She wanted to run and scream from her own feelings and her own thoughts. She began shaking uncontrollably. She screamed Philip's name. He ran up the stairs, taking two at a time, with Frank following close behind him. Alice stayed downstairs while she tried to comfort Sophie.

Philip held her tight while Frank stroked her hair, asking. "Now, lass, what's this all about?"

Hannah clung to the man who had caused her breakdown, terrified that she was losing her mind, and because she did not want to be left alone in the room with her terrifying thoughts and feelings.

Frank went back down to Alice, very badly shaken over what he had just witnessed.

"Alice, we need to collect the boys after school and take all three children to ours. We can't let them see their mother like that. I'll pop back once the children are in bed and give Philip a couple of hours break. We'll speak to James and Gill later and get them on board. I'm afraid a lot is going to fall on you, my love. I can only take a week off work. And I'm sure Philip won't be able to afford to lose more than a week's wages."

"I'll be fine Frank, let's just take it a week at a time."

Alice packed the children's things into two holdalls so that once the boys were collected from school, they, along with Sophie, could be taken straight to their grandparents' house.

It was explained to them that they would stay at Nanna's until Mummy was a bit better. They accepted it without too many questions. It was a real help that all the children loved being at Nanna's house. It was cosy and warm, and there were always treats and lots of cuddles whenever they stayed there.

Philip did his best to keep Hannah calm during the hours that followed. Frank had called round for an hour after the children were in bed, but there was not much he could do.

Philip had eaten the meal that Alice had sent round, but they had not been able to get Hannah to eat anything. Frank left feeling heavy-hearted, praying that she would recover

. Later that evening, Philip had given Hannah another glass of watered-down whiskey, against his better judgement when the medication had not calmed her enough.

He had not realised that since going back to him in September, Hannah's mental health had been suffering, as she struggled against anxiety and depression while trying to keep a brave face.

The doctor called in at nine the following morning, just before Alice had arrived to give Philip a break.

Frank had taken Sophie home with him after dropping the boys off at school.

The doctor told Philip that he was prescribing an anti-depressant that had a strong sedative effect. The sedative effect would take effect immediately, but the anti-depressant side of the medication would take about three weeks to kick in, and from then on, Hannah's condition should start to improve.

Philip was asked to stop the other tablets because she would not be able to take both medications simultaneously.

The doctor was happy that Hannah's condition had not got any worse overnight, so he said he would call again the following morning. He instructed Philip to ring the surgery if she got any worse.

Philip allowed Hannah to stay in bed over the forty-eight hours that followed because the strong medication was knocking her out. He reasoned that if she was sleeping, she wasn't suffering those awful symptoms. He made sure to keep her neck covered with a scarf so that no one saw the bruising to her throat that had now fully come out. He had stopped his mother from removing it at one point, and she had given him a strange look.

When Hannah was awake, she felt like she was living in hell! She experienced unwanted scary thoughts that would invade her mind unexpectantly. Everything felt unreal, and she suffered crippling panic attacks. But most of the time, she was in a drug-induced sleep, which Alice agreed was giving her mind a chance to heal.

Later in the week, the GP had advised Philip to get Hannah up for at least two or three hours in the afternoons.

"Maybe get her out for a short walk, to get some fresh air. Perhaps she could watch some light television or do some other activity that she enjoys."

Hannah clung to Philip during the first two weeks that followed her breakdown. She needed someone with her every minute and could not cope with being left alone for even a few minutes.

Philip was glad that she no longer looked at him with pure hatred and that she hadn't been carted off to the nearest mental institution. His main worry was that she might not get better and what would that mean for their future? Their children's future? What if she ended up in a mental hospital for the rest of her life? he asked himself. It was more than he could bear to think about. His hope was that if she did get well, she would forgive him and stay.

Both Philip and Frank had to go back to work the following week. Philip bumped into Rachel more than once or twice his first day back at work because she worked for the same taxi firm, but he could not bear to look at her.

Hannah had high morals, and she had remained faithful to him despite all that he had put her through. She was never meant to find out about Rachel. It wasn't even an affair. It had just been sex! He had been shocked when Hannah had walked into the pub and had caught him red-handed.

He remembered the blind rage he had been in when he had got home that evening, because he believed Hannah had made him look a right idiot in front of Rachel and his mates. The intensity of his anger, that night, meant it had been a miracle that he had managed to stop himself from choking Hannah to death.

He had never used sexual violence against her before that night, but he had been aroused to the point of no return, and now he could hardly believe himself what he had done.

Alice was an absolute brick, giving Hannah her full support day in and day out while she slowly recovered.

The medication kicked in after three weeks, as the doctor had said it would, and very slowly, Hannah began to recover. But the road to recovery was long and arduous. There were times that she felt sure she would not make it, and there were times when Philip believed that as a family, they would not survive.

He would sometimes lose patience with Hannah, and his children.

He had never had to put anyone ahead of himself before. So, he found himself leaning very heavily on his family for support. The truth was that had it not been for the unwavering support of Frank, Alice, James, and even Gill, then Philip and Hannah would have gone under.

Chapter Eleven

The children were returning to school after the Christmas holidays. It was five weeks since Hannah's breakdown. She was taking her boys to school for the first time since it had happened with the support of Alice. Hannah had hardly been out of the house at all during the last five weeks, and when she had, she had been with Philip each time.

Hannah and Alice were going to Debbie's for a cup of coffee after dropping the boys off. Debbie was desperate to see Hannah. She had not seen her since Hannah had taken the boys to school with Philip at the beginning of her illness.

It had been Alice who had taken Harrison and Ethan to and from school leading up to the holidays. Debbie had made a point of exchanging greetings and passing the time of day with Alice. She had deliberately tried to befriend the woman, because she had been desperate to find out how Hannah was. Alice had begun to trust the young woman, and so, she had begun to confide in Debbie regarding the state of Hannah's mental health.

Debbie had rung Alice the week before the new term was to begin, to invite her and Hannah around to hers the first morning of the new school term.

When she had met the two of them on the corner of her street that morning, Debbie had been stunned at Hannah's appearance. The once very animated Hannah, who had a talent for making people laugh, was very withdrawn. Her face was much thinner, and she had dark circles under her eyes. She looked far too thin, having lost a lot of weight, that she could ill afford to lose.

The three of them went back to Debbie's house after the children had been dropped off at school. They each had a cup of coffee and some left-over Christmas cake. Sophie had milk and biscuits as she sat on her

Nanna's knee. Hannah hardly spoke a word, except to say thank you for the coffee and cake and then goodbye as they left.

Debbie had never seen such a deterioration in someone in her life. She was left feeling terribly upset, and so angry at Philip, that she wished him dead, for what he had put Hannah through When Kenny got in from work that evening, Debbie had cried in his arms.

"I don't think Hannah will ever be the same again," she told him. "You should have seen her, Kenny. She looks terrible! She is stick-thin, she's lost what little confidence she had. She couldn't even give me eye contact, and we've been close friends for ages! She'll be stuck with him forever if she doesn't recover."

Kenny held Debbie while she continued to cry. "There is nothing that you can do other than be there for her," he told her. "Her mother-in-law is doing a good job of looking after her, so she is not completely at her husband's mercy. If she can start going out a little with Alice like she did today, she may start to get back on her feet a little."

"I do hope so, Kenny. I can't bear to see her like that. He must have done something awful to her for her to have had such a bad breakdown."

Debbie dried her eyes, blew her nose, and went to get supper ready.

That morning when Hannah and Alice had got back from Debbie's, Philip was up and was drinking a cup of tea in the living room.

"Where have you two been?" he snapped at his mother.

"We've been having a cup of coffee with one of Hannah's friends."

"Debbie?" he said with more than a hint of agitation in his voice.

"Yes, she's a nice woman, I like her."

Philip had one eye on Hannah, who was sat on one of the armchairs with her arms wrapped around herself, rocking slightly, wishing that she could shake herself out of whatever she was in the grip of.

"Don't be telling that nosey cow any of our business!" Philip snapped again.

"Of course, I'm not going to do that." Alice lied. She had told Debbie everything about Hannah's breakdown, her medication, the slow recovery, etc, yet she had given her son a glowing report over his devotion to getting Hannah back to good health. Debbie knew it was a mother's blind love for her son that was speaking. She knew much more about Philip than Alice realised.

Philip turned his attention to Hannah and snapped. "Hannah, have you taken your medication this morning?"

She turned towards him and nodded.

Alice was furious at the way he had just snapped at Hannah. "You don't have to talk to her like that, she is still very poorly!"

"Well, tell her to stop rocking like some retard!"

Alice was livid. "If you want her to get better, then you had better not speak like that in front of her! What is wrong with you this morning? Stop snapping the head off everyone!"

He gave his mother a filthy look. Hannah stopped rocking. She was back under his full control. She was far too ill to cope with the children on her own. She needed to be supported in everything she did, even with the simplest of tasks. Philip was trying harder than he ever had since they had married, because he was still riddled with guilt and remorse over what he had done to her. It was still their secret for now.

He did not believe for one second that he had raped her because, as far as he was concerned, a married woman's role was to provide her husband with sex. It was his right to demand it whenever he wanted it, or so he believed. He had admitted to himself that he had hurt her badly, but he had not raped her. Of that, he was convinced.

After Helen had voiced her concerns to both May and Pat, they had tried to contact Hannah but had got Philip on the end of the telephone instead. He had told them that Hannah was terribly ill and would not be attending the Thursday group for the foreseeable future. They had left it until the Christmas school holidays and had tried to make contact again and had been delighted to have got Alice on the telephone while Philip was out working. They had arranged to call round to see Hannah on the Friday of the new term.

They arrived at one-thirty in the afternoon while Sophie was having her afternoon nap.

When they saw Hannah that afternoon, they had not even tried to hide their feelings of shock, at the marked difference in her appearance. She had always been thin, but now she looked anorexic. The light had gone out of her eyes. Her clothes hung on her, and her hair was scraped back in a rough ponytail. She struggled to make eye contact and hardly spoke a word all the time they were there. They managed to convince Alice that although Hannah was extremely ill, she would still benefit from attending the group each Thursday and that it would help her with her recovery. So, it was arranged that May would collect Hannah and Sophie the following Thursday, to take them to the group, and then she would drive them both back home afterwards.

Once they were outside, May, broke down, while Pat whispered the words, "What has he done to her?"

Neither of them had expected such a noticeable change in Hannah's appearance. They did, however, take some comfort in the knowledge that Hannah's husband's family were heavily involved with her care and that she had not been left totally at his mercy.

Very slowly, as the months passed by, Hannah grew stronger, and she began to get back to some kind of normality, although she remained fragile.

As she started to do more and more for herself, Alice spent less time with her and more time at home, catching up with things that she had had to let slide while she had supported her daughter-in-law. She and Frank still had the children from Saturday afternoon until Sunday evening to give the young couple some time to relax together.

They had resumed marital relations many weeks after that awful night. Philip had not wanted to cause a relapse in her recovery by insisting on his rights as a husband, so he had not gone near her for weeks, but eventually, desire and the need for sex had got the better of him. He had told Hannah that it was her duty as his wife.

The first attempt had been a total disaster because Hannah had been so tense that she could not go through with it. But eventually, they had made love again many weeks after that dreadful night.

But Hannah hated it! She had not the slightest interest, in that side of her marriage, and wished he would just leave her be when they were in bed together. The memory of that awful night, would stick with her for the rest of her life, so, how could she be expected to enjoy that side of their relationship, knowing what Philip was capable of.

As the summer months progressed, Hannah's friends were pleased to see her becoming more like her old self.

She had started going out with Debbie and Helen every Monday afternoon to the coffee shop near the school. Hannah had eventually told each of them what had taken place the night she had followed Philip to the pub.

Both Debbie and Helen had been disgusted and had urged her to leave at the first opportunity, warning her that it would only be a matter of time before Philip did something like it again.

Although Hannah knew that it was a possibility, she just did not have the emotional strength to leave. She felt sure that she didn't have the strength, just now, to bring three children up alone. Although on the outside she appeared to have made a good recovery, on the inside, she remained fragile.

Hannah's faith in the existence of an almighty God, had remained intact. Her faith had helped her through the darkest days of her recovery. Philip had often mocked her for her faith in the past because he was an atheist and believed anyone who believed what was written in the Bible was a weirdo. So, when Hannah had started to attend a weekly Bible study group, he was more than annoyed. The truth was, he did not like his wife having any involvement in anything that didn't involve him. He believed he should be the centre of her world and so, he had put obstacles in the way to stop her from attending the group as regularly as she would have liked.

Frank and Alice had stopped having the children overnight on Saturdays as Hannah became ever stronger, but they did carry on having them through the day, each Saturday, to give Hannah a bit of respite each week.

Philip had taken up drinking on a Sunday lunchtime again, much to Hannah's disappointment. After drinking too much, he would come home in a bad mood and go straight up to bed to sleep it off.

He had come home one Sunday and had called Hannah a madwoman and had told her that she belonged in the loony bin before storming upstairs to bed. His cruel mockery of her illness had made her cry. She was not completely well yet, and she feared she might have a relapse if

Philip were to go back to his old ways. When he had eventually got up, he had apologised and had told her that he had not meant it, but Hannah had still been terribly upset by his outburst.

It was late December when she discovered that she was pregnant again. She and the children had all had a stomach bug. Philip had managed to escape it. After she had recovered, she had asked Philip to use protection, telling him that her pill would not be as effective due to the bug. He had refused, telling her that it did not feel the same and that she would be fine. She had hoped that she would not get pregnant, but she had.

Hannah had been devastated by the test results because the last thing she needed was another baby. She knew Philip would be furious once he found out about the pregnancy even though it was his fault. And she certainly did not want to bring another child into this mess!

The doctor had reduced her medication to a safer dose because of the pregnancy. He had also offered her a termination, but Hannah had told him it was out of the question.

It was nearly a month from the positive test results before she dared to tell Philip.

"YOU HAD BETTER GET RID OF IT!" he had shouted at her when she had finally told him.

"No, I can't do that, Philip. You know what I believe." She prayed silently that she would have the courage to stand up for what she believed to be right.

"I am telling you right now that you are going to get rid of it!" he told her through gritted teeth.

She had not seen him as angry as this since the night he attacked her before her breakdown. She felt sick with fear as she shook her head, while trying to be as brave as she could be. She told him. "Philip, I asked you to use a condom, but you refused. It is not my fault that I am pregnant. I do not want another baby, I really don't, but I cannot do what you are trying to force me to do."

She was afraid that Philip would beat her black and blue, for daring to stand up for herself, but he didn't. But neither did he speak to her again for the rest of the evening.

The next few days were difficult. Philip stomped around the house with a face like thunder and shouted at the children over absolutely nothing. Even Sophie, who was nearly three, knew to be quiet when Philip was behaving that way.

Hannah feared that she might have a relapse, believing that she did not have the emotional strength to cope with Philip's behaviour.

She knew she had to speak to someone about the pregnancy, or she would go mad. She decided to talk to Helen. She loved having Debbie as a friend, but she could be a little too forceful with her opinions, whereas Helen was not. Hannah poured everything out in Helen's kitchen one afternoon. She told her how devastating it had been to hear Philip insist that she had an abortion, when it was his fault, she was pregnant.

Is that really not an option?" Helen asked carefully. Hannah told her it wasn't.

"Hannah, do you think that you are doing the right thing by staying with Philip? You are more than capable of looking after the children on your own, including the one you're carrying. I was pregnant with Jason when I left my ex-husband. And you know what? It's been a lot easier bringing my kids up on my own than it would have been if I had had him to cope with him day in and day out as well."

"I hear what you're saying, Helen, but I don't feel emotionally strong enough to leave Philip just now."

"You are much stronger than you know. Look what you've come through this year. That takes guts and determination! YOU CAN DO IT... You can!"

Hannah looked down at the floor as she thought about what Helen was saying, but she felt within herself that she was not strong enough to take that step just yet.

Eventually, much to Hannah's embarrassment, everyone learned of her pregnancy.

Philip did not bring up the subject of a termination again, but he made sure that she knew that he was not happy about the pregnancy. As the pregnancy progressed, he started to drink more heavily and would come home in the foulest of moods, after a heavy session

He had never hit Hannah when she had been pregnant with her other children, but he had hit her several times during this pregnancy. Even while she had been heavily pregnant.

She had not known how she had kept her sanity during those months. But the intensity of her loathing towards her husband grew as her pregnancy progressed.

Things just went from bad to worse once Liam was born at the back end of July. He had been born six weeks early and had stayed in the neonatal unit until he was strong enough to be discharged.

He had been quite sickly during the first week of his life, to the point that Hannah had been anxious as to whether he would survive, whereas Philip had appeared not to care. During the second week he had greatly improved and had been discharged at the end of it.

As she held Liam in her arms, after his birth, she made a silent promise to him that he would not see the violence that her other children had. She told herself that as soon as she had recovered from the birth, she would find her way to a refuge, as far away as was possible. She would wait until she had had her six-week postnatal check-up, and then she would find some way to get herself and her children away from the monster that she had already wasted nine years of her life on.

Her doctor increased her medication after Liam had been born because he was concerned that the changes in her hormones might bring on some of her old symptoms. But if anything was going to bring back those symptoms, it would be Philip's cruelty.

It was the August bank holiday when things came to a sudden head. Philip rarely had a Saturday off, and so he had gone out drinking all afternoon with his cronies. Hannah was dreading him coming home because she knew what he would be like, when he got home.

Liam had been home for just over two weeks, and Philip had mostly ignored him. Hannah's heart broke for her youngest child. He did not deserve a father who hardly acknowledged his existence!

She often thought about the time she had got herself and the children to a place of safety. Almost two years had gone by since then. She felt ashamed, when she thought about all the pain and suffering that could have been avoided if she had not put Philip's feelings ahead of her own.

She felt a terrible guilt over all the awful things her other children had seen during their young lives. It made her want to weep for them.

The truth was, she would have been long gone by now if it had not been for the terrible breakdown she had suffered.

It was four in the afternoon, and Hannah was at the sink chopping vegetables for tea when she saw Philip walking up the garden path. She knew straight away that he had had a lot to drink and that by the look on his face, he was in a foul mood. Her heart began to beat faster, and her legs trembled. She knew what was going to happen once he walked through the door. The children were playing in the other room.

Philip wore that all too familiar smirk on his face when he saw her looking at him through the kitchen window. She knew that look, it meant she was in for a severe beating. She felt sick and dizzy with fear as he flung open the back door.

"What's wrong with your face?" he roared at her as she stood frozen to the spot, while she feared for her life. He had that awful half-smirk, half-grin expression on his face that he always had just before he was about to attack her.

"I said, what's wrong with your face... BITCH?"

"Nothing!" she told him as her hands trembled, and her heart hammered in her chest.

He mimicked her, "Nothing!" before grabbing her hair and throwing her to the floor. As she lay on the floor, he kicked her in her back. She had given birth to his child only four weeks earlier, and here he was kicking her, as if she were a man, he was having a drunken brawl with in the street.

Sophie ran into the kitchen and began screaming hysterically at the sight of her mother struggling for breath as she lay on the floor. Hannah watched in horror as Philip spun around and slapped Sophie across her face, sending her flying into the kitchen door. Hannah struggled to her feet and ran at him. She grabbed his hair with both her hands. He swung his fist, it hit her side of the face, knocking her to the floor. She felt disorientated for a few seconds, but she managed to scramble to her feet once more. She ran towards the kitchen sink, where she grabbed the knife that she had been using earlier.

"GET OUT OF HERE NOW, OR I WILL KILL YOU!" she screamed at her husband.

She was shaking from head to foot, and her eyes were wild. "I mean it. I will kill you with this knife if you don't get out of here," she told him as her voice took on a quieter but more meaningful tone.

Philip saw something in her that day that he had never seen before, and for the first time, Hannah saw fear in the cowardly and pathetic face of her husband. He stormed out of the kitchen and marched upstairs to bed, telling himself that she will have calmed down by the time he got back up.

Hannah let enough time pass by to make sure that Philip was asleep, and then, taking nothing but her medication along with milk and nappies for the baby, she gathered her children to her and walked out of her front door for the very last time. She left the front door slightly ajar so that the sound of the door being closed didn't wake Philip. She no longer cared if Philip was to kill himself this time. He had attacked her child, and that was the last straw. She knew that she would have killed him to save her children from the monstrous bully that was their father. And God knows he would have deserved it, she told herself.

"Where are we going Mummy?" Ethan asked.

"We are leaving Daddy and going somewhere where we will be safe. It isn't safe for us to live with Daddy any more. "Hannah's voice was heavy with emotion.

"I'm glad we're leaving him, Mummy," Ethan told her as his little chin quivered.

"I am too. I hate him!" Harrison told her passionately.

Hannah did not chastise her eldest son over his comment. After what her children had witnessed that day, they were entitled to be angry. Their father was an animal!

Yes, there were times when he could be loving, even a little tender, but the bad times far outweighed the good times.

Hannah believed things had become critical. Either she would lose her sanity completely, or she or Philip would end up dead, if she didn't leave now. Philip had crossed a line today, when he had turned his violence towards one of their children. It was time to leave and never return, no matter what the cost.

Sophie sat on the front of Liam's pram, sucking her thumb in silence. Hannah noticed that her little girl had a mark on her left cheek from where Philip had hit her.

Twenty minutes after walking out of her marriage, Hannah, walked into the police station with her children.

She had finally found the courage to leave the house, where she had been physically, mentally, and sexually abused by the man she had once loved.

She left the pram parked outside and carried Liam in her arms as he slept. The young officer who was manning the desk looked up with surprise as he looked at the waif in front of him, who appeared to have a tribe of children with her.

"Can I help you, madam?" he asked while taking note of the bruise on her cheekbone. Hannah quickly explained what had taken place that afternoon and how she needed to get herself and her children to a place of safety, far enough away so that her husband would not find them.

"I'll just show you to one of the interview rooms, and then I'll get one of our female officers to speak to you"

The young officer spoke in a gentle tone of voice, showing Hannah that he had sympathy for her situation.

Hannah was shown into a small room where the young officer offered her a chair. "Someone will come and have a chat with you very soon. Can I get you a cup of tea and maybe a biscuit for the kiddies?

"That would be lovely. Thank you."

Once the policeman had left the room, Hannah's children all huddled around her in silence as Liam continued to sleep in her arms. Several minutes later, the young officer arrived with the tea and biscuits, accompanied by a senior female officer.

Hannah was handed the cup of tea and the biscuits were offered to the children., but they were all too shy to take one, so the plate was left on the desk.

As the young officer, was leaving the room, Hannah thanked him. "My pleasure," he told her with a wink.

The female officer had taken a seat opposite Hannah.

"I'm Senior Constable Burns, but you can call me Katherine," she told Hannah as she shook her hand. "It looks like you've been having a tough time of it," she said quietly, as she scanned the faces of the children.

Hannah tearfully told Katherine all that had gone on that afternoon and how relieved she was to be in the safety of the police station.

The constable pushed a box of tissue towards Hannah.

"I must look a right sight," she told Katherine.

"Do you want to press charges against your husband, Hannah?"

"No. I just need to get to a place of safety. I need to get as far away as possible, because my husband has warned me several times that if I leave him, he will find me and then kill me."

"Has he indeed? Just a ploy to frighten you into staying with him, I reckon." Katherine patted the back of Hannah's hand. "I'm just going to make a phone call. I shouldn't be more than a few minutes. Katherine smiled at the children before leaving the room.

After she had gone, the children all took a biscuit from the plate as Hannah finished her cup of tea, while her hands shook. It was teatime and so, the children were very hungry.

"Naughty Daddy," Sophie suddenly blurted out, pushing out her bottom lip. Harrison repeated what he had told his mother earlier.

"I hate him, I really do."

Hannah sighed. Ethan said nothing, as he chewed on a biscuit.

Hannah felt nauseous. She was anxious as to whether there would be a refuge with an available room for her and the children. She might need to come up with a plan B, she told herself. She knew Helen would put them up for a few nights, even if it meant them all sleeping on the living room floor. Philip did not know Helen or where she lived. As Hannah was chewing it all over in her mind when, Katherine opened the door.

"Good news," she announced with a smile, "there is a refuge just over fifty miles away that has a room big enough for you all. There is a social worker on her way as we speak."

"But it's the bank holiday. I thought that the social services offices would be shut today."

"They have an emergency out of hours number, and I think getting you and all these lovely children to a place of safety is an emergency. Now, I have noticed that your little girl has a mark on her face?"

Ethan spoke up. "Daddy did it. He hit Sophie because she was screaming, because Daddy was hitting Mummy."

Katherine's heart went out to the little boy as his bottom lip and chin quivered at the memory of it. Ethan's beautiful brown eyes swam with tears, making Katherine feel desperately sad for all that he must have witnessed during his young life.

"Are you certain that you don't want to press charges against your husband, Hannah?"

"Believe me, it will be punishment enough when he finds us gone"

It seemed like no time at all had passed when the social worker arrived for them. As they walked past the front desk, the young officer at the desk called out to Hannah, "All the best love."

Hannah looked over towards him, nodded her head and smiled for the first time that day.

Fortunately, the pram could be folded small enough to fit in the boot. Hannah and her children were all soon settled in the car. Liam had started to stir and would be due a feed and a nappy change very soon.

Katherine stood guard over them as they got settled in the car. Her eyes scanned the road for anyone who might be parked up and watching. She tapped on the passenger door window. Hannah wound the window down. "If you change your mind about pressing charges, then just call here, and I will deal with it personally."

Hannah nodded as a huge feeling of relief washed over her. She was free at last. As the car drove away with them all in it, Hannah felt a huge weight lift off her shoulders.

She smiled for the second time that day, when an hour later, they arrived at the women's refuge.

Three hours after Hannah had walked out, Philip woke up. The house was quiet, so he assumed that the children were all in bed. Slowly the events of that afternoon came back to him, causing him to groan deep within himself with shame and regret for what he had done to Sophie.

He remembered Hannah holding the knife. The wild look in her eyes and the chilling sound of her voice when she had threatened to kill him. He fully believed that she would have carried out the threat had he not left the kitchen right there and then.

He knew he had stepped over yet another line.

He wondered to himself whether Hannah would have calmed down yet.

After several minutes he got up to use the bathroom. While he was coming out of the bathroom, he noticed that the boys' bedroom door was open. Harrison's bed was empty. He quickly went into the room and saw that Ethan's bed was empty too. He ran into Sophie's room and found her bed empty. He was gripped by a growing fear, as he ran downstairs.

He quickly checked each room and found them all empty. The front door was open. He saw two of their neighbours out in the street, they appeared to be engrossed in conversation. He ran out to them. "Have you seen my wife and my kids?" he asked frantically.

"I saw her going out of the street with them all, but that was about three hours ago... Is there something wrong?" The neighbour asked. Philip did not stop to answer. He ran back into the house. He knew she had left him as he sank to his knees. "No... No... No!" he cried out loud, as his world came crashing down. The house that was usually full of the sound of children was now silent except for the sound of his own weeping.

After several minutes, he rang his mother, hoping beyond hope that Hannah might be there, but his mother was as shocked as Philip was. He continued to weep. His mother told him that she and Frank would be over very soon.

"Frank, Hannah's left Philip again."

Frank turned the TV off as he digested what Alice was telling him. She frantically wrung her hands and began to cry.

Frank's heart ached, at the thought that he may never see Hannah or his grandchildren ever again. He knew that she would not make the same mistake in going back to Philip a second time. No, she had her children with her, and that was all she needed.

For Alice's sake, not Philip's, he agreed to take Alice to be with her son.

Philip was in shock. He was knelt doubled, on the floor, crying. "Where are you, Hannah?" he said out loud as his tears continued to flow.

When Hannah and the children arrived at the refuge, they were met by two of the staff. She thanked the social worker who had driven them there.

She was shown to her room which was on the first landing.

The house was a large three-storey detached property. The room was a little bit shabby but clean. There were two sets of bunk beds, a small cot, and two chests of drawers, but no wardrobe. It didn't matter because the only clothes they had were the ones they were wearing. They didn't even have a coat because it had been a very warm day, and Hannah had left in such a hurry. She was shown a tiny bathroom that was to be shared with another family of three whose room was on the same landing as hers.

Once back downstairs, she found one of the residents cooking egg and chips for her and her children since they had not eaten properly since lunchtime.

Another resident had changed Liam's nappy and was about to give him a bottle.

Hannah found the same feeling of camaraderie existed here as it had in the first refuge, she had stayed in.

The refuge was smaller than the other one and could only accommodate four families at a time. That did not matter, they were safe, they had a roof over their heads and clean beds to sleep in.

As Hannah and the children tucked into the meal that had been cooked for them, Hannah realised that she was very hungry. She cleared her plate, as did her children.

After they had finished eating, the children were taken into the TV lounge to meet the other children who lived in the refuge with their mothers, while Hannah was shown where everything was.

A doctor arrived not long after they had eaten to check Sophie over. After several shakes of his head over what Philip had done to the little girl, he told Hannah that Sophie was fine, and then he left.

After he had left, Hannah felt completely drained both physically and emotionally. She got her children into bed at seven. When she got back downstairs, she found the other mothers rummaging through bags of second-hand clothes, trying to find some items that might fit Hannah and her children. They were all so kind and friendly.

Hannah knew she had made the right decision to leave Philip, and for the first time in an awfully long time, she felt a sense of happiness inside.

Between Hannah and the other three women, eleven young children were living in the refuge. Thankfully, all the mothers were strict about bedtime It gave the women a chance to enjoy some peace and quiet in the evenings and some adult conversation.

When she had been getting the children ready for bed, Harrison had asked her, "Mummy, are we going to live here forever?"

"Not forever, Harrison, because we will eventually get a place of our own, but we might have to stay here for quite a long time."

He then said, "I don't really hate Daddy. I'm just scared of him when he shouts and when he hits you. Will we ever see him again?"

Hannah thought about how loyal children were, even towards a bad or abusive parent.

Do you still want to be able to see him?" she had asked her eldest son.

"Only if he's not shouting."

Hannah had explained to her children that it might be a long time before they saw their father again. They all appeared to accept it, without questioning why.

Her heart ached for all that they had been through. She knew she should have got them out much sooner, the thought filled her with a terrible feeling of guilt and remorse.

Later that evening, Philip had been taken to his mother's house. Alice had been too afraid to leave him alone, because he was rambling on and on, about doing away with himself, if Hannah could not be found. He didn't mention the children at all.

Once they had gone inside, he and Frank had drunk nearly a bottle of whiskey between them and had almost had a fight as Frank once again told Philip several home truths. Alice had taken the whiskey bottle from the two of them and had locked it in the drink's cupboard, telling both men that them getting drunk and killing one another was not going to solve anything.

She had rung the police earlier to report Hannah and the children missing, only to be told that they were not missing. They had been in the police station earlier and had been taken to a safe house, and no, she was not allowed to know where they had been taken, and neither was her son.

She suddenly had an idea, she told Frank and Philip that if they went to the police the next morning and explained that Hannah had mental health problems and was on medication for it, the police might understand that the children needed to be back in the care of their father. Alice knew Hannah would never leave them, and so if they could get the children back home, Hannah would have to go back to Philip if she wanted to keep her children. Philip felt hopeful that his mother's plan might just work. Frank had taken himself off to bed, disgusted with them both.

Chapter Twelve

Philip and Alice arrived at the police station at nine o'clock the following morning. They spoke to an officer, who had not been handling the front desk, but had been in the police station the day before. He had heard about the young woman who had been taken, along with her children, to a refuge, after seeking help from the police.

Philip spoke to the officer first. "I am here concerning my wife. I believe she was here yesterday with our young children. What the police do not know is that my wife is not of sound mind. She is on strong medication and is not fit to be on her own with the children." Alice, who had been nodding as Philip spoke, interrupted him,

"My grandchildren need to be returned to the care of their father immediately!"

The officer asked them to wait while he got someone to speak to them. They went and sat in the waiting area. Alice patted the back of Philip's hand. "I think this will all be sorted out quickly, and you'll have them all back by the end of today."

Philip felt hopeful.

The officer found Katherine at her desk. "Hey, Kath, you know that little lass that was in here yesterday with the kiddies?"

Katherine looked up, immediately, concerned. The other officer continued, "Well, I've got her husband and his mother at the front desk. They are saying that she's some kind of nut job, and the kiddies are not safe with her."

"I certainly did not get that impression when I spoke with her yesterday." Katherine answered.

The officer shrugged his shoulders.

"I'll come through and talk to them in a minute, Mick. Show them into interview room three and tell them I will be through in a couple of minutes."

Mick did as he was asked and took Philip and his mother through to the interview room. After several minutes Katherine walked into the room, shook their hands, and introduced herself before asking each of them for their name.

Alice spoke first. "We are extremely concerned for the welfare of my grandchildren."

Katherine eyed Philip up and down as Alice spoke of her concerns. "Hannah has recently suffered a severe breakdown and is on medication. She is not strong enough to cope with the children on her own. Now, if you could get in touch with her and ask her to get in touch with either my son or myself so that this can be sorted out quickly, we would appreciate it."

Katherine allowed Alice to finish speaking before speaking herself. "First of all, Mrs Johnson, I have to tell you that I can't force Mrs Turner to ring you or your son." She noticed Philp shuffling in his seat, suggesting some agitation. "And I must tell you this. I spoke at length with Mrs Turner yesterday, and I saw no evidence to suggest, that she was mentally unbalanced in any way, what I *did* see was a frightened young woman with evidence of domestic abuse on her bruised face."

Alice gasped as she brought her hand up to her mouth. Philip's face dropped, and Katherine saw.

"Mr Turner, are you happy to carry on this conversation with your mother present, or would you rather she waited by the front desk?"

Realising that things might be said that he did not want his mother to hear, Philip asked her to go and wait for him by the front desk. On leaving the room, Alice began to realise that Philip had not told her everything that had gone on the day before. She knew that he sometimes hit Hannah, but she had no idea of how much Hannah had suffered at Philip's hands and that if the children were in danger from anyone, it was him and not their mother.

Once Alice had left the room, Katherine told Philip that she would try to speak to Hannah, but she could not insist Hannah ring him or anyone else if she did not want to.

Katherine noticed, the change in Philip's demeanour. It showed her that here was a man, who could quickly turn, if he didn't get what he wanted.

"What about my kids?" Philip asked, becoming noticeably more agitated.

"Mr Turner, your wife is in a place where there are professional staff, who give support to the families who reside there. If they were to notice any strange behaviour from her, I am quite sure that they would seek medical advice. Now, I will see what I can do, and I will be back shortly."

Philip leaned back in the chair with his hands on his forehead before running them through his hair. He waited impatiently.

As Katherine went through to use the phone, she called over to another senior officer. "Kev, I want you in interview room three with me, after I've made this call, just in case Mr Turner turns nasty."

"Sure, just give me a shout when you're ready."

Katherine rang the refuge. "Hello, may I speak with Hannah Turner please?"

Julie, who had taken the call, called Hannah, and told her someone was on the phone and wanting to speak to her. Hannah's stomach lurched. She went into the hall and picked up the telephone. "Hello," she said in a timid voice.

"Don't be alarmed, Hannah. It's Katherine, the police officer you spoke with yesterday."

Hannah held her breath, had Philip done something to himself?

"I have your husband and his mother here. They have asked me to contact you, to ask if you will get in touch with one of them. Now, no one is going to force you to do that. If you don't want to speak to them, then you don't have to."

"I don't want to speak to either of them. They'll use emotional blackmail to get me to go back like they did the last time."

"That is your decision to make, Hannah. But what I need to tell you, is that they are both claiming that you are mentally unstable and that you are taking medication after suffering a severe breakdown."

Hannah was both alarmed and angry. Her biggest fear was that her children may be taken off her if Philip could prove that she was mentally unstable. So, she told Katherine, "It is true that I had a breakdown quite a while ago, but I'm a lot better now, and I am taking much less medication than I was doing."

Her voice sounded emotional as she continued, "I am more than capable of looking after my children, and I will make a full recovery if I don't have to live with that monster," she finished close to tears.

"I believe you, Hannah," Katherine said.

Hannah continued, "Did he tell you that he raped me?"

Kathrine closed her eyes as she listened.

"I thought he was going to kill me, I really did! He squeezed my throat so that I could hardly breathe, and then he brutally raped me."

The other three women in the refuge could not help but overhear Hannah, because the telephone was just outside the room where they were sitting. They all looked from one to the other in shocked silence.

Hannah went on, "He smirked and grinned at me as he threatened to snap my neck or choke me to death. I was petrified! He held one of his hands across my mouth so that I couldn't scream while he did things to me. It was the last straw, and I suffered a breakdown." Hannah wept as she spoke of the attack. The other women wept too, as they listened.

Katherine struggled to keep her voice steady. "I am so sorry that you have had to relive that awful experience, Hannah. I think you are a woman of great courage. Don't ever go back to him. Men like that do not change, because they can't. You have made the right decision in getting yourself and your children out of that situation. I am going to speak with your husband now, and I will tell him that you do not want to speak to him or his mother."

"Thank you for listening to me," Hannah said, gratefully.

"You are more than welcome. Bye, Hannah, and please take care of yourself."

Katherine would never forget Hannah for as long as she lived. In the years that followed, she occasionally saw Philip with different women. Women that looked a certain type. Women who were very unlike the young girl she had helped escape from the man that had made her life hell on earth. She took great satisfaction in knowing that Hannah had never gone back to him. And she liked to imagine, that Hannah, had made a success of her life, without him in it.

After her conversation with Hannah, Katherine needed a moment or two to compose herself before calling Kev over to accompany her in going back to speak to the monstrous Mr Turner.

"Do you know what, Kev? Rape within marriage, ought to be a criminal offence?"

Kev nodded his head in agreement, concluding in his mind that Katherine must be referring to the man he was about to meet.

Katherine took a deep breath before entering the room where Philip was waiting. She broke the news to him that Hannah was not willing to speak to him nor his mother.

"What about my kids?" he demanded to know.

"One of your children had a bruise on their face yesterday, and one of your little boys was adamant that it was you who had put it there. What can you tell me about that, Mr Turner?" Katherine asked.

"She pulled a knife on me. Did she tell you that she threatened to kill me? I'm allowed to defend myself!"

"By hitting your children, Mr Turner?"

Katherine watched as Philip became more and more agitated. She continued. "Your wife has just told me that you brutally raped her while she feared for her life, and it was that attack that caused her breakdown… What do you have to say to *that*, Mr Turner?"

Kev, the other officer, was listening and watching Philip's reactions carefully.

"A man cannot be accused of raping the woman he is married to. I can have sex with my own wife whenever I want!" Philip threw back at Katherine.

"Mr Turner, let me tell you this. If a husband pins his wife down on a bed, and then holds his hand over her mouth to prevent her crying out for help, while he forces her to have sexual intercourse with him, then that is rape in my book, whether the law recognises it or not!" Katherine, hurled back, her eyes blazing.

Philip quickly stood up, almost knocking the chair over that he had been sitting on. His face was red, his breathing fast and shallow.

His first thought was to slap the officer's face, but he managed to just control himself enough not to. He looked at her with hatred, while Katherine calmly looked him straight in the eye. He stormed out of the interview room with his fists clenched on either side of him.

"Well!" said Kev.

"Give me a minute, Kev." Katherine closed her eyes as she calmed her thoughts.

"You were brilliant, Kath. What a lousy lowlife!"

"Kevin, those words are not strong enough to describe the likes of him, but he's got what he deserves," Katherine told her colleague, with a look of satisfaction.

Philip stormed out of the police station with his mother quickly following behind. He ignored her questions as he marched towards his taxi. He jumped into his taxicab and roared off, leaving his mother to find her own way home. He was in such a blind rage, that it was a miracle that he hadn't killed himself or anyone else as he sped back to his mother's house. When he got back, he found the key to the drink's cabinet. He took the bottle of whiskey out of the cabinet, that he and Frank had almost finished the night before, and poured what was left of its contents, down his throat.

If Hannah had been there at that moment, he would have battered her!

His mother had flagged a taxi down and had arrived home several minutes after Philip. She scolded him for leaving her. Philip ignored his mother as he paced up and down her living room, unable to calm down. Frank came in from the garden where he had been weeding. When he saw Philip, he asked Alice what was going on.

"I don't know what the police have said, but it has really upset him," she told Frank,

"She, the little bitch of a wife, has told the police that I raped her! How can a man be accused of raping the woman he is married to?"

Alice's eyes almost popped out of her head, "What a wicked thing to accuse you of," she said, shaking her head.

"Why would she make up something like that?" Frank questioned

"Because she is an evil, vindictive, little witch!" Philip was in such a rage that the veins in his neck were bulging, and saliva sprayed from his mouth as he ranted.

"No, I'll not have you call her that, not in this house!" Frank told him firmly.

Philip stormed out of his mother's house and went straight to the pub, where he got paralytic drunk.

Alice was beside herself while Frank went back out to the garden.

He remembered what he had said to Philip after Hannah had suffered the breakdown. "The truth will out," he had told Philip. And here it was! Frank believed that if Hannah had told the police that Philip had raped her, then that is what had happened. Hannah was no liar!

He wished Hannah well in his heart and hoped that she would have the strength to not go back to Philip. If she was to have any future, then she needed to be rid of him for good.

Frank knew he would miss her and the children for the rest of his life, but it was a price he would gladly pay for Hannah to find peace, and hopefully some happiness.

Alice rang Hannah's mother, hoping that she might have been in touch with them and that they might know where she was. Hannah's mother told her that they hadn't heard from Hannah in weeks. The two women promised to let the other know if they heard from her.

Later that day, Sue rushed to the door as soon as she heard Richard coming through it. "Guess what? Our Hannah has left her husband and has taken all the kids with her. Philip and his mother have been to the police and have been told that no one must be told of Hannah's whereabouts. Alice is terrified that she'll never see her grandchildren again."

Richard took his work jacket off, before saying anything. Turning to his wife, he said, "He must have been knocking our Hannah about for the police to have said, no one is to be told where she is. Just let him show his face up here, and I'll swing for him. Let's just hope she gets in touch soon, even if it's just to let us know that she's all right."

As Richard finished speaking, he stroked his chin, which he always did when he was thinking. Sue was hoping that he wasn't thinking of taking Hannah and her children in. They didn't have the room, and Sue did not want the inconvenience!

Philip woke up on the living room floor later that evening. He had been so drunk that he had no idea how he had managed to get himself home. He knew that he had to pull himself together, or either he would kill himself with the drink or lose his job.

He felt as if he had been hit over the head with a sledgehammer, as he took himself through into the kitchen. He poured himself a pint of water and drank it straight down before walking over to the kitchen table, where he sat down. He stared out of the window towards the children's swing that he had put up two summers ago.

He could see in his mind's eye, Hannah laughing as she chased the three children around the garden. He could picture them laughing and squealing as she caught each one in turn.

He rubbed his pounding head as the pain in his heart began to overwhelm him. "Where are you?" he whispered out loud. "I can't stand it here without you."

His earlier rage had subsided, although he was still stunned that Hannah had told the police what he had done to her. He had denied it, of course, but she had spoken the truth. He *had* brutalised her most appallingly. He wished once more that he could turn the clock back, so that it had never happened, but of course, that was impossible.

He had to find a way to get her back. It was the not knowing that was driving him insane. He had threatened to kill her, if she left him, but his threats had been just to frighten her into staying with him, and it had worked for a time. And, now she was gone, and he knew he would never get over it, and so, he would have to find a way to get her back, and then he would never let her out of his sight, so that she could never do this to him again.

His thoughts travelled back to when he first met her. She had been very petite, just a little over five feet and she had not grown an inch since then.

Of course, he had known that she was too young for him and that she had still been a child when he had coerced her into sleeping with him. He had wanted her, and he had been determined to have her. He had realised as he got older, that what he had done was a serious crime, and he had been lucky to have not ended up in prison when he had got Hannah pregnant when she was only fifteen.

He had failed her in so many ways, and she had not deserved any of it. She had remained faithful to him throughout all the years that he had played around. But it had always been her that he went back to. "Always her," he whispered.

He would do anything right now just to have her back and hold her in his arms.

He broke down and wept for a long time. He had never experienced pain like the pain that he was suffering, but he knew deep down that he had finally got what he deserved.

Chapter Thirteen

A couple of weeks, after leaving Philip, Hannah and the children were transferred to a refuge in the town where Hannah had grown up. She had rung to let her family know that she and the children were safe and well. Her father had answered the phone, and he and her younger sister Linda, had talked her into going back to her hometown where her family could help her and protect her from Philip. Richard had promised to put the fear of God into him if he even dared to go near her.

The staff at the refuge, where she had been during that first two weeks, had been amazing. They made all the arrangements for Hannah to be transferred up to Yorkshire. On the day she was leaving, they had taken her and the children to the bus station and had stayed with her until the bus had finally set off. She had thanked them for all the help and support that she had received from them.

She had given Alice a very brief call to tell her that they were all okay. Alice had started with the same tearful tale that Philip was not coping, so Hannah had simply put the phone down. The number could not be traced as a protection for all the women and children who lived in the refuge.

It had been arranged that a support worker would meet Hannah at the bus station. Val had been told to look out for a young waiflike girl with three small children and a young baby. As soon as Val had seen Hannah, she had known who she was straight away. Hannah was relieved when Val introduced herself. And minutes later, they all piled into Val's car.

It was before the days of compulsory seat belts and child car seats.

Hannah had little in the way of clothing for each of them, and she had had to leave the baby's pram behind with the promise of a donated one when she reached the other refuge.

The evening before, Philip had decided to ring her mother again, with the hope that she might now have some news of Hannah's whereabouts. Richard picked up the telephone. Philip had not been expecting that. "Hello, Richard. I'm just calling to ask if you have heard from Hannah?" Philip spoke as politely as he could.

"Yes, we have heard from her. She and the children are all fine."

"Has she told you, her whereabouts.?" Philip asked hopefully.

"No, I have no idea where she is just now. But if I do get to find out, I will not be telling you. I know all about what you have been doing to her. And I am telling you right now, that if you go near her or threaten her in any way, my sons and I will come after you, and we will tear you limb from limb, and that, my lad, is a promise. Now have you got that?"

Philip slammed the phone down. He was furious! He knew that Hannah's father and her brothers could all handle themselves and that he would never dare take any of them on. And so, he felt as if he had hit another brick wall.

Richard warned the whole family that under no circumstances were they to tell Philip or his family that Hannah would soon be back in Yorkshire.

After Philip had put the phone down on Richard, he sat and wept tears of self-pity, anger, and frustration. He was desperate, to find her, but he could not. No-one had any information to her whereabouts, and it was driving him insane!

He had gone back to work a few days after Hannah had left, but his heart was not in his work, and he could not concentrate on anything. He thought about her every second of the day and dreamed of her when he was asleep. He had dreamt the other night that she was back, and she had been sorry for what she had put him through. It had seemed so real, but then he had woken, and the harsh reality had hit him hard. Philip was not usually a crier, but he had probably cried more than he had done in his entire life since Hannah had left him.

Hannah and the children had arrived at the refuge, close to her hometown late afternoon. It was a large, dark, and foreboding building, and Hannah could see the anxiety on her children's faces. The building was divided into three houses, the largest of them being in the centre. It could house six families, whereas the two either side could house only four families.

"I'm not living here!" Ethan announced loudly.

"Ethan, we have to for now. It will be all right, I'm sure," his mother told him.

They all followed Val through the large front door and were shocked to see that instead of the clean and bright shelter they had just come from, this one was scruffy, dirty, and had an unpleasant odour. Rough-looking women were lounging about and using the foulest language as they roared at their unruly children, who were jumping all over the furniture. Hannah wanted to turn around and go straight back to where they had just come from. She felt afraid, as her heart sank to her feet. Her children all huddled as close to their mother as they could possibly get as they looked at the scene in front of them with fear in their hearts.

Val had seen Hannah's reaction, and so she quickly took her and the children to show them their room. It was a large room, with four beds, a cot, a large wardrobe, and a large chest of drawers. It was clean and smelt a lot better than the room downstairs.

Sophie started to cry. "I don't like it here, Mummy,"

Harrison's chin wobbled, as his eyes filled with tears. "Mummy, can't we go back to the other place?"

Val was already cuddling Sophie, and now she put her arm around Harrison to comfort him

"Kids, we have to live here for now, but it won't be for very long. We'll get a place of our own, and we will all be fine. I promise!" she told them, trying to convince herself too.

Val put on her brightest expression, "I bet you are all hungry. Let's go and have some cheesy beans on toast," she told the children to try to cheer them all up. They were all hungry, so they all followed her downstairs, with Hannah following with the baby.

"I like lots of cheese on my beans," Ethan told Val with the grumpiest look on his face. He made her want to laugh, but she kept her face straight. Ethan was such a passionate little boy for a six-year-old. Harrison had always been a much calmer child than his younger brother.

Val made tea for them all, while Hannah made up a couple of bottles for Liam. She had put him down in the pram that she had been given on their arrival when they got back downstairs. Thankfully, Liam was a very placid baby and was easy to care for. After they had all eaten, Val showed Hannah where everything was.

Her children would not stay in the room with the other families. They followed Hannah about like little lost sheep. Hannah wanted them with her anyway because she was afraid that one of the wild children they had seen earlier, might hurt one of them.

After Val left to go home, Hannah grabbed her children and fled with them to the safety of their room. She fed and changed her baby and then got herself and the other three changed for bed. It was a little after seven, but she was so very tired from the travelling and the upset over their new living conditions and knowing Liam would wake in the early hours to be fed, she decided to go to bed at the same time as her children.

As she lay in bed, she tried to think positively about her situation. *It is not forever*. She told herself. At least there will be an end to this.

Going back to Philip was not an option. He had proved that he could not control his violent and unreasonable temper.

Hannah surprised herself that she was hoping he would be all right and that he would not harm himself. But, if he did, she knew she would be able to live with it because she had given him every chance to mend his ways, and it had made her ill. She believed her conscience would be clear, but still, she wished him no harm.

She prayed for the strength to cope with her new surroundings as she drifted off to sleep.

The next morning the children had slept later than usual, and Hannah was grateful for the extra hour in bed because she had been awake for nearly an hour with Liam in the night. He had been grisly after his feed, so she had gone downstairs with him. The kitchen had been a mess, with dirty cups and plates everywhere. She had felt extremely downhearted about her situation while wishing she had never set eyes on Philip Turner.

After she had got herself and the children washed and dressed, Hannah took them all downstairs and into the kitchen to have breakfast.

There was a young woman of around her own age in there. She was drinking a cup of coffee.

"Are you the new lady?" she asked in a very polite, well-spoken voice.

"Yes, we arrived yesterday. I'm Hannah, and this is Harrison, Ethan, and Sophie."

"I'm Karen, and this is Amy. She's a bit shy, and she doesn't speak much."

Hannah smiled at the little girl who was partly hidden behind her mother.

"What do you think to the place?" Karen whispered.

Hannah looked around, before saying quietly, I've just come from a refuge in the midlands, and it was nothing like this." She kept her voice low. "I don't know if I'll be able to cope."

Karen, looked at Hannah sympathetically, "Well, it's a lovely day, why don't we take the children to the park after breakfast? It's just across the road."

"The kids will love that," Hannah said, her mood lifting a little.

After breakfast, they were just going through the door when they bumped into Val. She had just arrived. She was so glad to see that Karen and Hannah had found one another because she had been a little worried that Hannah might be tempted to go back to her husband if she couldn't cope with being where she was. But Hannah would not, under any circumstances, go back to Philip, she would have found another refuge if she had to.

Val told her that she needed to see her when they got back to go through some paperwork with her concerning a school for the boys, registering with a doctor, sorting out benefits, etc.

"We'll be back in an hour," she told Val. Hannah had cheered up considerably since meeting Karen.

It was a beautiful morning with lots of early autumn sunshine. The children all played happily. Sophie and Amy had appeared to have taken to each other and were holding hands as they played. Liam was kicking his legs as he lay in the pram. He was now smiling and cooing, and as his mother smiled down at him, she felt glad that at least one of her children would never have to watch his mother being kicked and punched in front of him.

Debbie and Helen had both been delighted that Hannah had finally escaped her dreadful marriage. They had made her promise to keep in touch.

Hannah was going to miss them both, but it was a price she would have to pay for her freedom. Still, she was determined that the two women who had been her support network after Ursula had moved away would always remain part of her life, and hopefully once it was safe to do so, they might meet up occasionally

When they got back to the refuge, Val had arranged for all of Hannah's children, including Liam, to be looked after in the playroom by their two trained play specialists

Once all the papers had been filled in and signed and appointments made, Val told Hannah that two rooms were becoming vacant in one of the other houses. She said she thought that both Hannah and Karen would get on very well with the two families who were living there now, but they would have to wait another fortnight, before they could move into the vacant rooms. Hannah could have kissed her; she was so elated.

"Have you told Karen yet?" Hannah asked.

"No, I'm going to have a word when we've finished in here. Please keep the news between you and Karen for now if you don't mind?"

Later that afternoon, Hannah and Karen went to the shops to buy a few groceries. They were both delighted that they were moving to a cleaner, less noisy environment.

Turning to Hannah, Karen told her, "I can't believe that someone of my age has four children."

"I started when I was very young, I'm embarrassed to say. I'll tell you all about it once the children are out of earshot."

"How many years did you stay with him?"

"Too many!" Hannah sighed from the pleasure of knowing she was free at last. "Let's have a cup of coffee together tonight once the children are all in bed, and we can tell each other everything."

"It's a date! "Karen told her with a smile.

The next fortnight went by quickly. Hannah and Karen quickly settled into their new surroundings. All four families got on very well. They shared the housework, cooking, and babysitting. Life in the new house felt warm and safe as Hannah and her children began to recover from the horrors of their former life. The children hardly mentioned their father during the five months that they were there.

They were rehoused three weeks after Karen and Amy. The house was a bit shabby, but Hannah felt that she could make it nice little by little. It was their own home. Never again, would she have to feel terrified in her own home.

She knew life was not going to be perfect, but at least she was free. Free to live her life. Free to make her own decisions and free of the constant fear she had lived with for far too long.

She stayed in touch with Karen for a long time, but after Karen remarried, and went to live in another part of the country, they eventually lost touch.

Chapter Fourteen
February 1984

Six months after leaving Philip, Hannah had to face him in court. He had found out where she was after Hannah's mother had let it slip to a tearful Alice one afternoon. Philip had applied to the court for access to his children, but what he really wanted was access to Hannah!

She walked into court that morning with her sister Linda on one side of her and her brother David on her other side. The boys were at school, and Hannah's younger children were being looked after by Hannah's youngest sister Lucy.

She really was not looking forward to seeing her soon to be ex-husband. She saw him immediately as she walked into court, but she pretended not to see him as her solicitor came over to have a word with her.

As Hannah, Linda, and David each took a seat in the waiting area, Philip's heart leapt at the sight of the woman that had not left his thoughts for a single second during the last six months.

She had put a little weight on which suited her. She took her coat off to reveal a smart but simple dress that showed off the lovely figure that she still had despite having had four children.

He had a longing to feel his arms around her, but he could not approach her because her brother David was glaring at him. As he caught her eye, he smiled at her. She did not smile back, she simply gave a small nod of her head to acknowledge that she had seen him, and then she turned away to speak to her sister. His heart sunk to his boots. He had been hoping to get her alone, to convince her to give their marriage another try. He would tell her that he would move to Yorkshire if that would make her happier. He realised that he was not going to get her on her own. Besides, the look that she had just given him had spoken volumes about her feelings towards him.

They entered the courtroom, and Hannah took a seat next to her solicitor, who specialised in working with victims of domestic abuse. Philip took a seat next to his.

Philip wanted monthly access to the children, but Hannah wanted him to have short, supervised visits.

He took the stand and put on an Oscar-winning performance of being a good husband and father. He brought up his concerns about Hannah's mental health and his concern as to whether she had the ability to care for four children on her own.

Hannah's face burned with anger. He had been the cause of her mental health problems, and he knew it. She was fully recovered now and no longer took medication.

He told the court that all he wanted was for them all to be back together because he still loved his wife deeply. Hannah's solicitor raised her eyebrows because she has seen and heard it all before.

When Philip turned to his wife and blubbered, "I don't want any of this Hannah, I just want us all to be back together again," she had put her hand on Hannah's and whispered. "They all cry, but he will never be anything other than the monstrous psychopath who made your life hell for years!"

Hannah looked back at him, and as she did, she lifted her chin in defiance, giving him a look of utter contempt that shook Philip to his core.

When it was her turn to take the stand, she exposed the lying, cheating dog for what he really was. She told the court about the night that he had brutally raped her. She explained to the court that it had been the last straw after years of abuse, and it was that that had caused her to have a nervous breakdown.

Her body trembled, and her voice shook with emotion as she relived the experience, but she held it together.

Philip had dared to shake his head as he listened, as if she was making it all up.

He knew now that the events of that awful night would remain with her for the rest of her life. They would remain with him too because no matter how much he denied it to other people, he knew it was the truth.

Alice had written a signed letter to say that the children could stay at their home with their father whenever he had them, hoping that that would give Philip more of a chance to get the result he wanted. The court allowed him to have the children for a weekend every month, and a whole week in the summer school holidays and at Christmas, on the condition that all the visits would be at his parents' home.

Hannah was disappointed with the court's decision, but she needn't have worried. Philip put little effort into seeing his children as the years went by.

Apart from seeing him while staying at their grandparents' home for a week in the summer and a few days at Christmas, they only saw Philip for an odd weekend once or twice a year.

The children adored their grandparents and really looked forward to the times that they spent with them. Philip would be there too, but it was Frank and Alice who made those visits special for the children.

Philip's children all had a difficult relationship with him, and one by one, they all eventually stopped having anything to do with him once they reached adulthood.

Hannah would occasionally get the odd letter or phone call from him as the years went by, to tell her that he still loved her and that life without her was worthless. She would tell him to leave her alone, and to only contact her when he needed to arrange access to his children.

He had remarried six years after she had left him, but it had only lasted two years, and Hannah could well imagine why.

Hannah had been an innocent child when she had met him and had been far too young to understand the type of man she had become involved with. He was a monster, who had almost succeeded in destroying her!

She would look back years after she had left Philip and realise that she had been sexually abused at the age of fourteen by a man who had convinced her that they were in love.

He had also convinced her that it was normal for couples who were in love to be sexually intimate with one another. The whole idea of it had frightened her, and she had only given in to him because she had been afraid of losing him.

How she wished she had never set eyes on him. How different her life could have turned out to be if only she had told someone when he had first begun to touch her sexually. If only she had run a mile.

But she had been desperate for someone to love her, and she had believed at the time that Philip did love her.

How wrong she had been to believe that he would take care of her, and that he would give her everything that she had missed out on during her childhood. No, he had conned her, and she had paid the price!

Chapter Fifteen
September 1993

It took a long time for Hannah to stop hating Philip over all the distress he had caused her during what should have been the happiest years of her life. He had robbed her of her youth and had let her down very badly. But as the years went on and she started to look more to the future instead of back to the things that she couldn't change, she started to let go of her hatred. Eventually, she felt nothing but pity for the sad individual who had lost so much because of his failure to change the behaviour that in the end, had ruined his own life.

Her experiences had made her the woman she was now. She was thirty-three and had become a strong-minded and very capable woman, who would take no nonsense from anyone. She had gone on to train as a childcare worker and had made a good career for herself, working on a children's ward for the NHS.

She had a close circle of friends whom she could rely on. She had a close relationship with her sisters but had never developed a close relationship with her parents because her mother simply didn't want it.

Her mother's mental health had improved now that she only had her two youngest children at home. Still, she continued to show the same indifference to her eldest daughters as she had done for most of their lives.

Hannah had attended counselling sessions a couple of years earlier, to work through her feelings and the issues she had with her mother. It had helped, and she had finally been able to put it to bed. She now fully accepted that she could not force her mother to be the person that she wanted her to be, if her mother did not want it. So, Hannah concentrated on the good relationships that she had in her life.

She had four amazing children. She had fantastic friends, a job she enjoyed, and her unbreakable faith in an almighty God!

She was proud of each of her children. They had all done well at school. Harrison was at college and was hoping to teach sports. Ethan was studying for his A-levels in the sixth form of high school. Sophie was at the same high school as Ethan, and Liam would be joining her the following year.

Ethan, the most sensitive of her children, had suffered from emotional problems and bed wetting for several months after they had left Philip. With professional help, he had come through it. He would go on to be a successful businessman in the future, causing his mother to be even more proud of him than she already was.

All of Hannah's children would go on to make a success of their lives. She was glad that she had eventually found the strength within herself to walk out when she did because it had given her children the rest of their childhoods to enjoy without having to watch their mother being beaten every other week, or sometimes every other day.

Hannah's house was always teeming with other people's children. Each of her children had their own circle of friends each, and so, when Friday or Saturday came around, she could end up with a houseful of other people's children staying overnight at her house., even though it meant them all being crammed into the children's bedrooms.

She loved it though. Her children could not have had friends stay over when they lived with their father because of his violent outbursts.

Alice had never really forgiven Hannah for walking out on Philip, and Frank had long given up trying to explain that she had done it not to just save herself but to save her children too.

Alice could not accept that her son was the monster that he was being portrayed as being. All she could see was the devastation that Hannah's walking out had caused him. He had never been the same since, and he had been a constant worry to her during that first year. In fact, Alice believed that Philip would never be totally over Hannah.

Hannah had not seen Frank nor Alice for many years now. She still felt a little sad about it occasionally because they had been exceptionally good to her. She had told them after leaving Philip that she would always remember their unwavering support and kindness. She often spoke to her children about how kind and supportive their grandparents had been towards her during those difficult years.

Hannah would have loved to be in the kind of rock-solid relationship that Frank and Alice enjoyed. Her experience of sex and marriage had made her overly cautious of men, and so she got on with her life and made the best of what she had.

She was still in touch with her old friends who had been such an important part of her life all those years ago. She saw Debbie and Helen at least twice a year. The two of them would travel to Yorkshire together and spend the weekend with Hannah and her children. They had become firm friends after Hannah had left, and they often spoke of her and all that she had gone through.

Like Helen, she was a survivor.

Helen was free to visit Yorkshire because her ex-husband had died eight years earlier in very tragic circumstances. His death had meant that she was out of danger. Still, her children were settled down south, and wherever her children were, that was where she wanted to be!

Hannah never visited the town where she had lived with Philip for obvious reasons, so that was why her two friends travelled to see her. They all spoke to one another on the phone often, and Hannah was grateful that their friendships had survived the distance between them.

She was still in touch with Dieter and Ursula. They spoke every two to three months, but she had only seen them twice in almost twelve years, and Hannah sometimes still grieved the closeness they had once shared.

What Hannah did not know was that her life was about to change forever. A new chapter was about to begin, and her life would never be the same ever after!

Chapter Sixteen

Hannah attended a Bible study group on Wednesday evenings with Sophie and Liam. Her two eldest two had stopped attending a couple of years before, after deciding that religion was not for them, and she had respected their decision.

The group was held at the home of two of Hannah's dearest friends, John, and Michelle. She had known them for just over four years, after they had moved into a house just around the corner from her. Michelle had a fantastic sense of humour, and she was kind. She had taken Hannah and her family under her wing, and Hannah considered Michelle to be her best friend. Michelle was loyal and trustworthy, and Hannah often confided in her if she had any worries.

Michelle had told Hannah that John's best friend, whom he had known since childhood, was moving back to the area after living away for five years, and that he would be staying at theirs for a few days. He shared the same faith as the three of them, so he would be at the Bible study group that evening.

Hannah hadn't really given it much thought as she knocked on Michelle's door.

"Come in, Hannah," Michelle called to her from inside. Hannah was always the first to arrive. Not only was Hannah a stickler for punctuality, but she liked to have a chat with John and Michelle before the others arrived.

There were ten of them that met there every Wednesday. It was a very relaxed and informal group, and they would often have cheese and wine afterwards while Michelle entertained them all, with her zany sense of humour.

Hannah had just sat down with Sophie and Liam when a tall, dark, and incredibly handsome man walked into the room. Hannah's heart leapt, and her stomach did a somersault all at the same time. She felt the colour rise in her cheeks when Michelle introduced them.

"This is Jonathan, Hannah. He's here to tie up some loose ends ready for his move back to the area."

His smile revealed a row of perfect white teeth. Hannah felt her cheeks begin to burn, when he said, "You must be Hannah, Michelle was just saying that you would be the first to arrive."

Her cheeks flushed a deep red. She hated the fact that she blushed so easily, especially, in front of the man she had just been introduced to.

"This is Sophie and Liam. Hannah's children. He smiled at them; they said a polite hello back.

Jonathan's eyes were dark and beautiful, and his skin crinkled at the side of them when he smiled. Hannah had to consciously tear her own eyes away from them.

Soon everyone else started to arrive, and he was quickly introduced to them all as it was almost time to start.

Just as everyone was seated and they were about to begin, Hannah and Jonathan both looked across at one another at the same time and then quickly looked away.

She was very conscious of his presence in the room and so, Hannah didn't join in the discussion She sat and listened to everyone else's comments and tried not to stare when Jonathan spoke.

Afterwards, John and Michelle brought cheese and biscuits in for everyone. Hannah mingled with other group members while trying to avoid Jonathan because he made her feel shy and incredibly nervous.

She had gone into the hallway, and was just untangling Sophie's and Liam's coats from everyone else's when a voice from behind her said, "Are you leaving already?" She spun round and looked up into Jonathan's face. She could see in the bright light of the hallway that his eyes were dark green.

"I've got work tomorrow, and the children have got school," she told him. She could have kicked herself for stammering like an idiot.

"Where do you work?" he asked, looking genuinely interested.

"At the hospital, just down the road. I have an early start, so I need to get home."

She was wishing that he would talk to someone else because she could feel her face turning red again, and she knew he could see.

He asked, "Are you a nurse?"

"No, I'm a nursery nurse," she answered. Her heart was beating fast, and her palms were beginning to sweat.

"Are they not the same thing?" he asked, looking puzzled.

No, they are not the same thing. I'm trained in childcare. Nurses are medically trained. I'm there to offer play therapy and to provide lessons for children who are in hospital in the long term."

She felt her mouth getting dry. Sophie and Liam had appeared and were both putting their shoes and jackets on. "We need to get home. It was nice to meet you," she told him, before fleeing outside without giving him the chance to say goodbye.

Sophie, wanted to laugh. She asked her mother, "Have you got the hots for Jonathan, Mum?

"Don't be so ridiculous!" Hannah protested a little too loudly, causing the children to giggle as they walked back to their own house. She hoped she hadn't given anyone else that impression, especially the man in question!

She lay in bed that night and found she could not stop thinking about him. She told herself that he probably had an exceptionally beautiful girlfriend somewhere. She was determined to put him out of her thoughts the next day as she went about her normal routine.

Three weeks later she saw him again. She had been invited to a barn dance that one of her friends had organised. Hannah was beginning to get out on her own, a bit more these days. Harrison had promised to look after the youngest two so that she could enjoy a night out with her friends. He was seventeen and mature for his age.

Hannah was wearing pale blue jeans, a white shirt, with a pale blue neckerchief around her neck. She had her hair tied up in a high ponytail that showed off her high cheekbones. She had no idea how good she looked as she scanned the room, looking for John and Michelle, who had not arrived yet.

She looked around for someone else to talk to. As she did, she saw Jonathan standing at the other side of the room, looking fabulous in denim jeans and a tee-shirt that did nothing to hide his physique. There were two young women from her congregation, talking to him and giggling, like a pair of teenagers.

Hannah, went to the bar and bought herself a glass of red wine. As she sipped her wine, she found that her eyes kept wandering over to where he was, so she walked towards the back of the room so that she would have her back to him.

Jonathan had seen Hannah walk into the venue, and now he watched her walk from the bar area towards the back of the room. He excused himself and followed her. She had just stopped to say hello to a young couple whose wedding she had attended a few weeks earlier when a voice from behind said her name. She turned around and found Jonathan looking down at her.

"Hello, Jonathan how are you?" she asked, trying to sound calm and confident.

"Good, thanks… I've just moved back to the area a few days ago, so I'm up to my ears in bubble wrap. I'm glad to be taking a break from it all, actually… You look really nice," he told her, causing the colour in her cheeks to rise, "I didn't know you were going to be here."

"And I didn't know you were going to be here either." The wine had given her a bit of Dutch courage. He laughed and Hannah noticed he had smiley eyes.

They stood and chatted for about ten minutes while Hannah took regular sips of her wine to calm her nerves.

One of the giggling girls from earlier suddenly appeared at Jonathan's side. Hannah was shocked when she threw her a mean look. Her name was Becky Summers.

"Jonathan, I need a partner for this dance. Will you be my partner?"

Before he could object, Becky practically dragged him away from Hannah, leaving Hannah speechless at the other woman's rudeness.

Becky stuck to his side for the rest of the evening, following him round like a lapdog. Hannah found herself disliking the young woman for her brazen conduct.

Jonathan hadn't tried to get her into conversation again, although their eyes had met briefly once or twice as the evening progressed.

At the end of the evening, Hannah was waiting for John and Michelle who were giving her a lift home, when Jonathan suddenly appeared from nowhere.

"Hi." Was all he said

"Hello," she said back, wondering where the 'clinging vine' had disappeared to.

"I'm waiting for John and Michelle," he told her.

"So am I. They're giving me a lift home."

At that both John and Michelle appeared.

"Hannah, do you fancy coming to ours for a little night cap?" Michelle asked.

"Yes, that would be nice, although I won't be able to stay long, it's getting quite late."

They walked out to the car park to Michelle's car. She told Hannah to get into the front with her while the two men got in the back. Hannah was surprised, she had assumed Jonathan would be going home in his own car.

"Jonathan's staying at ours tonight. His place still looks like Hiroshima," Michelle told her with a laugh. Hannah felt nervous, at the thought of spending time in his company.

"Eh, Jonny, Becky Summers was all over you tonight. Is there something going on with you two?" John asked.

"No, there isn't." Was Jonathan's immediate response, and he said it with a hint of irritation in his voice. It caused Hannah to raise her eyebrows.

"Well, I reckon she's set her cap at you. What do you think, Han?"

"I couldn't possibly say, it's none of my business," she replied, trying to sound like she didn't care.

The four of them walked into the house together. John and Michelle went into the kitchen to get some drinks and nibbles, leaving Jonathan and Hannah alone in the living room. Hannah sat in one of the armchairs and drew her legs up underneath herself. Jonathan sat in the chair directly opposite her.

"Did you have a good evening?" he asked.

"Yes, I did. Did you?"

He wrinkled his nose. "It was okay. Barn dances aren't really my thing if I'm honest."

"What is your thing?" she dared to ask.

"Lots of things."

"Such as?" The wine she had drunk that evening had given her more confidence than she would usually have.

He gave a light-hearted laugh before answering. "Good food, fine wine. Live music in dimly lit bars."

"What type of music do you like?"

"All kinds. I don't really have a favourite type."

"So, just about anything except barn-dance music?"

He nodded his head as a grin spread across his face.

"You have very nice teeth," she told him, and then wished she hadn't.

"So, have you," he told her with a smile.

They were both smiling at one another just as the drinks were being brought in.

The men had a large brandy each, and Michelle had poured a large gin and tonic for Hannah and herself.

Michelle was on form and had them all roaring with laughter. She was a natural comedienne and such good company! Before Hannah knew it, two hours had gone by.

"I'm going to have to get home, guys. It's nearly one in the morning."

"How are you getting home?" Jonathan asked, out of genuine concern, noticing that both John and Michelle had had a couple of drinks each.

"It's only two minutes away. I'll walk."

"Not on your own, surely?"

"I'll be fine."

"No, I can't let you walk home alone. I'll walk you home."

"Honestly, I will be fine," she told him, while secretly hoping that he would insist.

"Let him walk you home, Han, if it makes him feel better," John told her.

She and Jonathan put their shoes and coats on, and after saying good night to her friends, Hannah set off with him by her side. Three minutes later, they were outside Hannah's house.

John and Michelle lived in a nice house in a lovely street, but Hannah and her children lived in one of the council houses around the corner, which embarrassed her a little, knowing that Jonathan would see that she didn't live in a smart street like their friends.

"My house is just here," she told him.

"Oh, right," he grinned, "it really *is* only two minutes."

"Three minutes, actually! Thank you for walking me *all* the way home.

He narrowed his eyes at her, obviously amused, he asked, "Are you making fun of me?"

"I most certainly am not!" she told him, putting on an obvious pretence of being offended.

"I'll see you in the morning." He was smiling, and it made Hannah's heart flutter.

"You will… goodnight and thank you. It was kind of you to see me home."

"I'll wait here until you're safely indoors."

As she was about to close the door, she held her hand up and waved at him. He smiled and held his hand in the air, before turning to walk away.

Hannah sneaked quietly into the house because everyone appeared to be in bed. As she lay down, she let out a sigh, taking pleasure from the fact that he had insisted on seeing her safely home. She turned onto her stomach and smiled to herself as she thought about his lovely smile, his jet-black hair, and those beautiful dark-green eyes.

The next day Hannah arrived for Sunday morning worship with her two youngest children. As she walked towards the front, she saw Jonathan with Becky Summers. They talked and laughed with one another, while Becky appeared to be hanging on his every word, as she played with her long red hair in a flirtatious manner.

Hannah wondered if he had he lied to John when he told him that there was nothing between him and Becky? From where Hannah was standing, it didn't look as if he was pushing the young woman away.

Hannah walked right down to the front so that she had her back to them. She couldn't help but feel disappointed over what she had just seen.

"I see she's all over him again this morning, making a right show of herself," said a voice from behind. It was Michelle, who had felt sure that she had seen a spark of chemistry between hers and John's closest friends last night.

"I think he lied to John last night when he said nothing was going on between him and Becky. He doesn't look as if he's trying to get away from her, does he?" Hannah tried and failed not to let the disappointment show in her voice.

"I'll be really disappointed if he ends up with that pushy little madam!"

"Oh, Michelle, she's not that bad."

"She's not right for him, that's all I'm saying!"

After the service, Hannah mingled with members of the congregation and tried to stay away from Jonathan.

As she was leaving with Sophie and Liam, she accidentally caught his eye. He immediately smiled and put his hand up as if to say bye. Hannah returned his smile and waved back at him. Becky gave Hannah a filthy look, which didn't surprise her. It was obvious that Becky wanted him for herself.

Hannah gave herself a bit of a talking to when she got back home. She had lived without a man for more than ten years, and she must not allow another man to affect her this way. He had made no attempt to talk to her before or after the service, and yet he had laughed and chatted with Becky both before and after. She reasoned with herself that he could probably have any woman he wanted, so why on earth would he be the slightest bit interested in a mother of four?

She kept herself busy for the rest of the day, determined to try to keep him from her thoughts. When she found she could not, she rang her friend Debbie. She told her all about the tall, dark, good-looking man that had walked into her life so unexpectantly.

"Anyway, he seems keen on a young woman in my local congregation, and she seems determined to get him for herself. She's quite a bit younger than me and isn't dragging four children behind her. She's probably more his type. Oh, Debbie, what's wrong with me? Why am I letting him get to me like this? It's ridiculous!"

"Sounds like you've got quite a crush going on there." Debbie told her.

"That's what it is, Debbie... just a silly crush. At my age too. How ridiculous!"

"Hannah, you are still a young, attractive woman. Don't convince yourself that you aren't as good as the next woman just because you are a single mum. You have a lot to offer to any man, so, don't put yourself down."

Hannah changed the subject, and she and Debbie went on to talk about their children, and other aspects of their lives, before ending their conversation on a positive note.

As Hannah lay awake in bed that night, she decided that all she had to do was get on with her life, and her crush on Jonathan would eventually disappear. She would try to avoid him as much as possible until it had.

Chapter Seventeen

Hannah didn't see Jonathan for another two weeks. He had taken time out to paint and decorate his flat before starting his new job as a mechanical engineer. Hannah had gone to her Bible study group as usual, and on entering Michelle's living room, she found Jonathan in deep conversation with John. She purposely did not look at him as she walked straight into the kitchen where Michelle was, and there she remained until it was time to start. When she walked back into the living room, she kept her eyes down and took a seat. An elderly member of the group who had just returned to the group after a short illness, chatted with Hannah before things got started. She could feel Jonathan's eyes on her, and despite the unexpected ache in her heart, she did not look back at him. She was not going to allow any man to break her heart the way that Philip once had.

She remained quiet all the way through the hour-long discussion. It had not gone unnoticed by Michelle, who was a little concerned as to why Hannah was not her usual bubbly self.

Afterwards, Hannah deliberately avoided looking at Jonathan again.

She mingled a little before calling Sophie and Liam to come and get their coats and shoes on as she went into the hallway to wait for them. She had just finished putting her coat and shoes on when Jonathan appeared. *Oh, no,* she thought.

"Hannah, have I done something to upset you? You haven't looked at me or spoken to me all evening… What's wrong?" He looked her straight in the eye.

She was lost for words to begin with. She avoided meeting his eye, and said, "Of course, you haven't upset me, and I'm sorry if I've given you that impression." She looked away because she was embarrassed.

He was not convinced, her words were saying one thing, but her body language was saying the opposite. "I'd like us to be friends,

Hannah, so, if I've done something that has offended you, you would tell me?"

"Honestly, you haven't… I'm sorry if I've offended you."

Just then, Sophie and Liam appeared. They each started to put their coats and shoes on. They said goodbye to Jonathan, who was still standing in the hall.

"Bye, kids. Bye, Hannah," he told them.

"Bye," she said in almost a whisper as she walked out into the street.

Jonathan knew that something must have happened to cause Hannah to be so off with him, but he could not for the life of him think what it could be.

She could have cried as she walked back to her own house. She felt all churned up inside. Sophie and Liam could tell that their mother appeared a little upset, so the three of them walked home in silence

Hannah couldn't help but fret over what had taken place that evening as she removed her makeup. She was upset that Jonathan might think that she had been incredibly rude. She was just trying to protect herself, but she realised now that she had gone about it all the wrong way.

Because Hannah had only ever had one relationship with a man, she had no idea how to be around single men. And no idea how to deal with the attraction she felt for Jonathan. She was simply too inexperienced. She had never dated, during her youth, because she had married so young. She had a lot to learn and so, she told herself, that she must try and view Jonathan as just a friend. But she did not know how to be friends with single men, especially good-looking single men. She decided she would have to have a talk with Michelle and get her advice on the subject.

Just as she was about to go to bed, Michelle rang her. "What was the matter with you tonight, Hannah? I've never seen you like that before?"

"Oh, I've really offended Jonathan tonight, and I don't know what to do about it. The truth is that ever since meeting him for the first time, I've had this ridiculous crush on him. Please don't say anything to John. I feel so stupid about it at my age!"

"I won't say anything to John, you know that."

"Well, because he and Becky seem to be getting really close, I thought that it was best to avoid him until I get over it. But now he thinks I've been rude, and I'm so embarrassed. The truth is, Michelle, I have never had single male friends, and I don't know how to behave around him."

"He was hurt because he likes you. I'm not talking from a romantic aspect, but I know he admires you."

"Did he tell you that I'd blanked him?"

"Not me, but he did tell John that he didn't know what he had done to upset you."

"Oh no!" Hannah groaned, feeling utterly ashamed of herself.

"Just try to be his friend Hannah… Things will work out, in the long term."

"Really?"

"Yes, really!"

"Anyway, he's well out of my league"

"Why is he?"

"Oh, come on, Michelle. Why would someone who looks like Jonathan be interested in someone like me?"

"I can see why he might be… Don't underestimate yourself Hannah. Just be friends with him. He's a decent guy… I've known him a long time, and John's known him since they were kids."

"I'll apologise to him the next time I see him," Hannah said, biting her bottom lip and feeling absolutely dreadful over her behaviour.

The following Sunday, Hannah arrived for Sunday service. Not looking where she was going, she walked straight into Jonathan and almost knocked him over.

"Whoa!" he said, grabbing both her shoulders to steady them both.

"I'm so sorry," she told him while her cheeks burned yet again.

"It's okay," he told her with a look of amusement.

"I'm glad I've seen you. I want to apologise for the other evening. I wasn't feeling myself, and I'm so sorry if I offended you."

In a flash, Becky was at Jonathan's side, giving Hannah daggers. Hannah was annoyed at the intrusion of what was obviously a private conversation, so she carried on speaking to him as if Becky were invisible.

Becky's face was a picture when Jonathan told Hannah, "Becky's arranged for a group of us to go bowling, and then out for food afterwards this Friday. You're more than welcome to join us."

"I'll think about it," she told him, knowing she would not be joining them. She could not think of anything worse than having to watch Becky throw herself at him all night while she threw dirty looks in Hannah's direction.

"We'll be there at seven, if you can make it," he told her.

Becky looked as if she had a bad smell under her nose as she looked at Hannah, who simply raised her eyebrows at the young woman before walking away.

Friday evening came around quickly, and although Michelle had tried to talk Hannah into going, she had made her mind up not to go. She had decided that she would not ignore him, but neither would she seek his company either.

Jonathan arrived at the bowling alley ten minutes after seven. One or two were already there, one of them being Becky. There was no sign of Hannah yet. As more of their friends arrived, Jonathan kept a look out for her, and so did Becky, but obviously not for the same reason as Jonathan. After an hour, he realised she was not going to show.

All the attention that Becky was giving him was driving him crazy. She was beginning to be a real nuisance!

After they had finished bowling, he told everyone that he wasn't going out for food because he had a headache and had decided to have an early night instead. Becky put her hand on his arm. "Do you want me to come with you?"

"NO! I don't!" he snapped, quickly removing his arm from her grasp.

Becky looked as if she were going to cry. Michelle wanted to ring Hannah and tell her what had just happened, but she would have to save it for later.

Jonathan grabbed a beer as soon as he got in. He had been hoping all day that Hannah would show up, but she hadn't.

Jonathan's phone started to ring an hour after he got in., He knew it would be Becky. He had made the mistake of allowing her to have his number when she had asked for it two weeks earlier, and she had started calling him most evenings. He had done nothing to encourage her, or at least he thought he hadn't, but she just didn't seem to get the message, that he was not interested in her in that way.

He picked up the telephone. "Hello," he said.

"I'm just ringing to see if you're all right?"

"I'm tired." Was all he said back

"Aww, poor you!" Becky said in a silly baby voice that made him cringe.

"Becky, I need to have a chat with you."

"Really?" She sounded hopeful.

He took a deep breath. "I think we need to cool our friendship a little. I'm really sorry if I've led you on in any way, but I've only ever thought of you as a friend… I've got the impression over the last week, and please forgive me if I'm wrong, that you are looking for more than friendship… it's not something that I can give you. I am really sorry."

Becky felt like she had been punched in the stomach. "But Jonathan, I thought you felt the same way about me. I've been hoping that we would soon be more than just friends."

He was taken aback, "That was never my intention, Becky. I've never said anything to you that would suggest that I wanted you to be my girlfriend," she began to cry. "Becky, please don't cry. I should have said something before tonight."

"It's because of her, isn't it?"

"What? Who?"

"Hannah Turner. I've seen her batting her eyes and behaving all coy around you. She knows exactly what she's doing!"

Jonathan was gobsmacked. Becky's tone of voice had turned nasty, reminding him of his ex-wife, whom he had divorced five years earlier.

"None of this has anything to do with Hannah Turner."

"Yes, it has. You went home tonight, not because you had a headache, it was, because she didn't turn up."

Becky, I am not having this conversation."

"Are you going to ask her out?"

"I am not discussing that with you!"

"So, you are then, aren't you?" She accused him, her voice rising.

Jonathan was beginning to feel exasperated. "Becky, I hardly know Hannah, and even if I was thinking of asking her out, it really is none of your business."

"So, you *do* like her, don't you?" Becky accused him, raising her voice further.

I really am sorry, Becky, but I'm going to have to say goodnight." He put the telephone down carefully. Seconds later, it rang again. It was Becky.

"Goodnight Becky," he told her again. After hanging up, he left the phone off the receiver.

He had heard a different side to Becky's nature this evening, causing him to doubt that they would be able to remain friends. He hoped Becky wouldn't approach Hannah and accuse her of trying to steal him. That would be highly embarrassing for all concerned.

It was true that he hardly knew Hannah, but there was something about her that made him want to get to know her more. He liked her company, she could be really funny, then at other times, she appeared very shy.

It endeared her to him, the way she would blush so easily. The night she had joined him, John, and Michelle for a night cap after the barn dance had been a bit of a turning point. He had already found her attractive, but he had wanted to see more of her after that evening. He had offered to walk her home, mainly out of genuine concern for her welfare, but also because it would give him just another five minutes with her. But then the next time he had seen her, she had acted strange around him. He had felt invisible barriers go up all around her, causing him to wonder what on earth he had done.

He had spoken to John about it, who had explained that Hannah had been hurt and very badly let down by her ex-husband. He had advised Jonathan to get to know her slowly and gain her trust, as a friend.

On Sunday morning, Hannah turned up at their place of worship. Jonathan watched her walk in, and he also kept a watchful eye on Becky, just in case she approached Hannah, but to his relief, she didn't.

Michelle had already filled Hannah in on what had taken place between Jonathan and Becky on the Friday evening

Hannah went straight over to him, deciding she needed to get over her shyness around him "I'm sorry for not turning up the other evening, I was just too tired. I was in bed before ten," she told him.

He looked at her with genuine fondness. "No worries. I'm sure they'll be another time."

"Yes, ask me again, some other time." She was beginning to feel a little calmer around him.

He lowered his voice and leaned forward a little. "Actually, I thought you were avoiding me."

"No, really, I'm not. Please don't think that."

He smiled and held her gaze for just a little longer than was necessary, giving Hannah butterflies in her stomach.

"I'll see you on Wednesday evening if I don't get the chance to speak to you after the service."

Hannah smiled at him despite her blushes. Why did she have to blush like a teenager, she asked herself. It made her feel ridiculous, especially, since he must know, that she never seemed to blush around anyone else.

Becky stopped Jonathan after the service. "We need to talk."

"We have got nothing to talk about Becky," he told her with a sigh.

"I knew you were after Hannah Turner. I saw you with her earlier,"

Becky was clearly jealous of Hannah, Jonathan realised.

Aware that others might hear, Jonathan lowered his voice, "You are talking and behaving like someone who has a screw loose. There was never a 'me and you', and you have no right to question me this way."

He let out a heavy sigh. "Look Becky, I will admit to you that I do like Hannah. I like her a lot, but she doesn't know that, and I have no idea what she thinks of me. None of this is her fault. I never intended to hurt you. I believed up until just a couple of weeks ago that we were just friends. I only realised that you wanted more when you started ringing me every evening. I am so sorry if I somehow made you believe that I wanted more. It was never my intention!"

Becky stormed out through the open door, leaving Jonathan to wonder why he had not realised before now that Becky was a complete nut job.

Over the next couple of months, Hannah and Jonathan got to know one another better. They shared the same circle of friends, which meant that they would usually be at the same social gathering, at the weekends. And Hannah found herself becoming more comfortable around him.

Hannah liked Jonathan, not just for his looks, but because of who he was as a person. She saw how he interacted with the elderly people in the congregation and how he playfully teased the children. She had conversations with Michelle about him, all behind John's back.

Michelle assured her that he was a genuinely nice guy. She told Hannah that he had only been married to Adele for a year. She had turned out to be a bit of a psycho, who had not shown her true colours until after the wedding day. Michelle had also told Hannah that she and John had disliked her from the start.

Hannah continued to keep her guard up. She needed to protect her feelings, and did she want to get her heart broken.

She had not had a man in her life since leaving Philip, and it would be a terrible blow to her if the first man that she had an interest in after all these years was to let her down.

One Monday evening, Hannah was walking back from the supermarket with two heavy bags of shopping when the heavens opened, causing a heavy downpour. Hannah had neither an umbrella nor a hood. She speeded up her pace as the downpour continued. A car pulled up alongside her. The driver opened the front passenger door and called, "Hannah, get in."

To her horror, she realised it was Jonathan. She was completely drowned. Her clothes were ringing wet and so was her hair.

He hurriedly put her bags on the back seat as she climbed into the passenger seat. She wanted to the ground to open and swallow her! Her hair was stuck to the sides of her face and hung around her shoulders like rats' tails. She knew her mascara was running down her face as she tried to wipe it away.

Jonathan found it really funny, and was trying hard not to laugh. Knowing what women were like, he knew she would be mortified that he had seen her in the state she was in.

"I look a fright!" she suddenly blurted out.

That was it, he could no longer hold on to his laughter, and so, he burst out laughing. Hannah reached her arm out and playfully hit him. "Don't laugh," she told him, but then his laughter became contagious, and she began to laugh too. He passed her a handful of tissues, so she could wipe her face.

The rain had stopped by the time they reached her house, but Jonathan insisted on carrying her shopping to the door for her. He went back to his car, and Hannah went inside.

After she had got dried off and changed into a pair of pyjamas, she rang Michelle to tell her all about what she felt was the most embarrassing experience of her entire life. Michelle howled with laughter.

"I look like something the cat's dragged in! My hair looks like rats' tails, my mascara is smudged all over my face. I bet he thinks I'm really ugly now!"

"Well, if he doesn't, then he's definitely in love!"

"Don't have me thinking that, Michelle, when I'm trying to protect my feelings!" she said crossly.

"Okay, okay, keep your hair on," said Michelle.

As Hannah lay in bed that night, she found herself cringing over what had gone on earlier. She told herself that that would be the worst he would ever see her. She also wondered if Michelle was right. Did he like her more than she realised?

He did give her a lot of attention, but he had not asked her out. She wondered if she was reading too much into things. She hoped not, because she really liked him. In fact, she felt as if she was falling in love with him. And right now, she did not know what she would do with herself if it turned out that he did not have the same feelings for her.

Chapter Eighteen
January 1994

It was Saturday, just a few days after Hannah had got caught in the rain. She was attending the wedding of the daughter of a close friend with all four of her children. The five of them had been seated at the same table as John and Michelle. It had been a lovely wedding, and although it had been very cold, it had been bright and sunny all day.

It was now seven-thirty in the evening, and the guests who had been invited to the evening reception were all starting to arrive. Hannah knew that Jonathan had been invited. She had had butterflies in her stomach most of the day, and as the afternoon had progressed into the evening, they intensified, as she waited for him to arrive.

When he walked in, Hannah's heart leapt at the sight of him. She turned to Michelle and smiled. Michelle smiled back and gave her a wink

She had seen Jonathan as usual at Michelle's house on Wednesday evening. He had teased her about Monday's incident, and she had enjoyed his attention.

When Hannah had got home that evening, she felt sure that he had feelings for her, but the question was whether he would do anything about it. Meanwhile, she was still trying to protect her fragile heart!

He looked really good, as he walked into the room. He was wearing smart black trousers and an open-necked dark-green shirt. He was carrying a black jacket in his right hand. As he looked around for someone he knew, a familiar voice called to him.

"Jonny, over here." He looked across at John and then he noticed Hannah sitting at the same table, with Sophie and Liam. She was wearing a powder blue fifties style dress that was slightly off the shoulder. It had a broad belt around the middle, showing off her slim waist. Her hair was fastened up, accentuating her defined cheek bones.

He realised he was staring, so he looked around the table at the other guests. He was surprised to see two older teenage boys sitting at the table. He had never met either of them before, but he could clearly see that they each had a strong resemblance to Hannah, Sophie, and Liam.

"Can I introduce my eldest two to you, Jonathan? This is Harrison and this is Ethan."

They both said a polite hello, and as they did Hannah saw Jonathan's shocked expression that he then quickly tried to hide.

She had assumed that John or Michelle would have mentioned to him that she had two older boys. But now that she thought about it, they had never come up in any conversations that she had had with him either. She wondered what he was thinking now that he had just discovered that she had another two children.

He took a seat, between John and Ethan, and as he did, he turned to look at both Harrison and Ethan, and then back to their mother a couple of times as he tried to work out her age. He had guessed her to be around thirty, but that was only because she had a teenage daughter, otherwise he would have put her in her late twenties.

Jonathan guessed that Harrison and Ethan were probably in their mid to late teens, meaning she must be around his age or even a little older. He marvelled as to how she had stayed so slim, toned, and young-looking after having had four children.

After a short while, the music speeded up, and all Hannah's children went onto the dance floor to join their friends.

"Come on, my love, let's have a boogie," John told Michelle. "Come on, you two." He gestured towards Hannah and Jonathan. Hannah felt far too self-conscious to dance in front of Jonathan, and he wanted a few moments alone with her. So, they both shook their heads, much to John's frustration.

After they were left alone at the table, Jonathan moved from where he was sitting to sit next to her. Her heart was racing as he tilted his head and looked at her with admiration.

"You look really great!" he told her. His words caused her heart to race even more, especially when he turned in his seat so that he was facing her.

"You appeared surprised when I introduced Harrison and Ethan to you," Hannah said, as she took note of how the colour of his shirt brought out the colour of his eyes.

He raised his eyebrows and nodded. He turned to look towards the dance floor where Hannah's children were, and then he looked back at her. "You don't look old enough to be the mother of two young adults. Did you have your eldest one when you were like twelve or something?"

He was obviously joking, but Hannah asked herself, what he would think if he knew the truth about how young she had been when she had become pregnant with her first child.

The music slowed down. Hannah's children and their friends grumbled as they all left the dance floor. Michelle and John stayed on the dance floor so that they could enjoy a slow dance together.

"Will you have this dance with me?" Jonathan asked, his eyes were smiling. Hannah's heart leapt at the question.

"I would love to."

Once they were on the dance floor, John, and Michelle both looked over at the two of them, before exchanging a look between themselves.

As Hannah turned to face Jonathan, he put one arm around her waist and held one of her hands against his chest with his other hand. Waves of electricity swept throughout Hannah's entire body, making her feel a little breathless and dizzy as they slowly moved to the music. He smelled really good, and as she looked up at him, she thought about what an attractive man he really was. She could scarcely believe that she was being held by the man who had hardly left her thoughts during the last four months.

"Everyone will be talking about us," she told him with a light-hearted laugh.

"I don't care. Do you?" He looked amused.

She shook her head.

"We're not doing anything wrong. We are both free and single, and people will always talk," he told her with a smile.

He continued to look at her, and Hannah had to fight the desire to rest her head against his chest.

The song finished, and as the two of them walked back to their table, Jonathan absentmindedly held the palm of his hand against the small of her back, causing quite a few raised eyebrows amongst some of the wedding guests, who had been watching the two of them dance together.

Hannah's children all went back onto the dance floor as the music speeded up, while John and Michelle purposely left Jonathan and Hannah alone, while they mingled with the other guests.

Jonathan looked directly at Hannah. Her heart was beating at a rate of knots, as she watched his eyes move down to her lips for a few seconds and then back up to her eyes. He had turned in his seat again so that he was facing her. He went to speak, but then he appeared to hesitate for two or three seconds, and then he spoke.

"Hannah," He said tentatively, "have you any idea how I feel about you?"

The smile fell from Hannah's face as the blood rushed to her cheeks. Jonathan watched the smile fall from her face, but he continued. "I think about you all the time… forgive me if I'm coming on too strong… but, I would love to take you out some time."

His words gave her goosebumps! She swallowed hard before asking in a small voice, "Really? Would you?" She could feel her cheeks burning, as her heart hammered in her chest.

He nodded, "Yes, I would." He bit his bottom lip as he waited for Hannah to respond.

She found that her hands were trembling over the unexpected turn of events. She swallowed hard again. "That would be really nice," she told him.

Jonathan's face lit up, while Hannah tried to digest the enormity of the words that they had just exchanged. He looked down and stroked the back of her hand with his finger, causing her spine to tingle. "Can I take you out for dinner on Tuesday evening?" he asked her before lifting his head to look at her.

"Yes, I'd like that," she told him, smiling, while her heart continued to race.

"I'll pick you up at seven, if that's okay?"

"Can I ask you a question, Jonathan?" He looked at her quizzically. "Does it not bother you that I have four children?"

"I cannot lie," he told her, "I am surprised to discover that you had two more children hidden away, but no, it doesn't bother me, not at all." His smile faded. "Don't look now," he told her quietly, "Becky Summers is looking over in our direction, and if looks could kill, we would both be dead!"

"Oh dear!" Hannah said as she bit her bottom lip, while fighting the urge to turn around to see Becky's face.

Michelle and John both arrived back at the table. Michelle was hardly able to contain her excitement as she looked questioningly at Hannah, who beamed back at her, letting Michelle know everything she needed to know for now. Hannah knew Michelle would be on the phone once they were all home and would want a full running commentary of everything that had been said between her and Jonathan.

"Must be my round," Jonathan announced. "Will you come to the bar with me?" he asked, turning to Hannah.

She got up to follow him to the bar, and as she did, he put his hand against her waist, as he guided her through a large group that had congregated between the dance floor and the bar. The feel of his hand, warm against her waist, made her spine tingle with pleasure.

"Well," Michelle said to John as she beamed, "what do you think? That's all a bit unexpected..., do you think he's asked her out?"

"It's looking that way!"

"Oh, I do hope so!" Michelle said, holding her hands together as if she was praying. "Hannah's liked him for ages. But I just haven't told you that."

"He's liked her for ages too, and I just haven't told *you* that!"

The rest of the evening went by quickly.

Harrison and Ethan had returned to the table towards the end of the evening. As they did, they both grinned and nudged each other as they saw how their mother was looking at the tall, good-looking man, whom they had met for the first time that evening.

"Me-thinks our mother is in love!" Harrison told his younger brother with a grin.

"Me-thinks you are right!" Ethan said back. They were both grinning like a pair of Cheshire cats.

Hannah looked across at them both and gave them one of her looks. They both wiggled their fingers at her in a mock wave. She threw them a warning look, causing the pair of them to double up with laughter. Jonathan saw, and found it hilarious while pretending that he hadn't seen the exchange that had just gone on between the three of them.

In no time at all, the evening was at an end. Jonathan took Hannah onto the dance floor for the last dance under the watchful gaze of her children.

Both Sophie and Liam knew Jonathan well, and Sophie had been quite certain for some time that Jonathan really liked her mother. As she watched them, she knew that tonight was the beginning of something much more than friendship.

As the two of them moved to the music, Hannah felt as if her heart would explode with happiness.

She could now admit to herself for the first time how she really felt about the man who was holding her close.

She could finally put down the invisible barriers that she had kept up all around her since the evening she had first met him.

She felt as if she was floating along on a cushion of air as she left that evening. It had turned out to be so much more than she had expected. She and Jonathan were now moving forward in their relationship, and everyone who had been, there that evening knew it too. They had not left each other's side and had barely taken their eyes off one another since his arrival that evening.

Hannah's children teased her about it all the way home. She took it all light-heartedly and found herself laughing along with the four of them.

Michelle rang her as soon as she got in and wanted to hear every tiny detail of what he had said to her and what she had said back, etc. etc. She squealed with excitement when Hannah told her he was taking her out to dinner in a couple of days.

Hannah slipped between the sheets that night feeling gloriously happy. She was in love, really in love. It was not the childhood infatuation that she had felt for Philip that she had mistakenly thought was love. This was different, she had got to know Jonathan as a friend, and so she knew that he was a very different type of person to Philip.

Jonathan went to bed that night thinking only of her. When he had taken his shirt off, he had held it up to his face and breathed in the scent of her perfume that still clung to the fabric. He lay in bed, reliving that first dance, and thinking of the words they had spoken to one another afterwards as he slowly drifted off to sleep.

The following morning was Sunday. Hannah saw him as soon as she arrived, which set off the familiar butterflies, especially when he walked up to her with a big beaming smile on his face. She smiled up at him, not caring if anyone was watching.

"How are you this morning?" he asked

"I'm really good. I had a lovely time last night."

"Me too… do you and the kids want to sit with me this morning?"

She hesitated for a moment. That would tell everyone that they were now a couple, and they hadn't even been on their first date yet!

"Do you think it might be a bit too soon? You know what people are like," she answered in a hushed voice.

He turned around to look around the room before turning back to her. "People will talk no matter what. It's up to you, no pressure."

She decided that everyone who had been there last night, would already be discussing what had gone on between them, so what did it matter if they were seen taking seats together. She smiled up at him. "Okay, shall we find some seats?"

Her hand trembled a little as he took it in his and led her to where there were four empty seats in a row. As he did, Becky Summers walked past and hissed in his ear, "I don't know what you see in her!" He ignored the comment.

Sophie and Liam looked at Becky as if she had got three heads on hearing what she had just said to the man who they now realised was their mum's boyfriend.

John and Michelle watched the two of them taking their seats together. Michelle squeezed John's hand as they both smiled at one another. Michelle couldn't think of two people who were more perfectly matched.

When Hannah got in from work on Tuesday evening, she had her entire wardrobe out. She didn't want to be too dressed up, but neither did she want to dress too casually. She settled on a black pencil skirt, which she teamed with a fitted three-quarter sleeved cream blouse, with black patent shoes and a little patent black clutch bag.

She was excited but very nervous. Tonight, was going to be their first official date. Her first date in over nineteen years.

She would be spending an entire evening alone with Jonathan for the first time since they had met over four months earlier.

He turned up dead on seven. The kids had all eaten earlier, and she had told her eldest two to make sure that both Sophie and Liam were in bed by nine-thirty.

Jonathan had booked a table in a little French restaurant across town. He loved the ambience there, and the food was excellent. He had asked for the table next to the window because it was tucked a little away from the other tables, and so, it would give them more privacy.

When they arrived, they were shown to their table and given a menu along with a wine list. The waiter took their coats and went to hang them up.

"You look really nice. I love what you're wearing," he told her.

The compliment brought colour to her cheeks, and she thanked him. He looked really nice too. He was wearing a plum-coloured shirt that really complemented his dark features.

"I wouldn't have put that colour on someone with green eyes, but it really works," Hannah told him.

"My sister bought it for me. She has a thing about buying colours that bring out the colour of my eyes." He rolled them, before asking, "I know you prefer red wine, do you trust me to choose the right bottle?"

"Absolutely!" she smiled

He called the waiter over and ordered the one he thought she would like.

"Do you know, I was thinking on my way here that you really don't look old enough to have two children that are almost grownup."

"I'll be thirty-four tomorrow." She sighed.

"It's your birthday tomorrow?" he asked, with a look of surprise.

She pulled a face, "I'm almost middle-aged."

He laughed light-heartedly. "Forty is middle-aged, not thirty-four... How old are Harrison and Ethan?" he asked, looking genuinely interested.

Hannah blushed at the question. "Harrison will be eighteen in March and Ethan will be seventeen in July."

He looked thoughtful as he digested what she had just told him, while mentally subtracting Harrison's age from hers. At that the waiter came over with the wine and poured each of them a glass and asked if they were ready to order.

"Sorry, we haven't looked at the menu yet. Could you give us about fifteen minutes, please?" Jonathan asked.

"Of course, no problem." The waiter said as he walked away.

Hannah took a large sip of her wine. She decided that she should explain to him why she had given birth to her first child only two months after her sixteenth birthday. She took another sip of wine before speaking.

"I met my ex-husband when I was only fourteen. He was twenty-one." She paused and took another sip of wine before continuing. "I had had a very unhappy childhood, so when he showered me with affection and what I believed at the time to be love, I began to believe that he loved me. He led me to believe that he did without actually saying that he did. Does that make sense?"

"Yes, it does make sense," Jonathan told her as he lifted his glass to take a sip of wine

"When he first started touching me, I was alarmed and frightened, because I was not ready for that kind of relationship. Then over the following three weeks, he began to put a lot of pressure on me to go the whole way with him. He got really angry one evening and accused me of being a tease. I certainly was not teasing him. I was scared!" She started to feel emotional as Jonathan continued to listen attentively without comment. "I thought I would lose him if I didn't give him what he wanted. Basically, he bullied me into having sex with him long before I was ready. He convinced me that what we were doing was perfectly normal." She took another large sip from her glass while Jonathan had another sip of his. "He got me pregnant when I was fifteen, and we were forced to marry as soon as I turned sixteen. Harrison was born eight weeks premature the month after."

"Not a very good start to a marriage," he told her quietly.

She shook her head. "It was horrible. He abused me in every way you could possibly imagine, until I finally escaped when Liam was just a few weeks old."

"He was violent?" Jonathan asked her quietly.

"Not just violent… he was, and still is a monster! Please don't think badly of me."

Jonathan leaned towards her and put his hand on her arm.

"I don't think badly of you at all. You were a child, right? You were coerced into doing something that you didn't want to do by a grown man who would have known what he was doing was very wrong. It happens all over the world. Girls who are still children being exploited, dominated, and controlled by older men. Where on earth were your parents?" he asked, his eyes full of empathy.

"My parents tried to stop me from seeing him, but you know what it's like when you're a teenager, you believe that they are trying to ruin your life! I believed that he loved me, but I was wrong. I was just too young to realise it." She had another sip of wine. She was mortified that she felt close to tears.

She was worried that what she had told Jonathan might change his opinion of her, and he might even decide not to see her again, despite how understanding he appeared to be. He could see that she was emotional.

"You're upset," He said kindly, "shall we have a look at the menu, and then talk about something else?"

"I don't usually get upset when I talk about my dreadful ex-husband," she told him. In reality, it was also affecting her so because it really mattered to her what Jonathan thought of her.

"It's a very emotive subject, especially for the victim. Are you okay?" he asked, his face full of compassion.

Hannah nodded her head, too afraid to speak in case she burst into tears. Jonathan understood and purposely looked at the menu to give her time to get herself together.

In the end, they had a lovely evening. The food was some of the best that Hannah had ever tasted. They jumped from subject to subject, talking about all kinds of deep and interesting things. Hannah found Jonathan an interesting person to talk to. He had a depth and a warmth that made him even more attractive to her, while he had the same thoughts towards her.

After they had eaten and Hannah had drunk three large glasses of wine, Jonathan took her hands in his and told her.

"I think that you are an incredibly brave woman. I had no idea that you had gone through so much when you were so young. Bringing up four kids all by yourself must have been tough?"

"It's been a lot easier than it would have been if I had continued living with their father! I was afraid you would be put off once you knew about my underage pregnancy to a grown man."

"No," he told her, as he leaned forward. He gave her a light peck on her lips. "Never!"

"I've drunk too much wine."

"I know, but I won't tell anyone." He teased

As they left the restaurant, Jonathan took hold of Hannah's hand as they walked to his car. He had purposely only had one glass of wine because he was driving.

When they got back to Hannah's house, they sat in the car and talked for another hour. She could have sat there with him all night, but she had to go to work the next day so she told him she would have to go in. They arranged to meet again that coming Friday evening. Just as Hannah was about to climb out of the car, he took hold of her hand. "Can I take it that we are officially going out?".

"Is that what you want?" she smiled.

"Yes," he grinned.

"Then, we are!" She was still smiling. Her direct answer made him laugh.

"Goodnight, Hannah," he told her before giving her another light peck on her lips.

Hannah was floating on air as she got ready for bed. All the tension from earlier had now gone. She was glad that she had told Jonathan about what had happened to her, because she no longer had to worry about what he would think once he found out.

He had a clear understanding of how she had been exploited by Philip, and he did not think any less of her because of it.

She had a lovely warm feeling as she slipped between the sheets, where she quickly fell into a deep and contented sleep.

As Jonathan drove home, he thought about what Hannah had told him. He realised that she must have only been about six months older than Sophie was now when she had fallen into the hands of a man who had made her do things that she had not been ready to do.

He found it all so very appalling and felt that her parents should have taken better care of her. They had made her marry a man, who had turned out to be a wife beater, when she had been no more than a child, and Hannah had suffered years of abuse because of it.

He knew nothing of the difficulties, she had suffered while growing up. He would learn about that at some point in the future.

He knew that he loved her, and he knew too, that he could never hurt her.

Chapter Nineteen

Hannah and Jonathan had been seeing one another for over four months. The two of them were very much in love, and everyone who knew them could see it. Jonathan, had got to know her youngest two better and had enjoyed getting to know Harrison and Ethan. He felt Hannah had done a good job in bringing up her children. They were all well-mannered and pleasant to be around. He spent every Friday evening at Hannah's house. She would cook for them all, and after wards they would sometimes watch a film, or play scrabble or some other board game. The atmosphere was always light, and they would all end up laughing together at some point in the evening. Hannah took enormous pleasure at how easily her eldest two not only accepted Jonathan, but also how well the three of them got on.

Jonathan always went home at the end of the evening, because as devout Christians, sex outside of marriage was not for them.

Of all of Hannah's children, Jonathan was drawn more to Ethan. He had the same warmth and sensitivity as his mother.

Since turning sixteen Ethan had decided to stop seeing his father, even though it had meant not seeing other members of Philip's family, including his grandparents.

Philip had kicked off and had accused Hannah of turning his son against him. But Ethan had jumped to his mother's defence and had told his father over the telephone that it was his father's attitude and behaviour that had turned him against him, and that it had nothing to do with anything that his mother had said.

Jonathan realised that there were probably some deep issues going on inside Ethan, for him to forego his relationship with his grandparents by becoming estranged from his father.

Ethan had a long memory. It still hurt him that his mother had been treated so badly by his father, when he had been too little to defend her.

He had not forgotten what his father had done to Sophie the day their mother had taken them all to a place of safety.

The truth was that Ethan did not like his father at all and he did he not enjoy spending time with him.

He had often wished when he was younger that his Uncle James had been his father instead, because he was always kind and easy to be around, whereas his father was moody and very unpleasant.

Both Harrison and Ethan had told their mother separately that Jonathan was a great guy. He reminded them of their Uncle James, although the two men looked nothing like one another, but they both had the same kind and gentle nature.

One Saturday Jonathan took Hannah and her youngest two to the coast for the day, while her eldest two were on a camping trip with a group of their friends

On arriving they had had fish and chips for lunch, before taking a long walk along the beach.

After the walk Hannah and Jonathan had gone to sit on a bench as they watched Sophie and Liam running in and out of the sea. Hannah had warned each of them not to go too far out, and to stay near the edge. Her motherly concern for her children had made Jonathan smile. As they sat on the bench, he put his arm around her shoulder and pulled her a little closer. "I love you so much," he whispered in her ear.

"I love you too," she whispered back as she rested her head on his shoulder. After an hour had passed by the two of them walked back onto the beach and sat on the warm sand. Sophie came over to them and asked. "Can we go and get a drink, Mum? Liam and I are really thirsty."

"Actually, I'm quite thirsty too," Hannah said, turning to Jonathan she said. "Let's go and find somewhere to have a drink."

They found a not too busy tearoom not far from the beach. While they were having their drinks, Liam turned to his mother and asked. "Do you think you and Jonathan will get married, Mum?"

Hannah's face turned scarlet, and the look she gave her son told him that he had said something very wrong. Sophie thumped his arm and told him.

"You don't ask people who are going out, a question like that!" She rolled her eyes at her mother.

"Well, I didn't know that!" Liam told his sister. He had turned as scarlet as his mother had, and he was too embarrassed to look at Jonathan.

"Don't worry Liam, we all say silly things at times," Jonathan told him reassuringly.

Hannah wanted the ground to open and swallow her down over what Liam had blurted out in front of Jonathan.

"Boys are so stupid!" Sophie said, rolling her eyes again, before giving Liam another dirty look.

Jonathan felt really sorry for the eleven-year-old. He remembered only too well what it was like to have a stroppy teenage sister at Liam's age.

Jonathan's family knew that he had a special someone in his life. His mother had nagged him for weeks to let her meet his new girlfriend, but there was a reason why he had not introduced Hannah to his mother. But he knew he couldn't put it off forever, so he had arranged to take Hannah to meet her one Saturday afternoon.

On the way there, Jonathan had warned Hannah to take everything that his mother says with a pinch of salt, because she could be rather blunt with her comments. His words did nothing to calm Hannah's nerves.

They arrived just after one in the afternoon. Jonathan gave a light knock on his mother's front door and then walked straight in with Hannah. His mother appeared from the kitchen.

"Hello darling, this must be Hannah?" she said, while still smiling at her son. She was the only person that ever called him darling. His father and sister had always called him by his name.

"These are for you," Hannah told her with a smile.

She thought Emily was very striking, even though she was in her early sixties. Hannah could see that she must have been beautiful when she was younger. She had the same black hair, (although she had a few strands of grey in hers) and the same green eyes as her son.

"Oh, you didn't have to bring me flowers," she told Hannah without smiling, as she took them from her. "I'm just going to make some coffee. Please go through," she gestured to Hannah with her hand. Still no smile!

Hannah was already thinking that although Jonathan looked like his mother, they appeared to have very different personalities.

The two of them sat side by side on his mother's settee, as Hannah looked around at the tastefully furnished room.

Emily appeared several minutes later, with a tray of coffee and slices of homemade cake. She placed the tray on the coffee table, before pouring each of them a cup of coffee. Emily told Hannah to help herself to milk, sugar, and a slice of cake.

The three of them made small talk with one another for several minutes. Hannah, complimented Emily on her taste in furniture.

Still, she felt ill at ease in Emily's company, and so she shifted in her seat a little. She thought about Alice, and the lovely warm welcome she had received from her the first time they had met. There was nothing warm and welcoming about Emily Lawrence.

After twenty minutes had passed by Emily turned towards Hannah and asked very calmly, "How come you're not married at your age?"

Jonathan nearly choked on his coffee at his mother's incredible rudeness.

"I'm divorced," Hannah told Emily, as she shifted in her seat again.

"Divorced?" Emily said as she raised her eyebrows and lifted her chin, so that she was looking down at Hannah. She had taken on a supercilious air, as she looked from Hannah to Jonathan.

"Yes, divorced, Mum, like me!" He was looking at her with a look that said. 'Please don't start'. Emily ignored the look and raised her chin even higher.

"Any children?"

Answering the question for Hannah, Jonathan said, "She has four children, aged eighteen down to eleven."

Hannah took note of the irritation in his voice as she watched the expression on his mother's face change, and not in a good way.

"I hope you are not going to saddle my boy with four children!"

Jonathan looked at his mother incredulously. "Your boy! I'm thirty-six, and please do not insult my girlfriend."

"Well, she's hardly a girl if she has an eighteen-year-old." Emily snapped.

Hannah did not like the way the conversation was going and wanted to leave.

"Who I see at my age, is none of your business, Mum," he raised his voice a little, and Hannah knew he was annoyed.

Emily stood up and narrowed her eyes at him.

"None of my business? You are my son, and I do not want some little gold-digger getting her claws into you, so that you can provide for her and her offspring!" His mother was glaring at him, and ignoring the fact that Hannah was still in the room.

Hannah got up and rushed past Emily. She stopped, only to grab her sandals from the hallway, and did not stop to put them on until she was in the street.

Jonathan stood up and looked at his mother and shook his head. "I knew this was a huge mistake. How could you treat Hannah like that?"

His mother went to say something else, but he put his hand up and told her. "You've, said enough. Hannah did not deserve that. I won't be bringing her here again."

He walked out, leaving his mother standing where she was.

"You are a fool, Jonathan Lawrence!" she called to him as he quickly slipped his shoes back on before leaving.

When Jonathan got outside, he saw that Hannah was almost running down the street. He ran to catch up with her, and as he did, he found her in floods of tears. He wrapped her in his arms and held her close. "I'm so sorry, if I'd have known that she was going to behave like that, I would not have brought you to meet her. She promised me she would be on her best behaviour. I'm so, so sorry." After several minutes, he held her away from him and asked. "Will you wait here while I go and get the car?"

She nodded, as she wiped her eyes and nose on the back of her hand. When Jonathan got back with the car, she climbed in next to him. He handed her a packet of tissues that he always kept in the glove compartment.

"I must look terrible?" she said, as she wiped her eyes and her nose.

"No, you don't. You always look lovely… can we go to the pub near your house, and talk?"

"But I look a mess."

"No, you don't. You just look upset," he said gently.

Once inside the pub, Jonathan bought Hannah a large glass of red wine and a pint of beer for himself. He was anxious that his mother's spiteful nature would make Hannah think twice about their relationship. They found a quiet corner where they could talk. "Please don't let my mother's comments affect our relationship, Hannah."

"I can't believe she called me a gold-digger. Money has never been my priority in life, nor have I ever been materialistic."

"My mother is not a nice person at times. Don't take what she says too personally."

"That's very hard to do when she is so personal with her comments!"

"I know," he said quietly as he put his arm around her shoulder. He had begun twiddling with a strand of her hair, as he remembered his mother's incredible rudeness

She looked at him amused "You always do that when you sit next to me."

He looked at her in surprise. "Do what?"

"Play with my hair."

He smiled, he had not been conscious that he was doing it. He lent towards her and kissed her mouth. It was a proper kiss that aroused a passion in them both, that they had both been working hard to keep under control.

He pulled away from her. "I'm sorry, I shouldn't have done that."

"It was lovely," she told him, smiling.

He grinned. "It was, but we better not do it again!"

They stayed in the pub all afternoon. Hannah's youngest children were at each of their friends' houses and would not be back until much later. Her eldest two were not due back until late evening, which meant that Jonathan and Hannah had no rush to be anywhere other than with one another.

Jonathan told Hannah for the first time all that had gone wrong in his first marriage. She already knew everything about it because Michelle had sworn Hannah to secrecy, before telling her all the details of what had happened, between Jonathan and his ex-wife. Hannah did not let him know what she already knew as she sat quietly listening. She told him a little bit more about her own marriage, but she did not tell him about how she had been raped, by her ex-husband, nor did she tell him about how it had caused her to have a breakdown. She just wasn't ready to share that information with him just yet.

"Let me cook dinner for you." The wine had lowered Hannah's inhibitions. Her house was so close, that it seemed silly to buy food out when she could very quickly rustle up a spaghetti Bolognese. He ran a finger along the back of her hand.

"As much as I love your cooking, I don't think that's a sensible idea."

"What do you mean?" she asked with a frown.

"Because it would be too tempting if we were alone in your house. I don't think I could control myself. I don't think either of us could. You must know what I'm talking about?"

"Sorry, I wasn't thinking," she told him, realising the meaning of his words.

She looked up at him, as a wave of electricity swept through her over what he had just confessed.

"I suppose being in love and sexual desire go hand in hand," she told him.

He blew his cheeks out and nodded. "Yes, it does, so we need to be careful." Then he said, "Let's have something to eat in here, while we calm our passions!"

She laughed with him. It was good that they were comfortable enough with one another to talk about it. After all, they were both adults, with the same needs and desires as other adults. They just had to work harder at keeping such desires under control.

After Hannah had got back in that evening, she ran herself a hot bath and filled it with essential oils. As she lay inhaling the scent from the perfumed the oils, she thought about how lovely it would be to sleep in

Jonathan's arms night after night. That could only happen if they were to marry, and she did not want to rush into marriage.

Jonathan would be taking on a huge responsibility with her children if they were to marry, so he would need plenty of time if he were to come to that decision, and she had no intensions of rushing him.

Once Jonathan was back home, his thoughts turned to marriage too. He had been in love with Hannah long before he had asked her out, and he knew now that Hannah had felt the same way about him. There was nothing to stop them from getting married. They loved each other deeply and he knew he wanted to spend the rest of his life with her.

He thought about how he had always hoped to have a child of his own one day, but Hannah already had four and, so, he understood that she would probably not want another one.

Two of her children were adults now, and at fourteen, Sophie was not too far off becoming an adult either.

The telephone started to ring, interrupting his thoughts. It was his sister, Lynn.

"I've been ringing you all afternoon. Don't you ever listen to your voice messages?"

"I've only been in five minutes. Are you okay?"

"Mum's really upset. Apparently, you're going out with some slapper who has four kids."

Her words stung him, and he reacted. "Do not call Hannah a slapper, Lynn. She is anything but!"

"Look Jonathan, even if she's a genuinely nice woman, do you really want to take on another man's kids? You could have anyone. You've got everything going for you, good looks, great personality, a good job, and a property in a beautiful part of the country. Of course, she wants you, you're a good catch!"

"You don't know anything about Hannah, and she is no gold-digger. I love her. I mean I *really* love her, more than anyone I've ever met before."

"You've only known her five minutes, you would soon get over her if you ended it now."

"You're not listening, Lynn."

"Don't you care about Mum's feelings at all? You know that she worships the ground you walk on. Think about her feelings instead of just your own."

"Oh, that's rich, like she cared about Hannah's feelings when she called her a gold-digger to her face! I am not going to give her up, to please you and Mum, so you are both going to have to get used to it."

Before he had chance to say anything else, Lynn slammed the phone down on him.

Over the years his mother and sister had always shown little or no regard for what he wanted. It was always about what they wanted him to do. His mother had ruined a couple of his relationships in the past, because she viewed any woman that came into his life as competition for his attention.

He wished that his father was still here, he would understand his feelings and would want him to be happy. Jonathan's father had died of a massive heart attack seven years earlier and he still missed him every day.

His father had been his friend and his rock. And they had enjoyed a close relationship.

Jonathan knew without any doubt that his mother loved him, but her love smothered him and made him feel claustrophobic at times. His father had simply loved him. He would always talk any issues through with Jonathan, and then he would take a step back and allow him to make his own decisions.

His mother had always wanted to make all his decisions for him, and his father had often had to step in and tell Emily that she could not live Jonathan's life for him, and that she had to let him learn from his own mistakes.

Jonathan hadn't intended to fall for a woman who already had children, but he had. He wasn't just blindly walking into it, he had given it a lot of thought to it before asking Hannah out.

He had accepted that if he were to ask Hannah to marry him, it might mean never having a child of his own. She'd already been through all the sleepless nights, the nappies, and all the childhood ailments that children suffer as they grow. And now he was prepared to give up the chance of having a child of his own, to be with her, because he knew she was the one!

Chapter Twenty

A month had passed by since Hannah had had that awful encounter with Jonathan's mother.

She and Jonathan were going out for dinner that evening with John and Michelle, who were celebrating not just their tenth wedding anniversary, but also the fact that Michelle had just found out she was pregnant. They had been trying for over two years and had begun to think it was never going to happen. So, naturally, they were over the moon, that finally, Michelle was pregnant.

Hannah had gone into town that afternoon to buy herself a new dress for the occasion. She was walking along the high street when she spotted Jonathan's mother walking towards her. She was with another woman of around forty. Hannah put her head down and hoped that Emily wouldn't recognise her. As she got closer to them, she heard Emily say out loud, "Oh, look, here's the woman who has got her claws into my son."

The two of them stopped right in front of Hannah. Emily was looking Hannah up and down, as if she had a nasty smell under her nose. Hannah lifted her chin defiantly as Lynn stood quietly next to her mother and said nothing, but Hannah had detected her air of disapproval. Hannah said nothing as she walked past them, while looking straight ahead as she did so.

"Snotty cow!" She heard Emily call after her.

Hannah was quite shaken by the incident and was hoping she would not bump into them again as she continued to shop. She realised that the other woman with Emily must have been Jonathan's older sister, because she had seen the strong family resemblance.

It was mid-afternoon when Emily got home. She rang her son immediately. "Jonathan, I have just had a run in with that snotty girlfriend of yours. You should have seen how she looked at me and our Lynn!"

Jonathan closed his eyes and sighed. He knew all his mother's tricks only too well.

"Our Lynn and I, are both very concerned about you, and your involvement with that woman!"

"Her name's Hannah, Mum." He breathed in deeply and sighed again.

"Well, whatever. You can't do this to me Jonathan. It's bad enough that you are mixed up with that religious nonsense, now you're seeing her. What would your father think and say if he was here?"

"He would want me to be happy. Don't you want me to be happy, Mum?"

"You will be miserable if you take on another man's children." She was almost shouting, and Jonathan was finding it hard to remain civil.

"So, just because Hannah has children you are going to treat her like she's a leper. Well do you know what? I find your attitude towards her shameful. How would you feel if our Lynn had found herself in Hannah's position through no fault of her own? Would you consider her to be not good enough for any man that came along?"

Because she wasn't getting anywhere, Emily called down the telephone, "You are a fool, Jonathan!" Before putting the phone down.

Jonathan needed to calm his thoughts, so he took himself out for a run. As he ran, he told himself that even if Hannah didn't have children his mother wouldn't like her anyway.

The first serious relationship that he had was with a girl called Julie. They were both nineteen. He wasn't as devout in his beliefs back then and it had been his first sexual relationship. He was in love for the first time, and his mother had hated Julie with a passion.

He realised now that it had been pure jealousy. Julie had broken up with him after a year and a half, saying that she could not put up with his mother's nastiness any longer. He had tried to talk it out with Julie, but she had not been willing to make up with him because of his mother. She had warned him that he would never have a successful relationship while his mother was around.

He had been heartbroken for months. It was his first heartbreak, and at the time he had thought he would never get over it. A year later he had met Jackie, but he had ended up breaking up with her after six months. He had not got Julie out of his system, and so, he had found himself comparing the two of them constantly. His mother had not liked Jackie either.

She had been a sweet-natured girl, and Jonathan knew that he had broken her heart when he had broken up with her. It had been something that he had felt really bad about at the time, but his mother had appeared a little too pleased over the breakup, he remembered

He had gone on to have a couple of flings after that, that had not developed into anything permanent.

He had eventually met Adele through a work colleague when he was twenty-eight. He had liked the fact that she was a strong woman who could stand up to his mother. She had put his mother in her place a couple of times, and as their relationship progressed, Adele had put more and more space between them and Jonathan's family. And he had understood why at the time.

But after they were married, Jonathan had soon realised that she was just as sly and conniving as his mother was, but Adele had a violent temper too. Her true nature hadn't come out until after the honeymoon.

A year into the marriage, Jonathan, realising that he was in a toxic relationship, had walked out leaving everything he owned behind.

He had gone to stay with John and Michelle for a week while he got himself somewhere to live. Michelle had been alarmed to find Adele hanging around their house at all hours of the day and night. She had left threatening messages on Michelle's and John's car windscreens, and Michelle had been frightened by it all.

Jonathan had found himself a small flat to rent while he looked around for something better.

Adele must have followed him home one day, because she had started turning up at his flat late at night and would refuse to leave. In the end he had found another job, and somewhere to live a hundred miles away.

Only his family, and John and Michelle knew where he had moved to. They would visit him occasionally, but they had to be watchful, they did not want Adele to find him.

Jonathan had felt lonely many times during those first few months, and he had really missed his hometown even though he lived in a beautiful part of England.

Knowing Adele would continue to stalk him, if she were to find out where he lived, he could not risk her finding out, so, he had broken all contact with his other friends.

During those first few weeks, after he had moved away, Jonathan had taken long walks in the hills and around the lakes. He did a lot of thinking and meditating on life.

There was no light pollution where his cottage was, and he had spent many nights in awe of the millions of stars that were visible on a clear night. There was not one patch of sky that wasn't full of them.

He would spend summer evenings, sitting by the edge of the lake, watching the sunset, while ruminating about the complexity of the universe, and the way everything moved in perfect order.

. There was beauty all around him, it had all led him to the conclusion that none of it could have just happened by chance. There had to be an intelligent mind behind the design of it.

During that time, he long chats with John over the telephone about it all.

John and Michelle had both been devout Christians for many years and Jonathan had often had long chats with them about what they believed, but he hadn't taken any of it seriously until he had moved away. He had been a Christian all his life, but now he had a much stronger faith and reverence for God.

Five years after he had moved away, he had been delighted to hear from Michelle that Adele had remarried and was moving to Spain with her Spanish husband. After careful consideration he had put plans in place to move back to his old town.

When Jonathan got back from his run, he found a voicemail. It was from Lynn, telling him to have more respect for his mother's feelings. He deleted the message halfway through listening to it and took himself for a long hot shower.

. He had arranged to pick Hannah up at seven, and then he would pick John and Michelle up outside their house.

Later, as he pulled up outside Hannah's house, his heart jumped as he watched her. She was wearing a new dress, which showed off the curves of her body, including her ample bosom. She was unaware of how her hips gently swayed from side to side as she walked.

He could not tear his eyes away from her as he watched her walk around to the other side of the car. Yes, he was devout, but he was human too.

As she climbed into the car next to him, he asked, "What are you trying to do to me by wearing that dress, young lady?"

Her face dropped. "Is it a bit tarty?"

He gave a small laugh. "No, not at all, but it does show off your curves."

"Do you think I should go back in and change?" she asked anxiously.

"It looks really lovely. I was just teasing," he told her reassuringly, before setting off to drive around the corner to collect John and Michelle.

As the pair climbed in the car, John joked, "Drive carefully, if you don't mind driver, we have a baby on board."

Michelle giggled like a schoolgirl. Jonathan wasn't listening, he was still thinking about how amazing Hannah looked in that dress.

They pulled up outside the restaurant that John had booked. It was where he had proposed to Michelle, and it was their tradition to eat there every wedding anniversary.

Once they were all seated around the table, Michelle could not talk about anything else other than her pregnancy for the first hour. She told Hannah and Jonathan that she had taken three pregnancy tests, to make sure that she was definitely pregnant.

Joy radiated from her, as John beamed with equal joy, that they were finally having the baby they had both been longing for.

Michelle turned her attention to Hannah. "Would you ever consider having another baby, Hannah?" Michelle had unintentionally put Hannah on the spot in front of Jonathan.

"Mm... I suppose, if I was with the right man, then I might consider having just one more, if it was what he wanted."

She cringed inside, being keenly aware that Jonathan was sitting there and listening.

Jonathan immediately looked across at John, when she answered Michelle's question, and John understood the meaning behind that look.

"You see, Hannah, you had your babies with the wrong man, but I bet if you were to have one with someone like Jonathan, you would find it a totally different experience."

Hannah was mortified over what Michelle had just said in front of him, and Jonathan knew she would be. He gave John a look that pleaded with him to stop Michelle embarrassing them any further.

"Right, Michelle," said John, "let's change the subject." John gave her a subtle warning look.

Michelle didn't appear to hear or notice the look, or maybe she was suffering with baby brain, because she suddenly blurted out, "So, Jonathan, if you and Hannah get married, you'll be able to have a baby together."

Hannah blushed to her roots, and Jonathan quickly looked to John to step in.

"Michelle, stop it now with all this baby talk. Can't you see that you're embarrassing our friends?"

Michelle pulled a face at her husband as he quickly changed the subject.

But Jonathan had got the answer to the question that he had been pondering over, and that is why the two men now exchanged another look.

They went on to have a wonderful evening, once Hannah had recovered from her embarrassment.

Jonathan dropped John and Michelle off outside their house and turned down the offer of a cup of coffee, telling Michelle that he wanted to spend a bit of time alone with Hannah. Michelle was a little huffy with him about it, but Jonathan was insistent.

After their two friends had gone in and closed the door, Jonathan drove around the corner and parked up under the streetlamp outside Hannah's house. He turned around so that he was facing her. "What was

Michelle like earlier this evening, with all that talk of us having a baby together?"

Hannah blew her cheeks out, "I was so embarrassed! Talk about being put on the spot. She's usually more careful with people's feelings. She must be so caught up with the joy of being pregnant, that it's reduced her brain to mush."

Jonathan looked at Hannah enquiringly. "Did you mean what you said to her?"

"About having another baby?" she asked, frowning

"Yes."

"Why are you asking?" Hannah asked, while her heart raced.

"I was just wondering that's all… did you mean it?" he asked again, trying to sound like it was something you ask every day of the week.

"Yes, I did mean it."

She was wondering where the conversation was leading, but then he changed the subject.

"I was thinking of booking a table for Monday evening at our favourite restaurant. Do you think Harrison and Ethan would mind watching Sophie and Liam?"

"I don't think so, they've not had to babysit this evening, because Sophie and Liam are both at sleepovers tonight."

"I'll ring the restaurant tomorrow and try to book a table for Monday evening."

"Are we celebrating something?" she asked him, smiling, quizzically.

He looked amused., "It's just that we haven't been there for several weeks, and I want an evening where I have you all to myself. And it's our favourite place to eat."

Hannah beamed. She liked having him all to herself too. They chatted for another half hour before she told him, "I'd better go in its very late."

"Can I hold you for a minute, before you go in?"

She nodded. As he held her, he whispered words of love into her ear. Hannah felt her body respond. She pulled away from him breathlessly. He held her face in his hands. "Goodnight, my love," he told her.

After telling him goodnight, she got out of his car, and as she walked towards her front door, Jonathan watched her with admiration. Before closing the door, she turned around and blew him a kiss. He smiled broadly, before waving to her as he pulled away from the kerb.

They arrived at the restaurant at seven thirty the following Monday evening. Jonathan had managed to reserve the same table that they had sat at the first time he had taken her there.

"Good evening to you both." The manager said to them in his strong French accent. He had seen the two of them in his restaurant many times. He always took note of how much in love they appeared to be. He took their coats before snapping his fingers at one of the waiters to bring menus and the wine list across

"We'll have the usual wine, but can you give us twenty minutes or so to look at the menu, please?" Jonathan asked.

"Of course, not a problem. I will bring your wine."

The waiter was back within less than five minutes. He opened the bottle of wine and poured each of them a glass. They both thanked him in unison.

"You're a bit quiet tonight. Are you okay?" Hannah asked, looking concerned.

"Yes darling, I'm fine."

He was not fine at all. In fact, he'd been like a cat on a hot tin roof since getting in from his early shift that afternoon. He felt sick with nerves, and so he took a large gulp of his wine, causing Hannah to raise her eyebrows, Jonathan usually drunk his drinks slowly.

"I think I might leave the car here over night and get a taxi home. I'll get the taxi to drop you off first," he told her as he took another mouthful of wine.

"Something's wrong, Jonathan. What is it?" Her brows knitted together to form a deep frown.

"Honestly, I'm fine. Shall we have a look at the menu?"

Hannah picked up her menu, but she had a growing sense of unease. Jonathan did not appear himself at all. She hoped that he wasn't having second thoughts about their relationship because of his mother. Surely, he would not be so cruel as to bring her to their favourite restaurant to break up with her. She took a sip of her wine as Jonathan drained his glass and refilled it, before topping up her glass. He was starting to settle down and appeared to be more like himself again.

They ate their meal, and as they did, they talked, laughed, and smiled, and all had seemed well again. But after they had finished eating Jonathan appeared distracted. He was noticeably quiet, in fact, he had hardly spoken a word for over ten minutes. He excused himself and went to the toilet.

A minute later he stood in the gents' toilet. He blew out a large breath, and then he took a deep breath in, and then another one out. He used the urinal and washed his hands afterwards. Looking at his reflection in the mirror he whispered out loud to himself, "Just do it, you idiot!"

Meanwhile, back at the table Hannah felt close to tears. She knew there was something very wrong. She had never seen Jonathan behave the way he was this evening, and her feeling of unease had grown into full-blown anxiety.

Had his family convinced him that he was making a huge mistake by becoming romantically involved with a woman who had four children?

She watched him come out of the gents', and as she did, she fought to get her emotions under control. Jonathan sat back down at the table and took her hands in his. Hannah knew he was not himself, and now his expression was deadly serious.

"Jonathan, are you trying to break up with me?" *(Don't cry, don't cry)* she told herself.

He could not have looked more shocked. "No darling, absolutely not!"

Tears of relief fell from her eyes. Jonathan wiped them away, deeply concerned that she was crying.

Hannah cupped one of her hands over her mouth and nose as more tears fell. He handed her the car keys.

"Do you want to wait in the car while I pay the bill?" he asked her gently.

She nodded and got up from the table. She grabbed her jacket from the coat stand and fled outside.

Feeling like a total idiot for crying in public, she got into Jonathan's car and closed the door. She took a couple of tissues from the glove compartment to wipe her eyes and her nose, while she waited for him. As she waited, she wondered what explanation he was going to give her for his bizarre behaviour.

The restaurant manager had watched Hannah leave the restaurant in a hurry. "Is everything all right, sir?" he asked Jonathan, out of genuine concern.

"My girlfriend isn't feeling very well. Can I settle the bill, please?"

"Yes, yes, of course, sir."

Jonathan paid the bill and quickly went out to the car. He climbed into the driver's seat and immediately took Hannah into his arms. He kissed her face and stroked her hair.

"I'm sorry I've upset you. I have no intentions of breaking up with you, in fact just the opposite. I've been so incredibly nervous, all evening, and that's the only reason I've been acting weird."

"What do you mean?" she asked, feeling bewildered.

He looked at her lovingly. "How do you feel about getting married?"

Hannah was stunned! And then finding her voice she said, "I'm going to be sick."

"That's not quite the reaction that I was hoping for," he joked, but then, looking alarmed, he asked, "You're not *really* going to be sick, are you?"

She shook her head. "No, I'm not."

She swallowed hard before taking a deep breath. She had not expected a proposal from him that evening, and it had come as a shock. Jonathan held his breath as cold fear gripped his heart. She did not look as if she were about to say yes!

"There is something that I need to tell you… it's something that happened to me a long time ago, but I need to let you know about it, and if you still want to marry me, then ask me again… Do you remember the first time you took me out I told you that my ex-husband had abused me in every way you could possibly imagine?"

Jonathan nodded, dreading what she was about to tell him. Hannah continued, "He had at least two affairs while I was married to him. They may have been more, I'm sure there was. Anyway, as soon as I found out about the first one, he dumped the other woman, swearing that I was the only one that really mattered, and that it had only been a bit of fun and it had meant nothing. The second affair was confirmed when I followed him to the pub one night. I found them standing at the bar together. I threw a pint of lager over the other woman's head. She ran out of the pub, dripping wet, and in shock, over what I'd done, and then he marched out after her."

The image of Hannah throwing a pint over the other woman's head caused Jonathan to laugh out loud.

Hannah carried on. "I assumed that he would be spending the night with her. I was already in bed and had just dozed off when I heard him come into the bedroom. He was raging! I really believed that I was going to die that night."

Jonathan inhaled deeply, and slowly shook his head.

"After I told him that our marriage was over because I no longer loved him, he grabbed me by my throat and squeezed hard.

He smirked and grinned, and taunted me, while he threatened to either snap my neck or choke me to death. I was beyond petrified!" She paused and swallowed hard before continuing. "I panicked. I thought my children were going to be left without a mother, so, although I could barely speak, I begged him to let me go, but he appeared to be really enjoying it."

Jonathan was shocked, but he did not interrupt, as she continued.

"He finally let go of my throat.," She paused for a couple of seconds. Then he covered my mouth with his hand, so that I couldn't scream, while he subjected me to a violent sexual assault." She paused again just for a couple of seconds. He went on to rape me… It was absolutely terrifying. He really hurt me; you know… inside."

She saw the look of horror on Jonathan's face. "Oh, God, Hannah!" he groaned, "that is truly, truly terrible!"

She nodded her head, and then she realised she was crying. Talking about it to Jonathan was awful. She hadn't spoken about it for several years now, but the memory of it could still bring back the feeling of absolute terror she had felt that night at the hands of the man, who was not only her husband, but the man who had claimed he loved her.

Jonathan wrapped her in his arms, as she cried with her face against his chest. He quietly wiped his own eyes, not wanting Hannah to see.

After a while she pulled away from him and told him the rest. Of how it had been the last straw after years of abuse, and that she had suffered a massive breakdown that had taken her two years to fully recover from.

"I sometimes feel emotionally fragile, as if the breakdown has left me with a weakness. You know, like if you break an arm, and you are then left with a weakness in it.

Because you have asked me to marry me, you have the right to know that I've had mental health problems. But I also want you to understand why. If you've changed your mind, then I will understand."

Still recovering from the shock of what he had just been told, Jonathan told Hannah, "There is nothing wrong with your mind, my love. Anyone would have cracked under the pressure of what you were going through. Not just because of what he did to you that night, but because of all the years of cruelty you'd suffered because of him too. What a worthless piece of garbage! He should have done time for what he did to you, and for what he made you do when you were still a child."

Hannah could hear the contempt in Jonathan's voice, that he felt towards Philip.

"I promise you Hannah, that if you marry me, I will never intentionally hurt you, and I will always put your welfare ahead of my own."

"Do you still want to marry me?"

"Yes. I love you... I'm all in, Hannah... I will take whatever you bring to the table because I want to spend the rest of my life with you. Do you need time to think about it?" he asked quietly.

She shook her head, and without moving her face away from his chest, she whispered, "My answer is yes."

He hugged her tight, relieved that she had finally said yes.

"Let's make the wedding soon, how about early autumn?" he suggested as he lifted her face to look at her.

"Maybe the first week in October, before all the bad weather comes?" she suggested as she wiped her eyes dry.

"I think that sounds perfect."

He kissed her mouth tenderly, knowing how careful they were going to have to be during the next three months.

It was a very emotional end to a very emotional evening, but they were both smiling now.

Hannah could not believe that this man, with his beautiful eyes, and his beautiful smile was going to be her husband. They sat in the car for another hour discussing their plans, neither of them wanting the evening to end.

"Do you know what I'm really looking forward to?" he said,

"What are you really looking forward to?"

"Not having to go home at the end of each evening."

"I'm really looking forward to that too."

The thought of sharing a bed every night with Jonathan gave her goosebumps, and she knew waiting another three months was not going to be easy. But she also knew that Jonathan would be determined to do things properly.

They had been sat in the carpark for over two hours, and so Jonathan was able to drive Hannah home. He suddenly remembered the ring was still in his pocket. After all the emotion that the evening had brought, he had forgotten about it.

He had consulted Michelle the day before, regarding size, and style of ring, etc, and he had seen the ring he wanted Hannah to have within minutes of walking into the shop.

He had gone straight to the jewellers after finishing his early shift, that day He took the ring out of the box and put it on her finger. To his surprise it was a perfect fit.

"It's a beautiful ring. I absolutely love it," she told him.

She held her hand out to admire it with a beaming smile.

Jonathan's heart felt as if it would burst. After several minutes he told her," I had better get you off home. It's almost midnight, and I've to be up in less than five hours."

He had no idea how he was going to sleep after all that had taken place that evening. His emotions were still running high, and he knew it would take at least a couple more hours for him to settle down.

Chapter Twenty-one

It was now a week since Jonathan had proposed, and Hannah couldn't stop looking at the ring that shone on her finger.

Jonathan had arranged to see both his mother and sister that afternoon to try to get them both to understand that they would have to accept Hannah and her children, because they were going to be a part of their family very soon.

His mother was only too happy that the three of them should get together, because she saw it as an opportunity to talk him into ending his relationship with Hannah

They had arranged to meet at his mother's house at four in the afternoon. Emily had got Lynn to get there an hour before Jonathan, so that they could plan what they were going to say once he arrived. Lynn liked to please her mother. She knew that her brother, was her mother's favourite, and although Lynn loved him, she had lived in his shadow since the day he was born. So, she had become a people pleaser in her attempts to constantly win her mother's approval.

When Jonathan arrived and found Lynn already there, he knew what they had been up to. His mother came into the hallway to greet him when she heard him coming through the front door. She smiled. "It's lovely to see you, darling."

He had deliberately kept her at arm's length since the afternoon that she had been rude to Hannah. He kissed her cheek and then walked into the front room where Lynn was sitting on the settee. He asked, "How are you, Lynn?"

"I'm fine. How are you, stranger?"

"I'm good," he told her as he took a seat on the settee next to her.

Their mother came in with a tray of coffee. After putting it down on the coffee table, she poured each of them a cup before sitting herself opposite them both.

Jonathan braced himself, knowing this was going to be a difficult conversation.

"I need to speak with each of you regarding my relationship with Hannah." He saw his mother shift in her seat. He continued, "I'm not here to ask for your approval, I'm here to ask you not to be rude to her if you see her in town, or anywhere else."

"You didn't see how she looked down her nose at us!" his mother protested.

"Mum, I know you, we've been down this road before... why do you always have to try and meddle in my relationships? I'm not sixteen. I'm thirty-six. What I do with my life is my business. Would you prefer for me to go through life on my own and never experience the happiness that I feel when I'm with Hannah?"

His mother looked across at her daughter, who was sitting in silence with her arms folded and her legs crossed, and then she looked back at Jonathan. "I cannot accept that woman into this family, I just can't," she told him calmly.

"WHY?" he yelled back at her, frustration getting the better of him.

Lynn spoke up next, "Because she isn't good enough for you, and we don't want you to make another mistake," she told him, quietly.

He turned around and looked at her incredulously. "Of course, she's good enough for me. *You* don't even know her. You've never even had a conversation with her. How can you judge a person who you know nothing about?"

His mother spoke again, but this time she spoke in a very cold tone of voice. "I will not accept another man's children into this family, and that is my last word on the subject."

Jonathan swept his hands through his hair. He knew they were forcing him to choose between the woman he loved and them. He stood up and looked from one to the other.

"I know that you are trying to force me to choose, but if you push this, I will not choose you two... I love Hannah, and I need you to know this. I've already asked her to marry me, and she has said yes."

His mother looked as if she were about to have a cardiac arrest, as she clutched her chest. Lynn sat in stunned silence.

Jonathan looked at his mother with a pained expression and told her, "We will be married in the autumn and if your attitude remains the same, then you are not welcome to attend the wedding." He looked at his sister before adding, "Either of you."

He walked out, leaving the cup of coffee that his mother had poured for him on the coffee table. As he went through the front door, he could hear his mother having the usual hysterics she always had when she couldn't get her own way.

He hadn't arranged to see Hannah that evening, but he really needed to be with her, so as he left his mother's house, he drove in the direction of Hannah's.

After climbing out of the car, he took a moment to compose himself, before walking up the garden path. When Hannah opened the front door, she was surprised to see him standing there.

Taking note of the look on his face, she said, "It didn't go well then?"

He shook his head. "Are the kids around?"

"Two of them are out, and the other two are upstairs listening to music. Come through, we can sit in the back garden."

As they walked through Hannah felt a little anxious over what might have been said at his mother's.

Jonathan sat down on one of the garden chairs. He was both angry and terribly upset. Knowing his mother and his sister would never accept Hannah nor her children, he knew it would mean that his relationship with them would be forever changed.

Hannah came outside with a cold drink for each of them since the weather was hot and humid. She took a seat next to him. He put his arms around her as he explained what had gone at his mother's just minutes earlier.

"What do you want to do?" Hannah asked.

He frowned, "What do you mean?" he asked as he let go of her.

"If you marry me, you may lose them for good. Are you sure that's what you want?" She held her breath as she waited for him to respond.

He explained, "You are the most important person in my life. *They* have forced me to choose not you... please don't change your mind because of them. I've told them that if they don't change their attitude, they won't be invited to the wedding."

Hannah thought for a moment, and then choosing her next words carefully, she told him, "I can't have them there, Jonathan. It would ruin the day if they were there looking down their noses at me and my children. I don't want our wedding day to be ruined."

He nodded. "I completely understand. And you're right, they would ruin it."

He thought about his father and how different things would be if he were here. His father would give both his mother and Lynn a good talking to, and he would let his mother know how selfish she was being.

Jonathan was brought out of his thoughts by Hannah. She was saying, "Can we keep things small and simple? I don't have a lot of money to spend on a wedding."

"Oh, Hannah, you don't have to worry about money, I will pay for the wedding."

Hannah blushed, with embarrassment, over her financial situation.

Realising how she must be feeling Jonathan said, "Hannah, once we are married, what is mine will be yours. You shouldn't feel embarrassed. I will cover all the costs of the wedding and our honeymoon."

Her face brightened, "Honeymoon?"

"We must have a honeymoon!" He laughed.

"Where?"

"I'm keeping that as a surprise." He was greatly amused, by the expression on Hannah's face. "Anyway," he said, "Back to the wedding."

Hannah went on to explain, "The day is about us. A small wedding would be much more intimate and special."

"What about your family, won't they be put out, if they are not invited?

"Not if I explain the situation to them." She took his hand in hers. "What do you think of my suggestion?"

"I think under the circumstances, you are right. We'll keep it small, and we won't tell my mum or Lynn, until after the event."

Hannah could well imagine how that would go down with Emily, but she said nothing.

The date was set, and they drew up a list of the people that they both really wanted to be there. Hannah definitely wanted Ursula and Dieter to attend, if at all possible And Debbie, and Helen too. John and Michelle would be invited, along with the three work colleagues (and their wives) whom Jonathan had become friends with after he had moved away. And of course, all of Hannah's children, would have a play a part in it.

Jonathan had cheered up immensely with all the talk of the wedding. They went back indoors. Hannah had asked him to stay and have dinner with her, Sophie, and Liam. He sat at the table with a glass of wine and watched her cook, taking in every inch of her. Hannah knew he was watching her, and she was enjoying the attention.

No one ever looked at her the way Jonathan did, and Hannah had never been so deeply and so totally in love.

When she wasn't with him, she ached to be with him. At times she felt she must have died and gone to heaven. To have found this kind of love at her age, after the dreadful years of abuse she had suffered, still took her by surprise.

Jonathan now knew her life story, and now that he knew everything about her past, it had made him fiercely protective of her.

Once dinner was ready, Hannah called her youngest two down to get ready for dinner. They both appeared five minutes later.

"Hi Jonathan, are you having tea with us?" Liam asked.

"That's why Mum has set the table for four!" Sophie told him as she rolled her eyes. She had got to that age where her younger brother really got on her nerves.

"Sophie, you are really horrible to Liam at times. He was just being polite to Jonathan, that's all," her mother told her.

Jonathan remembered how Lynn had been like that with him when she was Sophie's age. He remembered, how he and John would deliberately wind her up, and how often she had screamed at them both, before stomping out of the room, after telling Jonathan that she hated him.

By the time she was nineteen she had decided that she liked him again. After that they had gone on to have a good relationship, but during the last five years they had drifted apart. Jonathan had moved away, and Lynn's husband and her two children took up most of her time.

He had always found it odd, that his mother had never interfered when it came to her daughters' relationships. It had seemed that Lynn could see whomever she pleased, whereas with him, his mother had always had nothing but negative things to say about anyone he was seeing.

He would make sure that she would never get the chance to interfere in his relationship with Hannah. Their relationship was far too important to him.

Chapter Twenty-two
October 1994

The three months since Jonathan and Hannah had become engaged had flown by. Everyone who had been invited had said that they would be able to attend. Philip's family did not know the date of the wedding. He had hardly seen anything of them since the afternoon that he had told them of his and Hannah's intension to marry. His mother had tried bringing the subject up with him again, but he had refused to have any further discussions about it with her.

Hannah had spoken to her family about why the wedding was going to be small, and that it didn't seem fair to invite them if Jonathan's family were not invited. They had been very understanding about it all. And they had told her to enjoy her day, and not to worry about anyone other than herself and her husband to be.

Her family had only met Jonathan once, at her parents' wedding anniversary celebration. They all had really liked him, but then again why wouldn't they? He was a great guy!

All Hannah's friends from the days when she had been married to Philip had travelled to the town where she lived, two days before the wedding. Hannah had arranged for them all to join her and Jonathan, for dinner that evening, so that they could get to know him a little bit before the wedding day.

Dieter and Ursula would be staying at Hannah's house. Debbie and her husband along with Helen and her youngest son, Jason would be staying with John and Michelle.

It had been arranged that Hannah's boys were going to stay in Jonathan's flat with him, the night before the wedding. The stress of seven people all trying to get ready for the big day, with only one bathroom between them would be an ordeal that the bride could do without.

John was to be Jonathan's best man for the second time. Sophie was to be the only bridesmaid, and Harrison, being the eldest son, would be walking his mother down the aisle. Ethan and Liam had been given the job of making sure that the guests, would be seated in the right places.

When Dieter had pulled up outside Hannah's house with Ursula seated next to him, Hannah had recognised them both immediately. They were in their late fifties now, and Hannah had noticed with a little sadness how much older they both looked since the last time she had seen them.

When Hannah had opened the front door, Ursula had rushed up the path to meet her. She had thrown her arms around Hannah, almost crushing her. "It's so good to see you my dear. You look so well, and I can see the glow of love in your face!" she had beamed.

Hannah had smiled as Dieter caught Ursula up. "It's so good to see you both. I'm so pleased you were able to make it. Come on in." she had told them.

As they'd followed Hannah into her house, she had shown them to her room. telling them that she would be sharing with Sophie.

"Are you sure, Hannah? Will you both have enough room?" Dieter had asked.

She had explained that Sophie has a set of bunkbeds for when she has friends stay over, and that the night before the wedding she would use Liam's room.

She had explained that the three boys would be staying at Jonathan's the night before. She told them, "Can you imagine all seven of us trying to get ready with only the use of one bathroom on the day?"

"Oh, Hannah, we are so pleased for you." Ursula had looked like a proud mum as she looked at Hannah.

While Hannah had made fresh coffee and sandwiches for her guests. Ursula had picked up the official engagement photo of Hannah and Jonathan. It was displayed on the cabinet in the small dining area. "Ooh, so very handsome! I hope he is a good man, Hannah," she had said,

Hannah had responded with the words, "He is a good man Ursula, and yes, he is very handsome."

"Only the best for you this time." Dieter had added with a wink.

Ursula had become very emotional. "When I think of what you suffered all those years ago… you were such a skinny, frightened little thing and now look at you. You look so healthy, and so well. Wherever that selfish pig is now, I hope that he is suffering!" she had said with strong feeling.

"I don't care where he is or what he's doing," Hannah had said. "The children only see him two or sometimes three times a year… Ethan refuses to see him these days, which has devastated Frank and Alice, especially Alice. You remember what a doting granny she is."

"Yes, I remember," Ursula had nodded with sadness, feeling genuinely sorry for Philip's mother.

They had talked nonstop for over an hour until the others arrived. Helen and her youngest son, Jason, had travelled up with Kenny and Debbie.

Hannah had quickly gone to the door to greet them as soon as she had seen Kenny's car pull up behind Dieter's hire car. As they had all piled into Hannah's house, she introduced Helen and Jason to Dieter and Ursula. Debbie and Ursula remembered one another, but it had been over twelve years since they had last seen each other.

When Hannah's children returned home one by one later that afternoon, Dieter and Ursula were blown away when they saw that Harrison and Ethan were now young men. It had made Ursula cry all over again, when she remembered what they had suffered as small boys.

Sophie could not remember the two of them living next door when she was little, and they were total strangers to Liam. He had seen them twice when he was little, but he did not remember them.

The noise in the house was deafening, with all the talk and laughter. So, no-one heard the doorbell, when Michelle called round to take Helen, Jason, Kenny, and Debbie to her house, so she had opened the door and let herself in.

Hannah could not have been more delighted that all her friends who had helped her through the worst years of her life were all now under her roof at the same time.

They were here to share her special day with the man she now realised was the only one she had ever truly loved. She had once believed she had loved Philip, but she had been wrong. She had been infatuated, but not in love. What she felt for Jonathan, was real, and unlike Philip, he loved her back, in the truest sense of the word.

When Debbie and Helen had seen his photograph, they had both teased her about how she had managed to bag such a catch. Hannah had pulled a face and stuck her tongue out at them, sending both women into fits of laughter. And she had laughed with them.

They were all meeting at the French restaurant (where Jonathan had taken Hannah, on their first date), later that evening. Jason was staying the night at Hannah's house with her children. Michelle and John weren't going because, Michelle, who was now five months pregnant felt extremely tired in the evenings, and she wanted to save her energy for the wedding day.

Jonathan was very apprehensive about meeting Hannah's old friends. He knew they would be comparing him to Philip. He decided he would take a taxi to the restaurant so that he could have a glass of wine to settle his nerves before meeting up with everyone.

The conversation was in full swing around the table when he arrived. Hannah saw him walk in. She smiled and waved. He saw her and smiled back as he walked over to the table.

"Is that him?" Debbie asked with her mouth wide open.

"I am here you know!" Kenny said to her, looking really put out.

Debbie appeared not to hear him, as she continued to stare at Jonathan as he was introduced to each of them. Helen could not help but laugh at Debbie, and Kenny's obvious irritation, that his wife could not take her eyes off Hannah's fiancé.

Jonathan took his seat next to Hannah. He moved a stray piece of hair away from her face, before giving her a light kiss on her mouth "You look wonderful, darling!" he told her.

Debbie, who was still staring, practically swooned, causing Kenny to tap her leg under the table.

Jonathan whispered in Hannah's ear. "I'm really nervous!" He had noticed Debbie staring and it had put him even more on edge.

"You'll be fine. Try to relax," she told him. He took a large sip of the red wine that Dieter had poured him.

Dieter had announced to everyone that he would be taking care of the bill, and they were all to have whatever they wanted to eat and drink.

As Jonathan tried to relax, he put one arm around Hannah and absentmindedly started twirling a strand of her hair around his finger. Helen feared that she would collapse with hysterical laughter as she watched Debbie's mouth drop open again. Kenny coughed loudly to let his wife know that he could see her.

As the evening progressed Jonathan relaxed and started to enjoy himself. He was enjoying listening to all their stories about what Hannah had been like as a young girl, and later as a young woman. They were all careful not to bring Philip's name up in conversation.

It was obvious to Jonathan that they all thought a great deal about her, and that they were still protective of her.

They each told him that they were thrilled that Hannah had found love and happiness at last.

Later, Dieter bought champagne to celebrate old friends coming together, and the making of new ones. Jonathan already felt like he had had too much to drink, and so he turned down the offer of a brandy as the evening was ending.

Helen had never seen Hannah look so radiant, so happy, and so animated. She could tell by how attentive Jonathan was towards her, and how he interacted with them all, once he had settled down, that he was no Philip Turner. She had recently met someone herself but was taking things very slowly. Her experience of marriage had been every bit as bad as Hannah's, and she wanted to be very sure before she gave her heart to someone. But she was so pleased for her friend's obvious happiness.

As she watched Hannah smiling, laughing, and talking in such a carefree animated way, she thought about how Philip had almost destroyed her. But she had come out on top. She was now with someone who Helen felt sure would give her all the love she deserved.

Ursula, who had had a little too much to drink, turned to Jonathan, and slurring her words just a little, she told him, "You look after my little friend. She is very dear to me, if you hurt her, I will come after you!"

Jonathan held both his hands up and told her. "I promise you I will never hurt her!"

"Ursula please don't talk to him like that," Hannah said crossly, immediately jumping to Jonathan's defence.

"I know, I know, but I have to say it anyway." She put her hand on Jonathan's cheek as if he were a child. "You come and visit us with Hannah and the children next year."

Jonathan looked at her with amusement and said, "Okay, that would be nice."

It was late when they all eventually left. Debbie told Jonathan that they could give him a lift home, as Kenny was driving, and they had a spare seat in the car.

"I think she's trying to steal him, Hannah," Kenny called to her with a wink.

"I'll make sure she doesn't," Helen told her.

Debbie was more than a little annoyed with them both for showing her up in front of Jonathan. She sulked as she took her seat inside the car.

Jonathan took Hannah to one side. "The next time I see you, you will be walking down the aisle."

"I can't wait," she told him. "Do you like my friends?"

"Yes, they're all great, except I think Ursula and Debbie are both a bit crazy!" he whispered.

Because he would not be seeing her until the day of the wedding, and knowing there was no danger of the two of them falling into bed together, he pulled Hannah into his arms and kissed her mouth. As he kissed her, Hannah, felt the heat rise inside of her, as she thought about the intimacy, they would soon share.

"See you the day after tomorrow." He winked and smiled at her before walking away to join the others in Kenny's car.

Hannah still hadn't recovered from that kiss when she climbed inside the taxi where Dieter and Ursula were waiting for her.

She kept herself busy the day before the wedding, to make the time pass by more quickly. She had relived the kiss from last night over and over in her mind. It had filled her with a longing that would only be satisfied once she was lying in Jonathan's arms.

At some point in the afternoon, Philip came into her mind. She thought about how he had taken advantage of her, of how he had stolen her innocence. She remembered how he had not cared, about how afraid, and reluctant she had been to give him what he had wanted, that first time. And neither had he stopped when she had cried out and told him he was hurting her

The memory of it sickened her now.

She was glad that after tomorrow she would no longer have his name. Tomorrow she would become, Hannah Lawrence. She would never again be called Hannah Turner.

The evening before the wedding, the men were going to Jonathan's for Mexican food and drinks. Liam was excited to have been included. John, Dieter, Kenny, and Jason were taking a taxi there and back. Jason was only fifteen, and so Helen had made Kenny and Dieter promise her that they would make sure that he didn't have any alcohol, much to Jason's disappointment. Hannah had told Jonathan the same, regarding Liam, and had asked him not to allow her older boys to drink too much, because she did not want either of them to be ill during the wedding.

The ladies were having a pamper night, and cocktails at Hannah's house. She was keeping a strict eye on Sophie who had been told she was only allowed one cocktail. Hannah was careful not to have more than two herself because she wanted to look her best the following day.

Harrison had confided in Jonathan a week earlier that he hadn't prepared a speech because he knew he wouldn't have the confidence to give it. Jonathan had told him not to worry about it. He was not good when it came to giving speeches himself. He had had a word with John, and it been decided that John would give his speech first, and then Jonathan would give his, and that would be it as far as speeches went.

At the end of the evening after everyone had left and the boys had all gone to bed, Jonathan sat on the settee and poured himself a large brandy. He had given both bedrooms up for Hannah's boys. He would be spending the night on his large and very comfortable settee.

He thought about the following day with a huge knot in his stomach. He knew he was taking on a huge responsibility with the children, and he hoped that he would not let them down. He had had a great male role model in his own father, and so he felt that if he could try to follow his father's footsteps, then he couldn't go far wrong.

Hannah was completely exhausted by the time she got into bed, and so despite her excitement, she quickly fell into a deep sleep

Chapter Twenty-three

Both the bride and groom woke early the next morning. Jonathan's flat looked like bomb had been dropped on it. He set about clearing all the mess away. He had just finished when Ethan walked into the kitchen, wearing his boxer shorts, still looking half asleep. "Morning."

"Jonathan turned to look at him. "Good morning. I wasn't expecting to see you, or anyone else for a couple of hours. Do you want some coffee, or some juice?"

"Just some orange juice for now, thanks."

"Help yourself, it's in the fridge." Jonathan was watching Ethan closely. He looked like someone who was nursing a bad hangover.

He had only let them him and Harrison have three cans of beer the night before because he had promised Hannah that he would keep a close eye on them all, especially since Ethan was only seventeen.

Are you all right, mate? You don't look too good."

"I've got a confession to make." Ethan said, meekly.

Jonathan frowned.

"Me and our kid sneaked a bottle of wine from your wine rack and drank it when we went to bed. My head's killing me, and I don't feel well… don't tell Mum, she'll go mad."

Ethan walked over to the settee and flopped down in a heap. Jonathan stood for a moment, drying his hands. Half a bottle of wine plus three cans of beer was a lot of alcohol for a teenage boy who wasn't used to drinking. He knew Hannah would go mad if she were to find out.

"Well, I'm not happy that you stole alcohol from me, but I'm glad you've owned up to it." And then with a sympathetic look he asked Ethan, "On a scale of one to ten, how bad do you feel?"

Ethan shrugged his shoulders. "Eleven!"

Jonathan smiled, inwardly. "You need to drink lots of water. I'm going to cook us all some breakfast, that should help you feel a bit better. Don't tell Liam. He might tell your mum."

"You're not going to tell her then?"

"She doesn't need to know on *this* occasion but drinking too much alcohol when you are not used to it is dangerous. If you had been sick, you could have choked! Keep drinking lots of water, while I go get shaved and have a shower."

Ethan went into Harrison and woke him up. Harrison was furious when Ethan told him that he had confessed about taking the bottle of wine.

"Why did you tell him? He wouldn't have even noticed it was missing!"

"Because I could tell that he knew that I've got a hangover. I'm not good at telling lies, my face always gives me away."

Harrison got out of bed and pulled a tee-shirt on over his boxer shorts. "What did he say?" he asked in a whisper.

"He was okay about it, really. He gave me a bit of a lecture about the dangers of drinking too much. He's not going to tell Mum, and he said to make sure that Liam doesn't find out because he'll probably tell on us both... Haven't you got a hangover?"

"Yeah, I've got a bit of one."

"Jonathan's put a big jug of water on the table. He said to keep drinking, and hopefully we might be feeling a lot better by lunchtime."

Harrison grinned. "Looks like we've got away with it, our kid," he joked, nudging Ethan in the ribs.

Ethan held his head. "Don't make me laugh, I feel really ill."

They took themselves into the kitchen and poured themselves a large glass of water each. Harrison drank his straight down and then poured himself another.

Jonathan wasn't annoyed really. It wasn't anything that he hadn't done when he was their age. He remembered the time when he and John had got really drunk on his dad's whiskey when they were sixteen. Jonathan had been sick all over the kitchen floor. His mother had gone crazy, and his dad had grounded him for an entire fortnight.

"How are you feeling?" Jonathan asked Harrison, as he walked from the bathroom drying his hair on a towel.

"Not that bad really. I'm sorry for stealing the wine," he said, shamefaced.

"Drink lots of water, and hopefully you'll both be fine by lunchtime. All I'm going to say guys is that your mum would be really upset if she knew what you'd done. She trusted me to look after you both. What if one of you had choked on your own vomit… can you see the position that you could have put me in?"

They both nodded and told him, "Sorry," in unison.

"Do either of you need any paracetamol?" he asked, looking from one to the other.

"Yes please." They both answered at the same time.

After giving them a couple of paracetamols each he asked, "Can one of you get a shower now, while I cook breakfast?"

Harrison offered to use the shower first, while Ethan sat slumped on the settee with his third glass of water.

Liam appeared, sleepy eyed in his pyjamas, with his hair stuck up in all directions. The sight of him made Jonathan laugh.

"Are we having a full English?" Liam asked joyfully, at the smell of bacon and sausages being cooked.

"Are you hungry?" Jonathan asked, laughing again because he knew that Liam was always hungry.

"I'm starving!" Liam told him as he sat up to the breakfast bar. "Can I have some of this orange juice?"

"Help yourself," Jonathan told him. Turning to Ethan, he asked. "Ethan, could you make some toast for everyone please?"

Ethan dragged himself from the settee, still wearing only his boxer shorts, and looking really sorry for himself.

Jonathan smiled to himself, he knew Hannah's boys were all good lads really, and he knew that Ethan would think twice about drinking so much ever again.

"Could I have a slice now, I'm starving?" Liam asked. At the age of eleven he was growing fast and was eating his mother out of house and home.

"Well, we're all going to be eating in less than ten minutes. Do you think you can wait Liam?" Jonathan asked kindly.

"Okay," said Liam, pleasantly.

By eleven-thirty they had all eaten and were all suited and booted. John arrived with two bottles of champagne. Against his better judgement, Jonathan, at John's insistence, allowed the boys one glass each, telling each of them that that was all they were allowed.

Meanwhile Hannah and Sophie had had their hair and makeup done. Hannah had forced half a slice of toast and a cup of tea down herself. She felt sick with nerves. Ursula kept wringing her hands, behaving like the anxious mother of the bride.

She had come through to Hannah's room with a bottle of champagne and three glasses. Hannah allowed Sophie just the one glass because she did not want a tipsy teenage girl staggering down the aisle ahead of her. Ursula opened a second bottle and poured herself a third glass and Hannah a second one. She became teary once more. "Oh, my dear, who would ever have thought all those years ago that we would be doing this today?"

She squeezed Hannah's hand and planted kiss on her cheek.

"Careful, Ursula, I've just had my hair and makeup done," she told her with a light-hearted laugh. And then looking at the older woman, with fondness, she told her, "You saw me through some hard times, Ursula. I was devastated when you went back to Germany. I thought I would never get over it!"

Shaking her head, Ursula told Hannah, "I was so worried about you and the children after we left."

"I missed you both so much, I cried for days. But I'm really glad you and Dieter can be here today. It's made it even more special."

While they were speaking, Harrison knocked on the bedroom door He had been dropped off by John, because he would be joining his mum in Dieter's hire car to the wedding venue.

"Can I come in, Mum?"

"Yes, come in, Harrison." Hannah turned, around and smiled at him. "Did you enjoy yourself last night?"

"Yeah, it was good. We've all had a massive breakfast at Jonathan's this morning."

Hannah beamed. "Did he cook for you all?"

"Yes, he did." Harrison was relieved that his soon-to-be stepfather was not going to tell Hannah what he and Ethan had done the night before. He knew she would have been both annoyed and deeply embarrassed by their behaviour. He left his mum with Ursula and went back downstairs to see Dieter.

Michelle arrived ten minutes later, to pick Ursula and Sophie up.

Sophie had been in her bedroom putting on her bridesmaid dress when Harrison had arrived home. It was apricot in colour, which really went with her colouring.

The dress was a fifties style like her mother's wedding dress. When she walked into the living room, Harrison told her, "Wait till Jason sees you in that dress!"

They were all very aware that Helen's fifteen-year-old son had a crush on Sophie. Sophie had enjoyed the attention from him the evening that he had gone to theirs, the night when all the adults had gone out together. She was looking forward to seeing him again later.

Hannah was in her room, putting on her wedding dress. It had three-quarter sleeves and a boat neckline. It was ballerina length and overlaid with lace.

She had gone for cream because she had not felt comfortable about wearing white. She had cream shoes to match. Her hair was fastened up with a few wispy curls around her face. She had a small bunch of calla lilies, which were tied together with a ribbon to hold as she walked down the aisle. Sophie was to carry a single calla lily, as she walked ahead of her mother.

The champagne had done a lot to settle Hannah's nerves. When she walked into the living room, she heard everyone gasp. Harrison's face lit up, "You look lovely, Mum!"

"So do you, Harrison. I feel so proud to have you walk me down the aisle today."

After telling Hannah how wonderful she looked, Michelle told Ursula and Sophie, "It's time we were off." She had a very definite baby bump now, but she looked lovely. She had decided to wear burnt orange since it was an autumn wedding.

Ursula had the biggest wedding hat Hannah had ever seen, and she looked lovely in her light-blue outfit with navy accessories.

John and Jonathan arrived with Ethan and Liam at twelve fifteen, just as the odd guest was starting to arrive. In the end he and Hannah had invited a few more, bringing the guest list to thirty.

The wedding was booked for one o'clock. Jonathan had had a third glass of champagne, but it had done little to help his nerves. He mingled for ten or fifteen minutes, and then he saw his friends from Cumbria arrive. They had hired a seven-seater car between them to travel to and from the wedding. He went straight over to them.

"It's great to see you all. I'm so glad you could make it."

They told them they had thought that they might not get there on time due to there being an accident at Scotch Corner.

"Well, I'm glad you're all here. Its' so good to see you all," he told them again.

After much backslapping and man hugs, Jonathan went and took his position at the front with John.

Ethan was doing a great job in showing everyone to their seats with a little assistance from Liam.

It felt like an eternity to Jonathan before the music started to play to announce the arrival of the bride.

His heart was hammering in his chest, as Sophie walked in first. She walked slowly down the aisle and took her seat at the front. Jason was straining his neck to get a better look of her. She saw him and gave him a shy smile and a little wave. Helen noticed and thought how cute they both were.

Jonathan exhaled slowly out of his mouth and took a slow deep breath in through his nose, in an attempt to calm his nerves.

Suddenly, she was there, on the arm of her eldest son. Jonathan felt as if his heart was going to beat right out of his chest as she walked down the aisle towards him. Their eyes shone with love as they looked at one another.

Hannah took her position next to him and took hold of his hand. She could feel his hand trembling, so she gave it a light reassuring squeeze.

There was a short wedding talk, before they each said their vows. They exchanged rings, and it was announced that they were husband and wife. Jonathan kissed his bride.

They had the usual photo shoot, before going onto the reception. After four courses and several glasses of wine, John gave his best man's speech, where in true best man style he told a couple of majorly embarrassing stories from his and Jonathan's schooldays, and from the time they had served their apprenticeships together. Hannah laughed as she pictured the scenes in her head, while Jonathan closed his eyes, screwed up his nose.

After John's speech Jonathan stood up and looked round at everyone. "I'm afraid I'm not one for giving speeches. I don't have the gift of the gab like my friend here," He said, turning to look at John, "so I'm going to keep this brief."

He looked around and smiled at everyone. "I would like to thank you all for being here today to share our special day. Some of you have travelled an awfully long way to be here, and both Hannah and I are really pleased that you've been able to make it."

Hannah watched him, knowing how nervous he was. "I would like to say thank you to Harrison, Ethan, Sophie, and Liam for welcoming me into your family. You've had your mum all to yourselves for such a long time and it must be difficult to have to share her with an outsider.

I think you are all great kids, and I'd like to thank you all for the part you've all played in making today special." He turned to face Hannah and smiled at her, lovingly. "I will never forget how beautiful you looked as you walked towards me today... I never believed that it was possible to be this happy, and I thank God every day for bringing you into my life.

I promise you that I will do my absolute best to make you happy... You are the love of my life, and I am so honoured to have you as my wife." He bent down and kissed her before sitting back down, amidst lots of cheers and applause from the wedding guests.

Debbie had hung onto his every word as she sniffed and wiped a tear from her eye, while Kenny tutted and sighed, showing his displeasure.

At nine-thirty in the evening Jonathan slid his arm around Hannah's waist and whispered in her ear. "Do you think we could leave now?"

"Don't you think it's a little early to leave our guests?"

"Absolutely not!" he whispered, his lips softly brushing against her ear as he spoke, sending shivers down her spine.

"They'll all know why we're going to our room early."

"I can live with that," he told her. Then with eyes that were smiling he looked into hers., "We are married! "He reminded her.

"Okay," she said as she smiled back. "But we'll have to say goodnight to everyone before we leave."

They thanked everyone and said goodnight before taking the lift to their room.

Hannah's heart was racing in anticipation of the night ahead. When they got to their room, she suddenly felt shy. She had not undressed in front of a man for eleven years.

Jonathan hung his jacket and his tie over the back of the chair before sitting down to take his shoes off.

Hannah sat down on the side of the bed and took her shoes off too. She trembled a little at the thought that they would soon be making love for the first time.

Jonathan walked over to her and pulled her to her feet.

"You're trembling," he said, looking concerned.

"I know, it's ridiculous, isn't it? I feel like it's my first time!"

"It *is* your first time," He told her with a kiss, and then added, "with me."

He took her into his arms and kissed her mouth so tenderly and so lovingly that she simply melted in his arms.

As he continued to kiss her, all the apprehension she had felt evaporated. She felt him slowly unzip her dress. As she held on to him, she could feel the toned muscles of his body beneath his shirt, and he smelled wonderful.

A while later, after making love, they lay in each other's arms, gently kissing and caressing one another.

"That was wonderful!" he whispered to her

"It was wonderful, really wonderful," she whispered back.

He had touched her so lovingly and so tenderly. He had kissed her mouth with such gentle kisses, that were followed, with more passionate kisses.

That night Hannah experienced for the first time in her life, the ecstasy of what making love was supposed to be like, as Jonathan took her to a place where she had never been with Philip.

He held her close to him as he stroked her back with his fingertips. "I love you Hannah, so very much."

"And I love you!" she told him, as a feeling of euphoria filled her entire being.

They lay wrapped in one another's arms, whispering expressions of love to one another, before they each drifted off into a deep pleasurable sleep.

At some point in the night they had stirred, and their arms had automatically reached for each other. Half-asleep, Jonathan's lips had found hers, and then fully awake, they had made love a second time.

Jonathan was the first to wake the next morning. He lay a while watching Hannah sleep, the memory of their lovemaking filling him with a feeling of pure joy and happiness.

He turned to look at the clock. It was eleven in the morning. They had missed breakfast and they had to check out by twelve. He turned back to Hannah and stroked her face, whispering her name a couple of times before she opened her eyes. "Good morning, darling," he said.

"Good morning," she whispered back to him, smiling at the sight of him.

"We've slept in, and we have to check out in less than an hour."

She was suddenly wide awake. Hoping she did not have awful morning breath she went to the bathroom to clean her teeth.

They each had a quick shower, and while Hannah attended to her makeup Jonathan pulled on a pair of jeans and a jumper. He quickly packed their things. Hannah put on a pair of jeans, a shirt, and a short-waisted jacket before tying her hair up.

They managed to get down to reception with less than five minutes to spare.

John had dropped Jonathan's car off as promised and had left the keys at reception.

"I hope everything was to your satisfaction!" the receptionist called back to them over her shoulder as she went to retrieve Jonathan's car keys.

Jonathan turned to Hannah, unable to suppress a grin that had spread across his face, before answering, "It couldn't have been more perfect. Thank you."

Hannah had to bite her bottom lip to stop herself from laughing, as the receptionist handed the car keys to Jonathan.

Once outside Jonathan threw their bags into the boot and suggested they find somewhere to have brunch.

Hannah had no idea where they were going for their honeymoon, because Jonathan had kept it as a surprise. All she knew was that she had not needed a passport.

Jonathan pulled up outside the cottage late afternoon. Hannah got out of the car and looked around at the spectacular scenery, that surrounded the cottage. It was in a secluded spot overlooking a large lake.

"This is so beautiful!" she told him.

He unlocked the door, swept her up into his arms and carried her over the threshold into a quaint open plan kitchen and lounge. It was beautifully decorated and tastefully furnished.

"Have a wander round while I get the bags," he told her.

She walked through the kitchen door and found a hallway that had a large double bedroom off to one side. There was a double bed in the centre, fitted wardrobes down one side and a bathroom to the other side.

She wandered back out just as Jonathan was bringing the bags through. He gestured with his head. "Come with me, I want to show you something." She followed him up the tiny staircase that went off the side of the lounge. When they reached the top of the staircase they walked into a beautiful, converted loft.

"This is our bedroom. The bathroom is over there."

"It's beautiful!" Was all Hannah could say as her eyes studied the room, and then realising that he seemed to know where everything was, she asked him, "Have you been here before?"

"Yes, I have," he said, as he lay across the centre of the bed, propping himself up on his elbow.

Hannah looked astonished. "When have you been here before?"

"I used to live here!" The look on her face made him smile.

"No, you didn't!" she said, incredulously.

She knelt on the bed, next to where he lay. "When did you live here?"

"Hannah... I own it."

She could not have looked more shocked. "You *own* it?"

"I bought it when I was fleeing from my ex-wife. I've made some money renting it out as a holiday cottage since leaving here last year. I pay a woman from the village takes care of the cleaning and other bits of stuff for me."

"I can't believe you own it! I love it. It's so quaint, and it feels like home."

"I'm glad you like it." He was still smiling at the surprise on her face. "Do you know?" he said, "I can't remember a time when I've ever been happier than I am just now."

"What about when you got married the first time?"

"It wasn't like this! This is much deeper, its much stronger, and making love to you last night was incredibly special!" He pulled her closer to him.

They kissed passionately, both loving the fact that they could enjoy one another now that they were married.

Hannah had never been loved like this. She had never really enjoyed the intimate side of her marriage, with Philip, but with Jonathan it was completely different. It was so beautiful and joyfully intimate. She thanked God in her heart for allowing her to experience true love, the kind of love that He had intended for a man and a woman to experience together.

Later, that evening, while enjoying a candlelit dinner in one of the local restaurants, Hannah asked Jonathan, "How could you bear to leave such a beautiful place?"

"The truth is, I was lonely. I missed my hometown, my friends, and my family. As beautiful as it is here, if you haven't anyone to share it with then it can be a lonely existence."

"Do you think your family will ever come round?" she asked, changing the subject.

"Wait till they find out we're married. They'll probably never speak to me again! Anyway, I'm not going to stand back while they treat you like a leper. It isn't right and it isn't fair."

"I'm sure they'll come round in the end because they love you. I'm sure."

Let's not talk about them right now, Hannah. Let's enjoy our evening," he said, not wanting talk of his family to spoil their evening.

After spending a wonderful evening together, they walked back to the cottage holding hands. Hannah felt as if was walking on air. She was with the man she adored, and she knew without any doubt that he adored her too!

Their honeymoon was the most glorious week of Hannah's life. They spent hours walking and talking in the hills. Jonathan took her to several unspoilt beauty spots, as he showed her some of his favourite places.

Some evenings they would sit on the ground at the water's edge, and watch the sun go down over the lake. It was something that Jonathan had done many times before, but always on his own. It filled him with such intense happiness to be sharing the experience with Hannah.

The last time he had sat in this spot alone was over a year ago, just before he had moved back home. He remembered how he had been thinking of her as he sat there that evening. In fact, he had thought of her several times after meeting her for the first time at the home of his friends.

He knew he would meet her again, not only because of her connection with John and Michelle, but also because they shared the same faith, and so it was inevitable that their paths would cross again. But he could never have guessed in his wildest dreams that just over a year later, they would be sitting here together as husband and wife.

The sun's reflection as it went down often made the lake look as if it was on fire, at other times, the water just glistened.

After the sun disappeared, they would get up, hold hands, and walk to the village, to eat in one of the several good restaurants that the village boasted.

Afterwards, they would walk back to the cottage, go to bed, and make love.

Chapter Twenty-four

The week passed by very quickly, and soon they were on their way back home.

It must have been how different her life with Jonathan already was, that caused Hannah's mind to wander back to those awful years she had wasted with Philip. It angered her, that he had felt it his right as her husband to treat her the way he had done. She had been a child, giving birth to children, a child who had become a battered wife.

She talked through her feelings with Jonathan, who showed patience and understanding, as she worked through them. He knew it was something that she had to do, so that she could finally lay it to rest, and they could move forward towards a wonderful future without the ghost of her past hanging in the shadows.

But nothing could take away Hannah's joy of being loved by a real man, a man who concerned himself with her happiness, a man who genuinely loved her with all his heart.

The newlyweds came home to the news that Philip had called to arrange to pick the children up the following Friday to take them to his mother's house for the weekend.

Hannah was a little alarmed about whether he had got wind of her getting married. She thought about the words he had spoken to her the night that she had believed he was going to kill her. He had said that he would never allow her to belong to another man. Was he coming up with evil intentions, to put an end to her happiness with Jonathan? She spoke to Jonathan about her fears once they were alone in bed that night.

"I'm scared, Jonathan. He once told me that he would never allow me to belong to another man. Don't you think it's strange that he's decided to come up just as we've got married? Do you think he's planning something?"

Jonathan turned to look at her, and, seeing the anxiety clearly on her face, he reassured her. "I will be here when he arrives, and there is no way I'm going to allow him to hurt anyone in this household, especially you. It could just be coincidental that he's got in touch the week that we got married. Try not to worry, Hannah, everything will be fine."

As it turned out it *had* been coincidental, because Harrison had gone on to explain that when he had told his father that his mother was on her honeymoon, it had been met with total silence for several seconds, before Philip had gone on to make the arrangements to pick them up at five o'clock the following Friday.

Sophie and Liam arrived back from John and Michelle's where they had spent the week while their mother had been on her honeymoon. Harrison and Ethan were old enough to stay at home together, albeit under the careful watch of Michelle.

Philip's car pulled up outside his children's home just before five, the following Friday evening. Ethan had taken himself off to one of his friends where he was spending the night, so that he didn't have to see his father. Hannah was upstairs making sure that the other three had everything they needed to take with them

Philip knocked on the front door and was taken aback when a tall, good-looking man opened the door to him.

Although Philip was only forty-one, he looked more like fifty-one, due to his heavy drinking and heavy smoking. He looked Jonathan up and down, taking note of the wedding ring on his finger. It was something that he had refused to wear himself for obvious reasons.

"Who are you?" he asked not too kindly. Of course, he knew exactly who he was speaking to, he was just being his usual arrogant self.

"I'm Jonathan, Hannah's husband."

The words 'Hannah's husband' cut through Philip like a knife.

Hannah always kept Philip at the door come rain or shine, but she had forgotten to tell Jonathan not to invite him inside He opened the front door wider and beckoned for Philip to come in. Philip looked all around as he entered the house. It was exactly how he had expected Hannah's house to look on the inside. Philip sat down in one of the armchairs while Jonathan sat himself down on the settee.

Hannah walked into the living room and stopped dead at seeing Philip sitting on her furniture.

Philip's heart skipped a beat when she entered the room, because he still believed he loved her. She had a glow about her, in fact he had never seen her looking so well.

Jonathan was watching how Philip looked at her, so when Hannah sat down next him, he put a protective arm around her. Philip wanted to scream with jealousy.

"The kids will be down in a minute," she told him.

As she looked at him now, she wondered how she had ever been attracted to him. How had she ever thought she loved him? He had a mean look about him, and she found him quite repulsive now, as he sat there in her living room.

Philip had no desire to make small talk with Jonathan, so he turned to Hannah and said, "You look really well, how are you?"

"I'm really well. We've just got back from our honeymoon. Jonathan has a cottage in the lakes, so we spent it there."

She turned to Jonathan who smiled back at her.

Philip couldn't stand it, he stood up and was just about to say that he would wait in the car, when the children all appeared, looking surprised to see their father in the house.

The children followed him out to the car. Jonathan and Hannah stood at the door to wave them off. Philip kept his eyes fixed straight ahead, because he could not stand the sight of Jonathan's arm around Hannah's waist, nor the way she was leaning into him.

Once they were back inside, Hannah told Jonathan, "I never let him inside the house." It had upset her to see her awful ex-husband in her home, sitting on her furniture.

"I'm sorry, but you never said."

"I know. I should have let you know before he arrived."

Jonathan wrapped his arms around her. "Well, my love, we have the entire night to ourselves. What would you like to do?"

"What would *you* like to do?" She smiled.

"I could take you out, or we could cuddle up on the settee, watch a film, drink wine and eat lots of chocolate."

"Let's do that. Let's enjoy a night in, just the two of us," she told him. She hugged him close, safe in the knowledge that Philip would have to get past Jonathan if he ever tried to harm her again.

At their grandparents' house, the children were not allowed to mention the wedding or Jonathan's name when their father was around. Frank had been delighted to hear that Hannah was happily married to a man that genuinely loved her. Sophie had told her grandfather all about how happy their mother had been since meeting Jonathan

"Pass my congratulations on to them both when you get back home… I'm glad she's found happiness. She was such an unhappy little lass when she was down here. She did the right thing getting out."

I know, Grandad, and yes, she is so happy."

"I wish I could have done more to help her." Frank said, sadly.

Sophie put her hand on her grandfather's. "But you *did* help her enormously, Grandad. She often speaks about how you and Nanna treated her better than her own parents did. She has always told us that you were a true ally! She appreciated all that you did for her."

Sophie's words brought a tear to Frank's eye.

"You should come up for a visit, both you and Nanna, I'm sure Mum would love to see you both again."

"Sophie, I would love to see your mum again, but she has a new life now. I'm sure her new husband would not want your mother's ex-husband's parents turning up on his front doorstep."

"I think he would be fine about it. He will understand that none of what happened down here, was yours or Nanna's fault."

Frank could see how much the news of Hannah remarrying was eating away at Philip, but Frank knew that he had got what he deserved.

Philip had murderous thoughts towards Jonathan. Of course, he would not act them out. Jonathan was a big strong man and could easily deal with any trouble that Philip tried to bring his way.

Philip's mind kept wandering back to that sweet fourteen-year-old kid he had met twenty years ago. He had known that she was far too young for him, but he had wanted her. Her tight, firm fourteen-year-old body had aroused him so much that he had not been able to keep his hands off her. That was no excuse, and he knew it. He knew that he should have walked away and found someone much closer to his own age.

He knew that he had treated her badly, and how much he had let her down during the years that she had been his. She belonged to someone else now, and he could not stand it! The memory of the way Hannah had looked at her new husband, and the way he had put his arm around her and had drawn her closer to him, was killing Philip.

She had glowed when she had walked into the room that evening, something she had never done when she was with him.

He could not get the image out of his head of Jonathan sleeping next to, and making love to the woman, who up until recently had never been touched by any man other than himself. It felt like she had left him all over again, causing him to weep again for his loss, just as he had done eleven years earlier.

During those first few months after Hannah had left him, there had been times when he couldn't breathe, so deep was his grief. He had often fantasised about the two of them getting back together at some point, even if he had to wait another ten years.

That was partly why his second marriage hadn't worked. Apart from him being a controlling bully, it was because he still wanted Hannah. He would have dumped his second wife Janet at a second's notice to be with Hannah again.

He was jealous over Jonathan's looks, and the love that had shone in Hannah's eyes, as she looked at her new husband. It was over, he finally had to accept that she would never be his again!

The following Monday he took his kids back home. He had been helping to carry some things to the door that Frank and Alice had bought their grandchildren. Jonathan had opened the door to them, while Hannah remained in the kitchen finishing off tea.

They all said goodbye to their father and went through to see their mother in the kitchen while Jonathan made sure that he kept Hannah's ex at the door this time. Just as Philip was about to walk away, he turned around, and slyly whispered to Jonathan. "Remember, I was there first. She's second-hand goods mate!" Then he smirked at Jonathan, who quietly closed the door behind him, and keeping his own voice low, he responded to Philip's vicious words.

Looking at Philip with utter contempt, he said, "Second-hand goods? How dare you insult Hannah, after everything you did to her!"

Philip went to say something, but Jonathan carried on speaking. "I know it must be killing you that she's with me now... I see how you look at her, with your grubby little mind, but even if she weren't with me, she would never entertain a lowlife like you. She's not the little girl who you once bullied and controlled. She's a strong-minded woman, and she will never be a second-hand anything!"

Philip wanted to rip Jonathan's head off, and Jonathan knew it. But Philip could only attack, smaller, more vulnerable people, like Hannah. Jonathan stood his ground and continued to look Philip in the eye as he told him, "I think it's time for you to leave. Shut the gate on your way out."

Philip was blazing with anger as he turned and marched down the garden path. He deliberately left the gate wide open as he walked through it. After Philip had pulled away, as he roared his engine angrily, Jonathan walked down the garden path and shut it.

He went back inside just as the kids were all carrying various items through to put on the table in time for dinner. The dining room where they all ate at mealtimes was small and Jonathan had already discussed with Hannah the idea of selling the cottage to buy a bigger house, with the promise that he would take her there for another weekend before any sale was finalised. They definitely needed more room, especially since he and Hannah were going to be trying for a baby once they had had several months to settle into married life

"Did you all have a good weekend?" he asked.

"We weren't allowed to talk about the wedding, or mention your name in front of Dad," Harrison told him.

Ethan who had sat down at the table looked up at his stepfather and said with feeling, "He's a creep."

Jonathan couldn't have agreed more, but of course, he kept his thoughts to himself.

He went through to the kitchen to help Hannah bring dinner through. "What were you and Philip talking about outside?" she asked as she handed him the oven gloves to carry the large casserole dish through to the dining room.

"I'll fill you in later when we're on our own."

Once they were all seated round the dinner table and tucking into the meal, Hannah announced that Nanna and Grandad were coming up to visit a week tomorrow, so any plans that any of them had would need to be changed.

She had already spoken to Ethan the day before, knowing that he might feel awkward about the visit. He had not been to see his grandparents in over a year. Hannah had assured him of their love and had told him that they would only be too pleased to see him.

Harrison had told him several months earlier that Grandad fully understood why Ethan had decided to cut ties with his father. Ethan had decided that it would be nice to see his grandparents without having to see his father at the same time.

Sophie had rung her mum and had discussed the idea of them coming up. Hannah in turn had discussed it with Jonathan, who had said that he would be okay with them visiting occasionally. So, it had all been arranged and they were expecting Frank and Alice at twelve the following Saturday.

Later that night, when Jonathan and Hannah were in bed, Jonathan told her of the conversation that had taken place between him and Philip.

"How dare he say that to you!" she told Jonathan indignantly.

"Just the words of a bitter and jealous man. He still wants you, and he knows he can't have you. The fact that I've come along has brought an abrupt end to any fantasy he still entertained about the two of you eventually getting back together."

"Really?" Hannah, frowned.

"It's written all over him… Don't you see how he looks at you?"

"I don't really pay any attention to him. He makes my flesh crawl!" Looking at Jonathan earnestly, she told him, "You have nothing to worry about where he's concerned. Don't let him get to you, he's a pathetic nobody!"

Jonathan pulled her closer. "I know that darling, but I don't like him looking at you the way he does."

"It doesn't matter how he looks at me, he can't have me. Besides, I just happen to be head over heels in love with you!"

Jonathan switched the lamp off, and as they snuggled under the duvet together, he told her. "I know, but I like to hear you say it."

Chapter Twenty-five

Frank and Alice arrived just before twelve the following Saturday. Jonathan was out at the supermarket with Sophie and Liam, getting some last-minute items. Harrison and Ethan had not long been up and were still getting ready upstairs. Hannah saw them pull up outside and although she hadn't seen them for nearly ten years, she would have recognised them anywhere. They were both in their early sixties now, but they didn't look much different from the last time she had seen them. She walked down the garden path to greet them. As soon as Frank caught sight of her, he became emotional. He had thought about Hannah, so often as the years had rolled on by, but he had believed that he would never see her again. Hannah became emotional too.

"Aww, lass, you look grand. Doesn't she look well, Alice?" said Frank.

Alice nodded. She had felt a bit strange at the idea of seeing Hannah with another man, but the thought of having some extra time with her grandchildren and being able to see Ethan was an opportunity that she did not want to turn down.

It had devastated Alice that Ethan was no longer seeing his father, because it had been a huge loss to her and Frank. She had been surprised at how Philip had appeared to accept it a little too easily.

Hannah showed them into her home. As Alice looked about, she told Hannah that she had a very pretty house.

Frank had to keep brushing a tear away that kept escaping from his eye. Here was Hannah, the girl he had missed so much over the last eleven years. She had felt like his own flesh and blood during her time with Philip, and to see her so well and so happy meant the world to him.

Jonathan arrived back with Sophie and Liam, just as Harrison and Ethan came downstairs to see their grandparents. Ethan felt a bit awkward at first but as soon as his Nanna saw him, she threw her arms around him and almost squeezed the life out of him. Frank told him. "It's lovely to see you, lad," before giving him a hug.

Jonathan held back, while everyone finished hugging and kissing. He then stepped forward and introduced himself to Frank and Alice.

"I've heard a lot about you, Jonathan. It's nice to put a face to the name," Frank said in his usual friendly manner.

Sophie and Liam made coffee for everyone to give the adults a chance to talk. There appeared to be no bad feelings towards Hannah now from Alice, as the two of them talked as if all those years apart had never happened.

They all enjoyed a lovely lunch together as they talked about so many things from years gone by. No one mentioned Philip that day. Frank had warned Alice not to bring him up, and he had also told her that what Philip didn't know couldn't hurt him. So, they had kept their trip to Yorkshire between themselves.

Later, Hannah made afternoon tea for everyone.

At six in the evening Frank announced that they had probably outstayed their welcome, and it was time to set off home, as it was a long drive. Frank shook Jonathan's hand as they were about to leave. "I can see you're a good bloke, Jonathan, look after my girl. Keep her happy."

"I will do my best. It's been lovely to meet you both. You're both welcome to come again. I really mean that!" he said, turning to look at Alice, who nodded and smiled at him.

They made their way back to the car, and as their family waved them off, both Alice and Frank shed a tear.

"What a nice bloke he is, Alice, and doesn't Hannah look well?"

"Yes, she does. She looks really well. I think she will be happy with Jonathan."

"Oh, yes, Alice, I think so too." Frank said, happily, turning to smile at his wife.

"Thank you," Hannah told her husband as they all went back inside. "I never expected to see either of them again."

"I really like Frank. He's exactly as you described him," Jonathan told Hannah, as he began to clear the table with her.

It would not to be the last time that Frank and Alice would visit Hannah's home. For the next ten years, they would make the trip to Yorkshire together twice a year, and Philip was never told.

As the years went by with Jonathan by her side, Hannah was able to finally let go of the past, as the two of them journeyed through life together. He never once made her feel afraid, unwanted, or unloved, and Hannah gave him the child he had wanted, a daughter, who grew up in the security of her parents' love, and the love of her older siblings.

As Hannah's children became adults and found love themselves, Hannah and Jonathan would eventually welcome several grandchildren into their lives.

Jonathan loved each and every one of them as if they were his own flesh and blood, just as Frank had loved his step-grandchildren, her children.

Jonathan was a real man, the kind of man that Hannah deserved to spend the rest of her days with, after all that she had suffered, during her childhood, and later as a young wife and mother.

The two of them remained lifelong friends with John and Michelle. And of course, they stayed in touch with Hannah's friends from her younger days.

As the years rolled by, Jonathan and Hannah's love grew ever deeper and ever stronger. They never tired of one another, never ran out of things to talk about, or laugh about.

Once all five children were grown up, they holidayed all over the world together, giving Hannah a life full of rich experiences that at one time, she could never have imagined would be hers.

They thanked God every day for the love they had found in one another.

Hannah had claimed her life back as her own the day she walked away from Philip, and now she shared her life with a man that she knew, without a single doubt in her mind, loved her beyond measure. Jonathan and Hannah were truly a match made in heaven!